AGATHA CHRISTIE

The legendary author of eighty-five internationally bestselling mysteries, Dame Agatha has been delighting several hundred million readers for more than fifty years with her classic novels of deduction. Don't miss these other thrillers from the peerless creator of two of mystery fiction's greatest detectives: the incomparable Hercule Poirot and the dauntless Jane Marple:

Postern of Fate • Death on the Nile • A Holiday for Murder • The Mysterious Affair at Styles • Poirot Investigates • The Secret Adversary

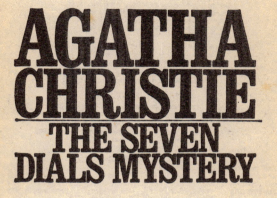

AGATHA CHRISTIE

THE SEVEN DIALS MYSTERY

BANTAM BOOKS
TORONTO • NEW YORK • LONDON • SYDNEY • AUCKLAND

This low-priced Bantam Book
has been completely reset in a type face
designed for easy reading, and was printed
from new plates. It contains the complete
text of the original hard-cover edition.
NOT ONE WORD HAS BEEN OMITTED.

THE SEVEN DIALS MYSTERY
A Bantam Book / published by arrangement with
Dodd, Mead and Company, Inc.

PRINTING HISTORY
Dodd, Mead edition published March 1929
    2nd printing .... March 1929
    3rd printing .... March 1929
Grosset & Dunlap edition published February 1930
    2nd printing .... November 1930
American Mercury edition published October 1942
    Bantam edition / January 1964

2nd printing .... April 1971	6th printing .... April 1972
3rd printing .... April 1971	7th printing .... June 1973
4th printing .. September 1971	8th printing .... March 1974
5th printing .. November 1971	9th printing .. September 1975

New Bantam edition / March 1976

2nd printing .... April 1976	6th printing .. September 1978
3rd printing ...... January 1977	7th printing .... August 1979
4th printing .... June 1977	8th printing ...... October 1980
5th printing .... May 1978	9th printing .... May 1981

Cover painting by Tom Adams

ISBN 0-553-14039-6

Published simultaneously in the United States and Canada

PRINTED IN THE UNITED STATES OF AMERICA

18 17 16 15 14 13

Contents

I	ON EARLY RISING	1
II	CONCERNING ALARUM CLOCKS	11
III	THE JOKE THAT FAILED	16
IV	A LETTER	25
V	THE MAN IN THE ROAD	32
VI	SEVEN DIALS AGAIN	37
VII	BUNDLE PAYS A CALL	43
VIII	VISITORS FOR JIMMY	48
IX	PLANS	54
X	BUNDLE VISITS SCOTLAND YARD	61
XI	DINNER WITH BILL	66
XII	INQUIRIES AT CHIMNEYS	73
XIII	THE SEVEN DIALS CLUB	82
XIV	THE MEETING OF THE SEVEN DIALS	89
XV	THE INQUEST	96
XVI	THE HOUSE PARTY AT THE ABBEY	102
XVII	AFTER DINNER	109
XVIII	JIMMY'S ADVENTURES	115
XIX	BUNDLE'S ADVENTURES	120
XX	LORAINE'S ADVENTURES	124
XXI	THE RECOVERY OF THE FORMULA	130
XXII	THE COUNTESS RADZKY'S STORY	137
XXIII	SUPERINTENDENT BATTLE IN CHARGE	146
XXIV	BUNDLE WONDERS	153
XXV	JIMMY LAYS HIS PLANS	159
XXVI	MAINLY ABOUT GOLF	167
XXVII	NOCTURNAL ADVENTURE	171
XXVIII	SUSPICIONS	176
XXIX	SINGULAR BEHAVIOUR OF GEORGE LOMAX	183
XXX	AN URGENT SUMMONS	190
XXXI	THE SEVEN DIALS	198
XXXII	BUNDLE IS DUMFOUNDED	203
XXXIII	BATTLE EXPLAINS	206
XXXIV	LORD CATERHAM APPROVES	216

CHAPTER I

On Early Rising

THAT amiable youth, Jimmy Thesiger, came racing down the big staircase at Chimneys two steps at a time. So precipitate was his descent that he collided with Tredwell, the stately butler, just as the latter was crossing the hall bearing a fresh supply of hot coffee. Owing to the marvellous presence of mind and masterly agility of Tredwell, no casualty occurred.

"Sorry," apologized Jimmy. "I say, Tredwell, am I the last down?"

"No, sir, Mr. Wade has not come down yet."

"Good," said Jimmy, and entered the breakfast room.

The room was empty save for his hostess, and her reproachful gaze gave Jimmy the same feeling of discomfort he always experienced on catching the eye of a defunct codfish exposed on a fishmonger's slab. Yet, hang it all, why should the woman look at him like that? To come down at a punctual nine-thirty when staying in a country house simply wasn't done. To be sure, it was now a quarter past eleven which was, perhaps, the outside limit, but even then——

"Afraid I'm a bit late, Lady Coote. What?"

"Oh! it doesn't matter," said Lady Coote in a melancholy voice.

As a matter of fact, people being late for breakfast worried her very much. For the first ten years of her married life, Sir Oswald Coote (then plain Mr.) had, to put it baldly, raised hell if his morning meal were even a half minute later than eight o'clock. Lady Coote had been disciplined to regard unpunctuality as a deadly sin of the most unpardonable nature. And habit dies hard. Also, she was an earnest woman, and she could not help asking herself what possible good these young people would ever do in the world without early rising. As Sir Oswald so often said, to reporters and others: "I attribute my success entirely to my habits of early rising, frugal living, and methodical habits."

Lady Coote was a big, handsome woman in a tragic sort of fashion. She had large, dark, mournful eyes and a deep voice. An artist looking for a model for "Rachel mourning for her children" would have hailed Lady Coote with delight. She would have done well, too, in melodrama, staggering through the falling snow as the deeply wronged wife of the villain.

She looked as though she had some terrible secret sorrow in her life, and yet if the truth be told, Lady Coote had had no trouble in her life whatever, except the meteoric rise to prosperity of Sir Oswald. As a young girl she had been a jolly flamboyant creature, very much in love with Oswald Coote, the aspiring young man in the bicycle shop next to her father's hardware store. They had lived very happily, first in a couple of rooms, and then in a tiny house, and then in a larger house, and then in successive houses of increasing magnitude, but always within a reasonable distance of "the Works" until now Sir Oswald had reached such an eminence that he and "the Works" were no longer interdependent, and it was his pleasure to rent the very largest and most magnificent mansions available all over England. Chimneys was a historic place, and in renting it from the Marquis of Caterham for two years, Sir Oswald felt that he had attained the top notch of his ambition.

Lady Coote was not nearly so happy about it. She was a lonely woman. The principal relaxation of her early married life had been talking to "the girl"—and even when "the girl" had been multiplied by three, conversation with her domestic staff had still been the principal distraction of Lady Coote's day. Now, with a pack of housemaids, a butler like an archbishop, several footmen of imposing proportions, a bevy of scuttling kitchen and scullery maids, a terrifying foreign chef with a "temperament" and a housekeeper of immense proportions who alternately creaked and rustled when she moved, Lady Coote was as one marooned on a desert island.

She sighed now, heavily, and drifted out through the open window, much to the relief of Jimmy Thesiger who at once helped himself to more kidneys and bacon on the strength of it.

Lady Coote stood for a few moments tragically on the terrace and then nerved herself to speak to Mac-Donald, the head gardener, who was surveying the domain over which he ruled with an autocratic eye. MacDonald was a very chief and prince among head gardeners. He knew his place—which was to rule. And he ruled—despotically.

Lady Coote approached him nervously.

"Good-morning, MacDonald."

"Good-morning, m'lady."

He spoke as head gardeners should speak—mournfully, but with dignity—like an emperor at a funeral.

"I was wondering—could we have some of those late grapes for dessert to-night?"

"They're no fit for picking yet," said MacDonald.

He spoke kindly but firmly.

"Oh," said Lady Coote.

She plucked up courage.

"Oh! but I was in the end house yesterday, and I tasted one and they seemed very good."

MacDonald looked at her, and she blushed. She was made to feel that she had taken an unpardonable liberty. Evidently the late Marchioness of Caterham had never committed such a solecism as to enter one of her own hothouses and help herself to grapes.

"If you had given orders, m'lady, a bunch should have been cut and sent in to you," said MacDonald severely.

"Oh, thank you," said Lady Coote. "Yes, I will do that another time."

"But they're no properly fit for picking yet."

"No," murmured Lady Coote. "No, I suppose not. We'd better leave it then."

MacDonald maintained a masterly silence. Lady Coote nerved herself once more.

"I was going to speak to you about the piece of lawn at the back of the rose garden. I wondered if it could be used as a bowling green. Sir Oswald is very fond of a game of bowls."

"And why not?" thought Lady Coote to herself. She had been instructed in her history of England. Had not Sir Francis Drake and his knightly companions been playing a game of bowls when the Armada was sighted? Surely a gentlemanly pursuit and one to which MacDonald could not reasonably object. But she had reckoned without the predominant trait of a good head gardener, which is to oppose any and every suggestion made to him.

"Nae doot it could be used for that purpose," said MacDonald noncommittally.

He threw a discouraging flavour into the remark, but its real object was to lure Lady Coote on to her destruction.

"If it was cleared up and—er—cut—and—er—all that sort of thing," she went on hopefully.

"Aye," said MacDonald slowly. "It could be done. But it would mean taking William from the lower border."

"Oh!" said Lady Coote doubtfully. The words "lower border" conveyed absolutely nothing to her mind—except a vague suggestion of a Scottish song—but it was clear that to MacDonald they constituted an insuperable objection.

"And that would be a pity," said MacDonald.

"Oh! of course," said Lady Coote. "It *would*."

And wondered why she agreed so fervently.

MacDonald looked at her very hard.

"Of course," he said, "if it's your *orders*, m'lady—"

He left it like that. But his menacing tone was too much for Lady Coote. She capitulated at once.

"Oh! no," she said. "I see what you mean, Mac-

Donald. N-no—William had better get on with the lower border."

"That's what I thocht meself, m'lady."

"Yes," said Lady Coote. "Yes. Certainly."

"I thocht you'd gree, m'lady," said MacDonald.

"Oh! certainly," said Lady Coote again.

MacDonald touched his hat and moved away.

Lady Coote sighed unhappily and looked after him. Jimmy Thesiger, replete with kidneys and bacon, stepped out on to the terrace beside her, and sighed in quite a different manner.

"Topping morning, eh?" he remarked.

"Is it?" said Lady Coote, absently. "Oh! yes, I suppose it is. I hadn't noticed."

"Where are the others? Punting on the lake?"

"I expect so. I mean, I shouldn't wonder if they were."

Lady Coote turned and plunged abruptly into the house again. Tredwell was just examining the coffee pot.

"Oh, dear," said Lady Coote. "Isn't Mr.—Mr—"

"Wade, m'lady?"

"Yes, Mr. Wade. Isn't he down *yet?*"

"No, m'lady."

"It's very late."

"Yes, m'lady."

"Oh! dear. I suppose he will come down *sometime,* Tredwell?"

"Oh, undoubtedly, m'lady. It was eleven thirty yesterday morning when Mr. Wade came down, m'lady."

Lady Coote glanced at the clock. It was now twenty minutes to twelve. A wave of human sympathy rushed over her.

"It's very hard luck on you, Tredwell. Having to clear and then get lunch on the table by one o'clock."

"I am accustomed to the ways of young gentlemen, m'lady."

The reproof was dignified, but unmistakable. So might a prince of the Church reprove a Turk or an infidel who had unwittingly committed a solecism in all good faith.

Lady Coote blushed for the second time that morning. But a welcome interruption occurred. The door opened and a serious, spectacled young man put his head in.

"Oh! there you are, Lady Coote. Sir Oswald was asking for you."

"Oh, I'll go to him at once, Mr. Bateman."

Lady Coote hurried out.

Rupert Bateman, who was Sir Oswald's private secretary, went out the other way, through the window where Jimmy Thesiger was still lounging amiably.

"Morning, Pongo," said Jimmy. "I suppose I shall have to go and make myself agreeable to those blasted girls. You coming?"

Bateman shook his head and hurried along the terrace and in at the library window. Jimmy grinned pleasantly at his retreating back. He and Bateman had been at school together, when Bateman had been a serious, spectacled boy, and had been nicknamed Pongo for no earthly reason whatever.

Pongo, Jimmy reflected, was very much the same sort of ass now that he had been then. The words "Life is real, life is earnest" might have been written specially for him.

Jimmy yawned and strolled slowly down to the lake. The girls were there, three of them—just the usual sort of girls, two with dark, shingled heads and one with a fair, shingled head. The one that giggled most was (he thought) called Helen—and there was another called Nancy—and the third one was, for some reason, addressed as Socks. With them were his two friends, Bill Eversleigh and Ronny Devereux, who were employed in a purely ornamental capacity at the Foreign Office.

"Hallo," said Nancy (or possibly Helen). "It's Jimmy. Where's what's his name?"

"You don't mean to say," said Bill Eversleigh, "that Gerry Wade's not up *yet?* Something ought to be done about it."

"If he's not careful," said Ronny Devereux, "he'll miss his breakfast altogether one day—find it's lunch or tea instead when he rolls down."

"It's a shame," said the girl called Socks. "Because it worries Lady Coote so. She gets more and more like a hen that wants to lay an egg and can't. It's too bad."

"Let's pull him out of bed," suggested Bill. "Come on, Jimmy."

"Oh! let's be more subtle than that," said the girl called Socks. Subtle was a word of which she was rather fond. She used it a great deal.

"I'm not subtle," said Jimmy. "I don't know how."

"Let's get together and do something about it to-morrow morning," suggested Ronny vaguely. "You know, get him up at seven. Stagger the household. Tredwell loses his false whiskers and drops the tea urn. Lady Coote has hysterics and faints in Bill's arms——Bill being the weight carrier. Sir Oswald says 'Ha!' and steel goes up a point and five eighths. Pongo registers emotion by throwing down his spectacles and stamping on them."

"You don't know Gerry," said Jimmy. "I daresay enough cold water *might* wake him—judiciously applied, that is. But he'd only turn over and go to sleep again."

"Oh! we must think of something more subtle than cold water," said Socks.

"Well, what?" asked Ronny bluntly. And nobody had any answer ready.

"We ought to be able to think of something," said Bill. "Who's got any brains?"

"Pongo," said Jimmy. "And here he is, rushing along in a harried manner as usual. Pongo was always the one for brains. It'd been his misfortune from his youth upwards. Let's turn Pongo on to it."

Mr. Bateman listened patiently to a somewhat incoherent statement. His attitude was that of one poised for flight. He delivered his solution without loss of time.

"I should suggest an alarum clock," he said briskly. "I always use one myself for fear of oversleeping. I find that early tea brought in in a noiseless manner is sometimes powerless to awaken one."

He hurried away.

"An alarum clock." Ronny shook his head. *"One* alarum clock. It would take about a dozen to disturb Gerry Wade."

"Well, why not?" Bill was flushed and earnest. "I've got it. Let's all go into Market Basing and buy an alarum clock each."

There was laughter and discussion. Bill and Ronny went off to get hold of cars. Jimmy was deputed to spy upon the dining-room. He returned rapidly.

"He's there right enough. Making up for lost time and wolfing down toast and marmalade. How are we going to prevent him coming along with us?"

It was decided that Lady Coote must be approached and instructed to hold him in play. Jimmy and Nancy and Helen fulfilled this duty. Lady Coote was bewildered and apprehensive.

"A rag? You will be careful, won't you, my dears? I mean, you won't smash the furniture and wreck things or use too much water. We've got to hand this house over next week, you know. I shouldn't like Lord Caterham to think—"

Bill, who had returned from the garage, broke in reassuringly.

"That's all right, Lady Coote. Bundle Brent—Lord Caterham's daughter—is a great friend of mine. And there's nothing she'd stick at—absolutely nothing! You can take it from me. And anyway there's not going to be any damage done. This is quite a quiet affair."

"Subtle," said the girl called Socks.

Lady Coote went sadly along the terrace just as Gerald Wade emerged from the breakfast-room. Jimmy Thesiger was a fair, cherubic, young man, and all that could be said of Gerald Wade was that he was fairer and more cherubic, and that his vacuous expression made Jimmy's face quite intelligent by contrast.

"Morning, Lady Coote," said Gerald Wade. "Where are all the others?"

"They've all gone to Market Basing," said Lady Coote.

"What for?"

"Some joke," said Lady Coote in her deep, melancholy voice.

"Rather early in the morning for jokes," said Mr. Wade.

"It's not so very early in the morning," said Lady Coote pointedly.

"I'm afraid I was a bit late coming down," said Mr. Wade with engaging frankness. "It's an extraordinary thing, but wherever I happen to be staying, I'm always last to be down."

"Very extraordinary," said Lady Coote.

"I don't know why it is," said Mr. Wade, meditating. "I can't think, I'm sure."

"Why don't you just get up?" suggested Lady Coote.

"Oh!" said Mr. Wade. The simplicity of the solution rather took him aback.

Lady Coote went on earnestly.

"I've heard Sir Oswald say so many times that there's nothing for getting a young man on in the world like punctual habits."

"Oh! I know," said Mr. Wade. "And I have to when I'm in town. I mean, I have to be round at the jolly old Foreign Office by eleven o'clock. You mustn't think I'm always a slacker, Lady Coote. I say, what awfully jolly flowers you've got down in that lower border. I can't remember the names of them, but we've got some at home—those mauve thingummybobs. My sister's tremendously keen on gardening."

Lady Coote was immediately diverted. Her wrongs rankled within her.

"What kind of gardeners do you have?"

"Oh! just one. Rather an old fool, I believe. Doesn't know much, but he does what he's told. And that's a great thing, isn't it?"

Lady Coote agreed that it was with a depth of feeling in her voice that would have been invaluable to her as an emotional actress. They began to discourse on the iniquities of gardeners.

Meanwhile the expedition was doing well. The principal emporium of Market Basing had been invaded and the sudden demand for alarum clocks was considerably puzzling the proprietor.

"I wish we'd got Bundle here," murmured Bill. "You know her, don't you, Jimmy? Oh, you'd like her. She's a splendid girl—a real good sport—and mark you, she's got brains too. You know her, Ronny?"

Ronny shook his head.

"Don't know Bundle? Where have you been vegetating? She's simply it."

"Be a bit more subtle, Bill," said Socks. "Stop blethering about your lady friends and get on with the business."

Mr. Murgatroyd, owner of Murgatroyd's Stores, burst into eloquence.

"If you'll allow me to advise you, Miss, I should say —*not* the 7/11 one. It's a good clock—I'm not running it down, mark you, but I should strongly advise this kind at 10/6. Well worth the extra money. Reliability, you understand. I shouldn't like you to say afterwards—"

It was evident to everybody that Mr. Murgatroyd must be turned off like a tap.

"We don't want a reliable clock," said Nancy.

"It's got to go for one day, that's all," said Helen.

"We don't want a subtle one," said Socks. "We want one with a good loud ring."

"We want—" began Bill, but was unable to finish, because Jimmy, who was of a mechanical turn of mind, had at last grasped the mechanism. For the next five minutes the shop was hideous with the loud raucous ringing of many alarm clocks.

In the end six excellent starters were selected.

"And I'll tell you what," said Ronny handsomely, "I'll get one for Pongo. It was his idea, and it's a shame that he should be out of it. He shall be represented among those present."

"That's right," said Bill. "And I'll take an extra one for Lady Coote. The more the merrier. And she's doing some of the spade work. Probably gassing away to old Gerry now."

Indeed at this precise moment Lady Coote was detailing a long story about MacDonald and a prize peach and enjoying herself very much.

The clocks were wrapped up and paid for. Mr. Murgatroyd watched the cars drive away with a puzzled air. Very spirited the young people of the upper classes nowadays, very spirited indeed, but not at all easy to understand. He turned with relief to attend to the vicar's wife, who wanted a new kind of dripless teapot.

CHAPTER II

Concerning Alarum Clocks

"Now where shall we put them?"

Dinner was over. Lady Coote had been once more detailed for duty. Sir Oswald had unexpectedly come to the rescue by suggesting bridge—not that suggesting is the right word. Sir Oswald as became one of "Our Captains of Industry" (No. 7 of Series I), merely expressed a preference and those around him hastened to accommodate themselves to the great man's wishes.

Rupert Bateman and Sir Oswald were partners against Lady Coote and Gerald Wade, which was a very happy arrangement. Sir Oswald played bridge, like he did everything else, extremely well, and liked a partner to correspond. Bateman was as efficient a bridge player as he was a secretary. Both of them confined themselves strictly to the matter in hand, merely uttering in curt short barks. "Two no trumps," "Double," "Three spades." Lady Coote and Gerald Wade were amiable and discursive and the young man never failed to say at the conclusion of each hand, "I say, partner, you played that simply splendidly," in tones of simple admiration which Lady Coote found both novel and extremely soothing. They also held very good cards.

The others were supposed to be dancing to the wireless in the big ballroom. In reality they were grouped around the door of Gerald Wade's bedroom, and the air was full of subdued giggles and the loud ticking of clocks.

"Under the bed in a row," suggested Jimmy in answer to Bill's question.

"And what shall we set them at? What time, I mean? All together so that there's one glorious what not, or at intervals?"

The point was hotly disputed. One party argued that for a champion sleeper like Gerry Wade the combined ringing of eight alarum clocks was necessary. The other party argued in favour of steady and sustained effort.

In the end the latter won the day. The clocks were set to go off one after the other, starting at 6:30 A.M.

"And I hope," said Bill virtuously, "that this will be a lesson to him."

"Hear, hear," said Socks.

The business of hiding the clocks was just being begun when there was a sudden alarm.

"Hist," cried Jimmy. "Somebody's coming up the stairs."

There was a panic.

"It's all right," said Jimmy. "It's only Pongo."

Taking advantage of being dummy, Mr. Bateman was going to his room for a handkerchief. He paused on his way and took in the situation at a glance. He them made a comment, a simple and practical one.

"He will hear them ticking when he goes to bed."

The conspirators looked at each other.

"What did I tell you?" said Jimmy in a reverent voice. "Pongo always *did* have brains!"

The brainy one passed on.

"It's true," admitted Ronny Devereux, his head on one side. "Eight clocks all ticking at once do make a devil of a row. Even old Gerry, ass as he is, couldn't miss it. He'll guess something's up."

"I wonder if he is," said Jimmy Thesiger.

"Is what?"

"Such an ass as we all think."

Ronny stared at him.

"We all know old Gerald."

"Do we?" said Jimmy. "I've sometimes thought that —well, that it isn't possible for anyone to be quite the ass old Gerry makes himself out to be."

They all stared at him. There was a serious look on Ronny's face.

"Jimmy," he said, "you've got brains."

"A second Pongo," said Bill encouragingly.

"Well, it just occurred to me, that's all," said Jimmy, defending himself.

"Oh! don't let's all be subtle," cried Socks. "What are we to do about these clocks?"

"Here's Pongo coming back again. Let's ask him," suggested Jimmy.

Pongo, urged to bring his great brain to bear upon the matter, gave his decision.

"Wait till he's gone to bed and got to sleep. Then enter the room very quietly and put the clocks down on the floor."

"Little Pongo's right again," said Jimmy. "On the word one all park clocks, and then we'll go downstairs and disarm suspicion."

Bridge was still proceeding—with a slight difference. Sir Oswald was now playing with his wife and was conscientiously pointing out to her the mistakes she had made during the play of each hand. Lady Coote accepted reproof good-humouredly, and with a complete lack of any real interest. She reiterated, not once but many times:

"I see, dear. It's so kind of you to tell me."

And she continued to make exactly the same errors. At intervals, Gerald Wade said to Pongo:

"Well played, partner, jolly well played."

Bill Eversleigh was making calculations with Ronny Devereux.

"Say he goes to bed about twelve—what do you think we ought to give him—about an hour?"

He yawned.

"Curious thing—three in the morning is my usual time for bye-bye, but to-night, just because I know we've got to sit up a bit, I'd give anything to be a mother's boy and turn in right away."

Every one agreed that he felt the same.

"My dear Maria," rose the voice of Sir Oswald in mild irritation, "I have told you over and over again not to hesitate when you are wondering whether to finesse or not. You give the whole table information."

Lady Coote had a very good answer to this—namely that as Sir Oswald was dummy, he had no right to comment on the play of the hand. But she did not make it. Instead she smiled kindly, leaned her ample chest well forward over the table, and gazed firmly into Gerald Wade's hand where he sat on her right.

Her anxieties lulled to rest by perceiving the queen, she played the knave and took the trick and proceeded to lay down her cards.

"Four tricks and the rubber," she announced. "I think I was very lucky to get four tricks there."

"Lucky," murmured Gerald Wade, as he pushed back his chair and came over to the fireplace to join the others. "Lucky, she calls it. That woman wants watching."

Lady Coote was gathering up notes and silver.

"I know I'm not a good player," she announced in a mournful tone which nevertheless held an undercurrent of pleasure in it. "But I'm really very lucky at the game."

"You'll never be a bridge player, Maria," said Sir Oswald.

"No dear," said Lady Coote. "I know I shan't. You're always telling me so. And I do try so hard."

"She does," said Gerald Wade *sotto voce*. "There's no subterfuge about it. She'd put her head right down on your shoulder if she couldn't see into your hand any other way."

"I know you try," said Sir Oswald. "It's just that you haven't any card sense."

"I know, dear," said Lady Coote. "That's what you're always telling me. And you owe me another ten shillings, Oswald."

"Do I?" Sir Oswald looked surprised.

"Yes. Seventeen hundred—eight pounds ten. You've only given me eight pounds."

"Dear me," said Sir Oswald. "My mistake."

Lady Coote smiled at him sadly and took up the extra ten-shilling note. She was very fond of her husband, but she had no intention of allowing him to cheat her out of ten shillings.

Sir Oswald moved over to a side table and became hospitable with whisky and soda. It was half past twelve when general good-nights were said.

Ronny Devereux, who had the room next door to Gerald Wade's, was told off to report progress. At a quarter to two he crept round tapping at doors. The party, pyjamaed and dressing-gowned, assembled with various scuffles and giggles and low whispers.

"His light went out about twenty minutes ago," reported Ronny in a hoarse whisper. "I thought he'd never put it out. I opened the door just now and peeped in, and he seems sound off. What about it?"

Once more the clocks were solemnly assembled. Then another difficulty arose.

"We can't all go barging in. Make no end of a row. One person's got to do it and the others can hand him the what-nots from the door."

Hot discussion then arose as to the proper person to be selected.

The three girls were rejected on the grounds that they would giggle. Bill Eversleigh was rejected on the grounds of his height, weight and heavy tread, also for his general clumsiness, which latter clause he fiercely denied. Jimmy Thesiger and Ronny Devereux were considered possibles, but in the end an overwhelming majority decided in favour of Rupert Bateman.

"Pongo's the lad," agreed Jimmy. "Anyway, he walks like a cat—always did. And then, if Gerry should waken up, Pongo will be able to think of some rotten silly thing to say to him. You know, something plausible that'll calm him down and not rouse his suspicions."

"Something subtle," suggested the girl Socks thoughtfully.

"Exactly," said Jimmy.

Pongo performed his job neatly and efficiently. Cautiously opening the bedroom door, he disappeared into the darkness inside bearing the two largest clocks. In a minute or two he reappeared on the threshold and two more were handed to him and then again twice more. Finally he emerged. Every one held his breath and listened. The rhythmical breathing of Gerald Wade could still be heard, but drowned, smothered and buried beneath the triumphant, impassioned ticking of Mr. Murgatroyd's eight alarum clocks.

CHAPTER III

The Joke That Failed

"TWELVE o'clock," said Socks despairingly.

The joke—as a joke—had not gone off any too well. The alarum clocks, on the other hand, had performed their part. *They* had gone off—with a vigour and *élan* that could hardly have been surpassed and which had sent Ronny Devereux leaping out of bed with a confused idea that the day of judgment had come. If such had been the effect in the room next door, what must it have been at close quarters? Ronny hurried out in the passage and applied his ear to the crack of the door.

He expected profanity—expected it confidently and with intelligent anticipation. But he heard nothing at all. That is to say, he heard nothing of what he expected. The clocks were ticking all right—ticking in a loud, arrogant, exasperating manner. And presently another went off, ringing with a crude, deafening note that would have aroused acute irritation in a deaf man.

There was no doubt about it; the clocks had performed their part faithfully. They did all and more than Mr. Murgatroyd had claimed for them. But apparently they had met their match in Gerald Wade.

The syndicate was inclined to be despondent about it.

"The lad isn't human," grumbled Jimmy Thesiger.

"Probably thought he heard the telephone in the distance and rolled over and went to sleep again," suggested Helen (or possibly Nancy).

"It seems to me very remarkable," said Rupert Bateman seriously. "I think he ought to see a doctor about it."

"Some disease of the ear-drums," suggested Bill hopefully.

"Well, if you ask me," said Socks, "I think he's just spoofing us. Of course they woke him up. But he's just going to do us down by pretending that he didn't hear anything."

Every one looked at Socks with respect and admiration.

"It's an idea," said Bill.

"He's subtle, that's what it is," said Socks. "You'll see, he'll be extra late for breakfast this morning—just to show us."

And since the clock now pointed to some minutes past twelve the general opinion was that Sock's theory was a correct one. Only Ronny Devereux demurred.

"You forget, I was outside the door when the first one went off. Whatever old Gerry decided to do later, the first one must have surprised him. He'd have let out something about it. Where did you put it, Pongo?"

"On a little table close to his ear," said Mr. Bateman.

"That was thoughtful of you, Pongo," said Ronny. "Now, tell me." He turned to Bill. "If a whacking great bell started ringing within a few inches of your ear at half past six in the morning, what would you say about it?"

"Oh! Lord," said Bill. "I should say—" He came to a stop.

"Of course you would," said Ronny. "So should I. So would anyone. What they call the natural man would emerge. Well, it didn't. So I say that Pongo is right—as usual—and that Gerry has got an obscure disease of the ear-drums."

"It's now twenty past twelve," said one of the other girls sadly.

"I say," said Jimmy slowly, "that's a bit beyond anything, isn't it? I mean a joke's a joke. But this is carrying it a bit far. It's a shade hard on the Cootes."

Bill stared at him.

"What are you getting at?"

"Well," said Jimmy, "somehow or other—it's not like old Gerry."

He found it hard to put into words just what he meant to say. He didn't want to say too much, and yet —He saw Ronny looking at him. Ronny was suddenly alert.

It was at that moment Tredwell came into the room and looked round him hesitatingly.

"I thought Mr. Bateman was here," he explained apologetically.

"Just gone out this minute through the window," said Ronny. "Can I do anything?"

Tredwell's eyes wandered from him to Jimmy Thesiger and then back again. As though singled out, the two young men left the room with him. Tredwell closed the dining-room door carefully behind him.

"Well," said Ronny. "What's up?"

"Mr. Wade not having yet come down, sir, I took the liberty of sending Williams up to his room."

"Yes."

"Williams has just come running down in a great state of agitation, sir." Tredwell paused—a pause of preparation. "I am afraid, sir, the poor young gentleman must have died in his sleep."

Jimmy and Ronny stared at him.

"Nonsense," cried Ronny at last. "It's—it's impossible. Gerry—" His face worked suddenly. "I'll—I'll run up and see. That fool Williams may have made a mistake."

Tredwell stretched out a detaining hand. With a queer, unnatural feeling of detachment, Jimmy realized that the butler had the whole situation in hand.

"No, sir, Williams has made no mistake. I have already sent for Dr. Cartwright, and in the meantime I have taken the liberty of locking the door, preparatory to informing Sir Oswald of what has occurred. I must now find Mr. Bateman."

Tredwell hurried away. Ronny stood like a man dazed.

"Gerry," he muttered to himself.

Jimmy took his friend by the arm and steered him out through a side door on to a secluded portion of the terrace. He pushed him down on to a seat.

"Take it easy, old son," he said kindly. "You'll get your wind in a minute."

But he looked at him rather curiously. He had had no idea that Ronny was such a friend of Gerry Wade's.

"Poor old Gerry," he said thoughtfully. "If ever a man looked fit, he did."

Ronny nodded.

"All that clock business seems so rotten now," went on Jimmy. "It's odd, isn't it, why farce so often seems to get mixed up with tragedy?"

He was talking more or less at random, to give Ronny time to recover himself. The other moved restlessly.

"I wish that doctor would come. I want to know——"

"Know what?"

"What he—died of."

Jimmy pursed up his lips.

"Heart?" he hazarded.

Ronny gave a short, scornful laugh.

"I say, Ronny," said Jimmy.

"Well?"

Jimmy found a difficulty in going on.

"You don't mean—you aren't thinking—I mean, you haven't got it into your head that—that, well, I mean he wasn't biffed on the head or anything? Tredwell's locking the door and all that."

It seemed to Jimmy that his words deserved an answer, but Ronny continued to stare straight out in front of him.

Jimmy shook his head and relapsed into silence. He didn't see that there was anything to do except just wait. So he waited.

It was Tredwell who disturbed them.

"The doctor would like to see you two gentlemen in the library, if you please, sir."

Ronny sprang up. Jimmy followed him.

Dr. Cartwright was a thin, energetic young man with a clever face. He greeted them with a brief nod. Pongo, looking more serious and spectacled than ever, performed introductions.

"I understand you were a great friend of Mr. Wade's," the doctor said to Ronny.

"His greatest friend."

"H'm. Well, this business seems straightforward enough. Sad, though. He looked a healthy young chap. Do you know if he was in the habit of taking stuff to make him sleep?"

"Make him *sleep?*" Ronny stared. "He always slept like a top."

"You never heard him complain of sleeplessness."

"Never."

"Well, the facts are simple enough. There'll have to be an inquest, I'm afraid, nevertheless."

"How did he die?"

"There's not much doubt; I should say an overdose of chloral. The stuff was by his bed. And a bottle and glass. Very sad, these things are."

It was Jimmy who asked the question which he felt was trembling on his friend's lips, and yet which the other could somehow or other not get out.

"There's no question of—foul play?"

The doctor looked at him sharply.

"Why do you say that? Any cause to suspect it, eh?"

Jimmy looked at Ronny. If Ronny knew anything now was the time to speak. But to his astonishment Ronny shook his head.

"No cause whatever," he said clearly.

"And suicide—eh?"

"Certainly not."

Ronny was emphatic. The doctor was not so clearly convinced.

"No troubles that you know of? Money troubles? A woman?"

Again Ronny shook his head.

"Now about his relations. They must be notified."

"He's got a sister—a half-sister rather. Lives at

Deane Priory. About twenty miles from here. When he wasn't in town Gerry lived with her."

"H'm," said the doctor. "Well, she must be told."

"I'll go," said Ronny. "It's a rotten job, but somebody's got to do it." He looked at Jimmy. "You know her, don't you?"

"Slightly. I've danced with her once or twice."

"Then we'll go in your car. You don't mind, do you? I can't face it alone."

"That's all right," said Jimmy reassuringly. "I was going to suggest it myself. I'll go and get the old bus cranked up."

He was glad to have something to do. Ronny's manner puzzled him. What did he know or suspect? And why had he not voiced his suspicions, if he had them, to the doctor.

Presently the two friends were skimming along in Jimmy's car with a cheerful disregard for such things as speed limits.

"Jimmy," said Ronny at last, "I suppose you're about the best pal I have—now."

"Well," said Jimmy, "what about it?"

He spoke gruffly.

"There's something I'd like to tell you. Something you ought to know."

"About Gerry Wade?"

"Yes, about Gerry Wade."

Jimmy waited.

"Well?" he inquired at last.

"I don't know that I ought to," said Ronny.

"Why?"

"I'm bound by a kind of promise."

"Oh! Well then, perhaps you'd better not."

There was a silence.

"And yet, I'd like— You see, Jimmy, your brains are better than mine."

"They could easily be that," said Jimmy unkindly.

"No, I can't," said Ronny suddenly.

"All right," said Jimmy. "Just as you like."

After a long silence, Ronny said:

"What's she like?"

"Who?"

"This girl. Gerry's sister."

Jimmy was silent for some minutes, then he said in a voice that had somehow or other altered:

"She's all right. In fact—well, she's a corker."

"Gerry was very devoted to her, I knew. He often spoke of her."

"She was very devoted to Gerry. It—it's going to hit her hard."

"Yes, a nasty job."

They were silent till they reached Deane Priory.

Miss Loraine, the maid told them, was in the garden. Unless they wanted to see Mrs. Coker—

Jimmy was eloquent that they did not want to see Mrs. Coker.

"Who's Mrs. Coker?" asked Ronny as they went round into the somewhat neglected garden.

"The old trout who lives with Loraine."

They had stepped out into a paved walk. At the end of it was a girl with two black spaniels. A small girl, very fair, dressed in shabby old tweeds. Not at all the girl that Ronny had expected to see. Not, in fact, Jimmy's usual type.

Holding one dog by the collar, she came down the pathway to meet them.

"How do you do," she said. "You mustn't mind Elizabeth. She's just had some puppies and she's very suspicious."

She had a supremely natural manner and, as she looked up smiling, the faint wild rose flush deepened in her cheeks. Her eyes were a very dark blue—like cornflowers.

Suddenly they widened—was it with alarm? As though, already, she guessed.

Jimmy hastened to speak.

"This is Ronny Devereux, Miss Wade. You must often have heard Gerry speak of him."

"Oh! yes." She turned a lovely, warm, welcoming smile on him. "You've both been staying at Chimneys, haven't you? Why didn't you bring Gerry over with you?"

"We—er—couldn't," said Ronny, and then stopped.

Again Jimmy saw the look of fear flash into her eyes.

"Miss Wade," he said, "I'm afraid—I mean, we've got bad news for you."

She was on the alert in a moment.

"Gerry?"

"Yes—Gerry. He's—"

She stamped her foot with sudden passion.

"Oh! tell me—tell me—" She turned suddenly on Ronny. "*You*'ll tell me."

Jimmy felt a pang of jealousy, and in that moment he knew what up to now he had hesitated to admit to himself. He knew why Helen and Nancy and Socks were just "girls" to him and nothing more.

He only *half* heard Ronny's voice saying gravely:

"Yes, Miss Wade, I'll tell you. Gerry is dead."

She had plenty of pluck. She gasped and drew back, but in a minute or two she was asking eager, searching questions. How? When?

Ronny answered her as gently as he could.

"*Sleeping* draught? Gerry?"

The incredulity in her voice was plain. Jimmy gave her a glance. It was almost a glance of warning. He had a sudden feeling that Loraine in her innocence might say too much.

In his turn he explained as gently as possible the need for an inquest. She shuddered. She declined their offer of taking her back to Chimneys with them, but explained she would come over later. She had a two-seater of her own.

"But I want to be—be alone a little first," she said piteously.

"I know," said Ronny.

"That's all right," said Jimmy.

They looked at her, feeling awkward and helpless.

"Thank you both ever so much for coming."

They drove back in silence and there was something like constraint between them.

"My God! that girl's plucky," said Ronny once.

Jimmy agreed.

"Gerry was my friend," said Ronny. "It's up to me to keep an eye on her."

"Oh! rather. Of course."

They said no more.

On returning to Chimneys Jimmy was waylaid by a tearful Lady Coote.

"That poor boy," she kept repeating. "That poor boy."

Jimmy made all the suitable remarks he could think of.

Lady Coote told him at great length various details about the decease of various dear friends of hers. Jimmy listened with a show of sympathy and at last managed to detach himself without actual rudeness.

He ran lightly up the stairs. Ronny was just emerging from Gerald Wade's room. He seemed taken aback at the sight of Jimmy.

"I've been in to see him," he said. "Are you going in?"

"I don't think so," said Jimmy, who was a healthy young man with a natural dislike to being reminded of death.

"I think all his friends ought to."

"Oh! do you?" said Jimmy, and registered to himself an impression that Ronny Devereux was damned odd about it all.

"Yes. It's a sign of respect."

Jimmy sighed, but gave in.

"Oh! very well," he said, and passed in, setting his teeth a little.

There were white flowers arranged on the coverlet, and the room had been tidied and set to rights.

Jimmy gave one quick, nervous glance at the still, white face. Could that be cherubic, pink Gerry Wade? That still peaceful figure. He shivered.

As he turned to leave the room, his glance swept the mantelshelf and he stopped in astonishment. The alarum clocks had been ranged along it neatly in a row.

He went out sharply. Ronny was waiting for him.

"Looks very peaceful and all that. Rotten luck on him," mumbled Jimmy.

Then he said:

"I say, Ronny, who arranged all those clocks like that in a row?"

"How should I know? One of the servants, I suppose."

"The funny thing is," said Jimmy, "that there are seven of them, not eight. One of them's missing. Did you notice that?"

Ronny made an inaudible sound.

"Seven instead of eight," said Jimmy, frowning. "I wonder why."

CHAPTER IV

A Letter

"Inconsiderate, that's what I call it," said Lord Caterham.

He spoke in a gentle, plaintive voice and seemed pleased with the adjective he had found.

"Yes, distinctly inconsiderate. I often find these self-made men *are* inconsiderate. Very possibly that is why they amass such large fortunes."

He looked mournfully out over his ancestral acres, of which he had to-day regained possession.

His daughter, Lady Eileen Brent, known to her friends and society in general as "Bundle," laughed.

"You'll certainly never amass a large fortune," she observed dryly, "though you didn't do so badly out of old Coote, sticking him for this place. What was he like? Presentable?"

"One of those large men," said Lord Caterham, shuddering slightly, "with a red square face and iron-grey hair. Powerful, you know. What they call a force-ful personality. The kind of a man you'd get if a steam-roller were turned into a human being."

"Rather tiring?" suggested Bundle sympathetically.

"Frightfully tiring, full of all the most depressing virtues like sobriety and punctuality. I don't know which are the worst, powerful personalities or earnest politicians. I do so prefer the cheerful inefficient."

"A cheerful inefficient wouldn't have been able to pay you the price you asked for this old mausoleum," Bundle reminded him.

Lord Caterham winced.

"I wish you wouldn't use that word, Bundle. We were just getting away from the subject."

"I don't see why you're so frightfully sensitive about it," said Bundle. "After all, people must die somewhere."

"They needn't die in my house," said Lord Caterham.

"I don't see why not. Lots of people have. Masses of stuffy old great grandfathers and grandmothers."

"That's different," said Lord Caterham. "Naturally I expect Brents to die here—they don't count. But I do object to strangers. And I especially object to inquests. The thing will become a habit soon. This is the second. You remember all that fuss we had four years ago? For which, by the way, I hold George Lomax entirely to blame."

"And now you're blaming poor old steam-roller Coote. I'm sure he was quite as annoyed about it as anyone."

"Very inconsiderate," said Lord Caterham obstinately. "People who are likely to do that sort of thing oughtn't to be asked to stay. And you may say what you like, Bundle, I don't like inquests. I never have and I never shall."

"Well, this wasn't the same sort of thing as the last one," said Bundle soothingly. "I mean, it wasn't a murder."

"It might have been—from the fuss that thick-head of an inspector made. He's never got over that business four years ago. He thinks every death that takes place here must necessarily be a case of foul play fraught with grave political significance. You've no idea the fuss he made. I've been hearing about it from Tredwell. Tested everything imaginable for fingerprints. And of course they only found the dead man's own. The

clearest case imaginable—though whether it was suicide or accident is another matter."

"I met Gerry Wade once," said Bundle. "He was a
friend of Bill's. You'd have liked him, Father. I never
saw anyone more cheerfully inefficient than he was."

"I don't like anyone who comes and dies in my
house on purpose to annoy me," said Lord Caterham
obstinately.

"But I certainly can't imagine anyone murdering
him," continued Bundle. "The idea's absurd."

"Of course it is," said Lord Caterham. "Or would be
to anyone but an ass like Inspector Raglan."

"I daresay looking for fingerprints made him feel
important," said Bundle soothingly. "Anyway, they
brought it in 'Death by misadventure,' didn't they?"

Lord Caterham acquiesced.

"They had to show some consideration for the sister's feelings."

"Was there a sister? I didn't know."

"Half-sister, I believe. She was much younger. Old
Wade ran away with her mother—he was always doing
that sort of thing. No woman appealed to him unless
she belonged to another man."

"I'm glad there's one bad habit you haven't got,"
said Bundle.

"I've always led a very respectable God-fearing life,"
said Lord Caterham. "It seems extraordinary, considering how little harm I do to anybody, that I can't be let
alone. If only——"

He stopped as Bundle made a sudden excursion
through the window.

"MacDonald," called Bundle in a clear, autocratic
voice.

The emperor approached. Something that might possibly have been taken for a smile of welcome tried to
express itself on his countenance, but the natural gloom
of gardeners dispelled it.

"Your ladyship?" said MacDonald.

"How are you?" said Bundle.

"I'm no verra grand," said MacDonald.

"I wanted to speak to you about the bowling green.

It's shockingly overgrown. Put someone on to it, will you?"

MacDonald shook his head dubiously.

"It would mean taking William from the lower border, m'lady."

"Damn the lower border," said Bundle. "Let him start at once. And, MacDonald——"

"Yes, m'lady?"

"Let's have some of those grapes in from the far house. I know it's the wrong time to cut them because it always is, but I want them all the same. See?"

Bundle re-entered the library.

"Sorry, Father," she said, "I wanted to catch MacDonald. Were you speaking?"

"As a matter of fact I was," said Lord Caterham. "But it doesn't matter. What were you saying to MacDonald?"

"Trying to cure him of thinking he's God Almighty. But that's an impossible task. I expect the Cootes have been bad for him. MacDonald wouldn't care one hoot, or even two hoots for the largest steam-roller that ever was. What's Lady Coote like?"

Lord Caterham considered the question.

"Very like my idea of Mrs. Siddons," he said at last. "I should think she went in a lot for amateur theatricals. I gather she was very upset about the clock business."

"What clock business?"

"Tredwell has just been telling me. It seems the house-party had some joke on. They bought a lot of alarum clocks and hid them about this young Wade's room. And then, of course, the poor chap was dead. Which made the whole thing rather beastly."

Bundle nodded.

"Tredwell told me something else rather odd about the clocks," continued Lord Caterham, who was now quite enjoying himself. "It seems that somebody collected them all and put them in a row on the mantelpiece after the poor fellow was dead."

"Well, why not?" said Bundle.

"I don't see why not myself," said Lord Caterham. "But apparently there was some fuss about it. No one would own up to having done it, you see. All the servants were questioned and swore they hadn't touched the beastly things. In fact, it was rather a mystery. And then the coroner asked questions at the inquest, and you know how difficult it is to explain things to people of that class."

"Perfectly foul," agreed Bundle.

"Of course," said Lord Caterham, "it's very difficult to get the hang of things afterwards. I didn't quite see the point of half the things Tredwell told me. By the way, Bundle, the fellow died in your room."

Bundle made a grimace.

"Why need people die in my room?" she asked with some indignation.

"That's just what I've been saying," said Lord Caterham, in triumph. "Inconsiderate. Everybody's damned inconsiderate nowadays."

"Not that I mind," said Bundle valiantly. "Why should I?"

"I should," said her father. "I should mind very much. I should dream things, you know—spectral hands and clanking chains."

"Well," said Bundle, "Great Aunt Louisa died in *your* bed. I wonder you don't see her spook hovering over you."

"I do sometimes," said Lord Caterham, shuddering. "Especially after lobster."

"Well, thank heavens I'm not superstitious," declared Bundle.

Yet that evening, as she sat in front of her bedroom fire, a slim, pyjamaed figure, she found her thoughts reverting to that cheery, vacuous young man, Gerry Wade. Impossible to believe that anyone so full of the joy of living could deliberately have committed suicide. No, the other solution must be the right one. He had taken a sleeping draught and by a pure mistake had swallowed an overdose. That *was* possible. She did not fancy that Gerry Wade had been overburdened in an intellectual capacity.

Her gaze shifted to the mantelpiece and she began thinking about the story of the clocks. Her maid had been full of that, having just been primed by the second housemaid. She had added a detail which apparently Tredwell had not thought worth while retailing to Lord Caterham, but which had piqued Bundle's curiosity.

Seven clocks had been neatly ranged on the mantelpiece; the last and remaining one had been found on the lawn outside, where it had obviously been thrown from the window.

Bundle puzzled over that point now. It seemed such an extraordinarily purposeless thing to do. She could imagine that one of the maids might have tidied the clocks and then, frightened by the inquisition into the matter, have denied doing so. But surely no maid would have thrown a clock into the garden.

Had Gerry Wade done so when its first sharp summons woke him? But no; that again was impossible. Bundle remembered hearing that his death must have taken place in the early hours of the morning, and he would have been in a comatose condition for some time before that.

Bundle frowned. This business of the clocks *was* curious. She must get hold of Bill Eversleigh. He had been there, she knew.

To think was to act with Bundle. She got up and went over to the writing desk. It was an inlaid affair with a lid that rolled back. Bundle sat down at it, pulled a sheet of notepaper towards her and wrote.

DEAR BILL,—

She paused to pull out the lower part of the desk. It had stuck half-way, as she remembered if often did. Bundle tugged at it impatiently but it did not move. She recalled that on a former occasion an envelope had been pushed back with it and had jammed it for the time being. She took a thin paperknife and slipped it into the narrow crack. She was so far successful that a corner of white paper showed. Bundle caught hold of it and drew it out. It was the first sheet of a letter, somewhat crumpled.

It was the date that first caught Bundle's eye. A big

flourishing date that leaped out from the paper. Sept. 21st.

"September 21st," said Bundle slowly. "Why, surely that was—"

She broke off. Yes, she was sure of it. The 22nd was the day Gerry Wade was found dead. This, then, was a letter he must have been writing on the very evening of the tragedy.

Bundle smoothed it out and read it. It was unfinished.

"MY DARLING LORAINE,——I will be down on Wednesday. Am feeling awfully fit and rather pleased with myself all round. It will be heavenly to see you. Look here, do forget what I said about that Seven Dials business. I thought it was going to be more or less of a joke, but it isn't—anything but. I'm sorry I ever said anything about it—it's not the kind of business kids like you ought to be mixed up in. So forget about it, see?

"Something else I wanted to tell you—but I'm so sleepy I can't keep my eyes open.

"Oh, about Lurcher; I think—"

Here the letter broke off.

Bundle sat frowning. Seven Dials. Where was that? Some rather slummy district of London, she fancied. The words Seven Dials reminded her of something else, but for the moment she couldn't think of what. Instead her attention fastened on two phrases. "Am feeling awfully fit . . ." and "I'm so sleepy I can't keep my eyes open."

That didn't fit in. That didn't fit in at all. For it was that very night that Gerry Wade had taken such a heavy dose of chloral that he never woke again. And if what he had written in that letter was true, why should he have taken it?

Bundle shook her head. She looked round the room and gave a slight shiver. Supposing Gerry Wade were watching her now. In this room he had died . . .

She sat very still. The silence was unbroken save

for the ticking of her little gold clock. That sounded unnaturally loud and important.

Bundle glanced towards the mantelpiece. A vivid picture rose before her mind's eye. The dead man lying on the bed, and seven clocks ticking on the mantelpiece—ticking loudly, ominously . . . ticking . . . ticking . . .

CHAPTER V

The Man in the Road

"FATHER," said Bundle, opening the door of Lord Caterham's special sanctum and putting her head in, "I'm going up to town in the Hispano. I can't stand the monotony down here any longer."

"We only got home yesterday," complained Lord Caterham.

"I know. It seems like a hundred years. I'd forgotten how dull the country could be."

"I don't agree with you," said Lord Caterham. "It's peaceful, that's what it is—peaceful. And extremely comfortable. I appreciate getting back to Tredwell more than I can tell you. That man studies my comfort in the most marvellous manner. Somebody came round only this morning to know if they could hold a tally for girl guides here—"

"A rally," interrupted Bundle.

"Rally or tally—it's all the same. Some silly word meaning nothing whatever. But it would have put me in a very awkward position—having to refuse—in fact, I probably shouldn't have refused. But Tredwell got me out of it. I've forgotten what he said—something damned ingenious which couldn't hurt anybody's feelings and which knocked the idea on the head absolutely."

"Being comfortable isn't enough for me," said Bundle. "I want excitement."

Lord Caterham shuddered.

"Didn't we have enough excitement four years ago?" he demanded plaintively.

"I'm about ready for some more," said Bundle. "Not that I expect I shall find any in town. But at any rate I shan't dislocate my jaw with yawning."

"In my experience," said Lord Caterham, "people who go about looking for trouble usually find it." He yawned. "All the same," he added, "I wouldn't mind running up to town myself."

"Well, come on," said Bundle. "But be quick, because I'm in a hurry."

Lord Caterham, who had begun to rise from his chair, paused.

"Did you say you were in a hurry?" he asked suspiciously.

"In the devil of a hurry," said Bundle.

"That settles it," said Lord Caterham. "I'm not coming. To be driven by you in the Hispano when you're in a hurry—no, it's not fair on any elderly man. I shall stay here."

"Please yourself," said Bundle, and withdrew.

Tredwell took her place.

"The vicar, my lord, is most anxious to see you, some unfortunate controversy having arisen about the status of the Boys' Brigade."

Lord Caterham groaned.

"I rather fancied, my lord, that I had heard you mention at breakfast that you were strolling down to the village this morning to converse with the vicar on the subject."

"Did you tell him so?" asked Lord Caterham eagerly.

"I did, my lord. He departed, if I may say so, hotfoot. I hope I did right, my lord?"

"Of course you did, Tredwell. You are always right. You couldn't go wrong if you tried."

Tredwell smiled benignly and withdrew.

Bundle meanwhile, was sounding the Klaxon impatiently before the lodge gates, while a small child came hastening out with all speed from the lodge, admonishment from her mother following her.

"Make haste, Katie. That be her ladyship in a mortal hurry as always."

It was indeed characteristic of Bundle to be in a hurry, especially when driving a car. She had skill and nerve and was a good driver; had it been otherwise her reckless pace would have ended in disaster more than once.

It was a crisp October day, with a blue sky and a dazzling sun. The sharp tang of the air brought the blood to Bundle's cheeks and filled her with the zest of living.

She had that morning sent Gerald Wade's unfinished letter to Loraine Wade at Deane Priory, enclosing a few explanatory lines. The curious impression it had made upon her was somewhat dimmed in the daylight, yet it still struck her as needing explanation. She intended to get hold of Bill Eversleigh sometime and extract from him fuller details of the house-party which had ended so tragically. In the meantime, it was a lovely morning and she felt particularly well and the Hispano was running like a dream.

Bundle pressed her foot down on the accelerator and the Hispano responded at once. Mile after mile vanished, traffic stops were few and far between and Bundle had a clear stretch of road in front of her.

And then, without any warning whatever, a man reeled out of the hedge and on to the road right in front of the car. To stop in time was out of the question. With all her might Bundle wrenched at the steering wheel and swerved out to the right. The car was nearly in the ditch—nearly, but not quite. It was a dangerous manoeuvre, but it succeeded. Bundle was almost certain that she had missed the man.

She looked back and felt a sickening sensation in the middle of her anatomy. The car had not passed over the man, but nevertheless it must have struck him in passing. He was lying face downwards on the road, and he lay ominously still.

Bundle jumped out and ran back. She had never yet run over anything more important than a stray hen. The fact that the accident was hardly her fault did not weigh with her at the minute. The man had seemed drunk, but drunk or not, she had killed him. She was quite sure she had killed him. Her heart beat sickeningly in great pounding thumps, sounding right up in her ears.

She knelt down by the prone figure and turned him very gingerly over. He neither groaned nor moaned. He was young, she saw, rather a pleasant-faced young man, well dressed and wearing a small toothbrush moustache.

There was no external mark of injury that she could see, but she was quite positive that he was either dead or dying. His eyelids flickered and the eyes half opened. Piteous eyes, brown and suffering, like a dog's. He seemed to be struggling to speak. Bundle bent right over.

"Yes," she said. "Yes?"

There was something he wanted to say, she could see that. Wanted to say badly. And she couldn't help him, couldn't do anything.

At last the words came, a mere sighing breath: *"Seven Dials . . . tell . . ."*

"Yes," said Bundle again. It was a name he was trying to get out—trying with all his failing strength. "Yes. Who am I to tell?"

"Tell . . . Jimmy Thesiger . . ." He got it out at last, and then suddenly, his head fell back and his body went limp.

Bundle sat back on her heels, shivering from head to foot. She could never have imagined that anything so awful could have happened to her. He was dead—and she had killed him.

She tried to pull herself together. What must she do now? A doctor—that was her first thought. It was possible—just possible—that the man might only be unconscious, not dead. Her instinct cried out against the possibility, but she forced herself to act upon it. Somehow or other she must get him into the car and take him to the nearest doctor's. It was a deserted stretch of country road and there was no one to help her.

Bundle, for all her slimness, was strong. She had muscles of whipcord. She brought the Hispano as close as possible, and then, exerting all her strength, she dragged and pulled the inanimate figure into it. It was a horrid business, and one that made her set her teeth, but at last she managed it.

Then she jumped into the driver's seat and started off. A couple of miles brought her into a small town and on inquiry she was quickly directed to the doctor's house.

Dr. Cassell, a kindly, middle-aged man, was startled to come into his surgery and find a girl there who was evidently on the verge of collapse.

Bundle spoke abruptly.

"I—I think I've killed a man. I ran over him. I brought him along in the car. He's outside now. I—I was driving too fast, I suppose. I've always driven too fast."

The doctor cast a practised glance over her. He stepped over to a shelf and poured something into a glass. He brought it over to her.

"Drink this down," he said, "and you'll feel better. You've had a shock."

Bundle drank obediently and a tinge of colour came into her pallid face. The doctor nodded approvingly.

"That's right. Now I want you to sit quietly here. I'll go out and attend to things. After I've made sure there's nothing to be done for the poor fellow, I'll come back and we'll talk about it."

He was away some time. Bundle watched the clock on the mantelpiece. Five minutes, ten minutes, a quarter of an hour, twenty minutes—would he never come?

Then the door opened and Dr. Cassell reappeared. He looked different—Bundle noticed that at once—grimmer and at the same time more alert. There was something else in his manner that she did not quite understand, a suggestion of repressed excitement.

"Now then, young lady," he said, "let's have this out. You ran over this man, you say. Tell me just how the accident happened?"

Bundle explained to the best of her ability. The doctor followed her narrative with keen attention.

"Just so; the car didn't pass over his body?"

"No. In fact, I thought I'd missed him altogether."

"He was reeling, you say?"

"Yes, I thought he was drunk."

"And he came from the hedge?"

"There was a gate just there, I think. He must have come through the gate."

The doctor nodded, then he leaned back in his chair and removed his pince-nez.

"I've no doubt at all," he said, "that you're a very reckless driver, and that you'll probably run over some poor fellow and do for him one of these days—but you haven't done it this time."

"But—"

"The car never touched him. *This man was shot.*"

CHAPTER VI

Seven Dials Again

BUNDLE stared at him. And very slowly the world, which for the last three quarters of an hour had been upside down, shifted till it stood once more the right way up. It was quite two minutes before Bundle spoke, but when she did it was no longer the panic-stricken girl but the real Bundle, cool, efficient, and logical.

"How could he be shot?" she said.

"I don't know how he could," said the doctor dryly. "But he was. He's got a rifle bullet in him all right. He bled internally, that's why you didn't notice anything."

Bundle nodded.

"The question is," the doctor continued, "Who shot him? You saw nobody about?"

Bundle shook her head.

"It's odd," said the doctor. "If it was an accident, you'd expect the fellow who did it would come running to the rescue—unless just possibly he didn't know what he'd done."

"There was no one about," said Bundle. "On the road, that is."

"It seems to me," said the doctor, "that the poor lad must have been running—the bullet got him just as he passed through the gate and he came reeling on to the road in consequence. You didn't hear a shot?"

Bundle shook her head.

"But I probably shouldn't anyway," she said, "with the noise of the car."

"Just so. He didn't say anything before he died?"

"He muttered a few words."

"Nothing to throw light on the tragedy?"

"No. He wanted something—I don't know what—told to a friend of his. Oh! yes, and he mentioned Seven Dials."

"H'm," said Doctor Cassell. "Not a likely neighborhood for one of his class. Perhaps his assailant came from there. Well, we needn't worry about that now. You can leave it in my hands. I'll notify the police. You must, of course, leave your name and address, as the police are sure to want to question you. In fact, perhaps you'd better come round to the police station with me now. They might say I ought to have detained you."

They went together in Bundle's car. The police inspector was a slow-speaking man. He was somewhat overawed by Bundle's name and address when she gave it to him, and he took down her statement with great care.

"Lads!" he said. "That's what it is. Lads practising! Cruel stupid, them young varmints are. Always loosing off at birds with no consideration for anyone as may be the other side of a hedge."

The doctor thought it a most unlikely solution, but he realized that the case would soon be in abler hands and it did not seem worth while to make objections.

"Name of deceased?" asked the sergeant, moistening his pencil.

"He had a cardcase on him. He appears to have

been a Mr. Ronald Devereux, with an address in the Albany."

Bundle frowned. The name Ronald Devereux awoke some chord of remembrance. She was sure she had heard it before.

It was not until she was half-way back to Chimneys in the car that it came to her. Of course! Ronny Devereux. Bill's friend in the Foreign Office. He and Bill and—yes—Gerald Wade.

As this last realization came to her, Bundle nearly went into the hedge. First Gerald Wade—then Ronny Devereux. Gerry Wade's death might have been natural —the result of carelessness—but Ronny Devereux's surely bore a more sinister interpretation.

And then Bundle remembered something else. Seven Dials! When the dying man had said it, it had seemed vaguely familiar. Now she knew why. Gerald Wade had mentioned Seven Dials in that last letter of his written to his sister on the night before his death. And that again connected up with something else that escaped her.

Thinking all these things over, Bundle had slowed down to such a sober pace that nobody would have recognized her. She drove the car round to the garage and went in search of her father.

Lord Caterham was happily reading a catalogue of a forthcoming sale of rare editions and was immeasurably astonished to see Bundle.

"Even you," he said, "can't have been to London and back in this time."

"I haven't been to London," said Bundle. "I ran over a man."

"What?"

"Only I didn't really. He was shot."

"How could he have been?"

"I don't know how he could have been, but he was."

"But why did you shoot him?"

"*I* didn't shoot him."

"You shouldn't shoot people," said Lord Caterham

in a tone of mild remonstrance. "You shouldn't really. I daresay some of them richly deserve it—but all the same it will lead to trouble."

"I tell you I didn't shoot him."

"Well, who did?"

"Nobody knows," said Bundle.

"Nonsense," said Lord Caterham. "A man can't be shot and run over without anyone having done it."

"He wasn't run over," said Bundle.

"I thought you said he was."

"I said I thought I had."

"A tyre burst, I suppose," said Lord Caterham. "That does sound like a shot. It says so in detective stories."

"You really are perfectly impossible, Father. You don't seem to have the brains of a rabbit."

"Not at all," said Lord Caterham. "You come in with a wildly impossible tale about men being run over and shot and I don't know what, and then you expect me to know all about it by magic."

Bundle sighed wearily.

"Just attend," she said. "I'll tell you all about it in words of one syllable."

"There," she said when she had concluded. "Now have you got it?"

"Of course. I understand perfectly now. I can make allowances for your being a little upset, my dear. I was not far wrong when I remarked to you before starting out that people looking for trouble usually found it. I am thankful," finished Lord Caterham with a slight shiver, "that I stayed quietly here."

He picked up the catalogue again.

"Father, where is Seven Dials?"

"In the East End somewhere, I fancy. I have frequently observed buses going there—or do I mean Seven Sisters? I have never been there myself. I am thankful to say. Just as well, because I don't fancy it is the sort of spot I should like. And yet, curiously enough, I seem to have heard of it in some connection just lately."

"You don't know a Jimmy Thesiger, do you?"

Lord Caterham was now engrossed in his catalogue once more. He had made an effort to be intelligent on the subject of Seven Dials. This time he made hardly any effort at all.

"Thesiger," he murmured vaguely. "Thesiger. One of the Yorkshire Thesigers?"

"That's what I'm asking you. Do attend, Father. This is important."

Lord Caterham made a desperate effort to look intelligent without really having to give his mind to the matter.

"There *are* some Yorkshire Thesigers," he said earnestly. "And unless I am mistaken some Devonshire Thesigers also. Your Great Aunt Selina married a Thesiger."

"What good is that to me?" cried Bundle.

Lord Caterham chuckled.

"It was very little good to her, if I remember rightly."

"You're impossible," said Bundle, rising. "I shall have to get hold of Bill."

"Do, dear," said her father absently as he turned a page. "Certainly. By all means. Quite so."

Bundle rose to her feet with an impatient sigh.

"I wish I could remember what that letter said," she murmured more to herself than aloud. "I didn't read it very carefully. Something about a joke—that the Seven Dials business wasn't a joke."

Lord Caterham emerged suddenly from his catalogue.

"Seven Dials?" he said. "Of course. I've got it now."

"Got what?"

"I know why it sounded so familiar. George Lomax has been over. Tredwell failed for once and let him in. He was on his way up to town. It seems he's having some political party at the Abbey next week and he got a warning letter."

"What do you mean by a warning letter?"

"Well, I don't really know. He didn't go into details. I gather it said 'Beware' and 'Trouble is at hand,' and all those sort of things. But anyway it was written from Seven Dials, I distinctly remember his saying so.

He was going up to town to consult Scotland Yard about it. You know George?"

Bundle nodded. She was well acquainted with that public-spirited Cabinet Minister, George Lomax, His Majesty's permanent Under Secretary of State for Foreign Affairs, who was shunned by many because of his inveterate habit of quoting from his public speeches in private. In allusion to his bulging eyeballs, he was known to many—Bill Eversleigh among others—as Codders.

"Tell me," she said, "was Codders interested at all in Gerald Wade's death?"

"Not that I ever heard of. He may have been, of course."

Bundle said nothing for some minutes. She was busily engaged in trying to remember the exact wording of the letter she had sent on to Loraine Wade, and at the same time she was trying to picture the girl to whom it had been written. What sort of a girl was this to whom, apparently Gerald Wade was so devoted? The more she thought over it, the more it seemed to her that it was an unusual letter for a brother to write.

"Did you say the Wade girl was Gerry's half-sister?" she asked suddenly.

"Well, of course, strictly speaking, I suppose she isn't—wasn't, I mean—his sister at all."

"But her name's Wade?"

"Not really. She wasn't old Wade's child. As I was saying, he ran away with his second wife, who was married to a perfect blackguard. I suppose the Courts gave the rascally husband the custody of the child, but he certainly didn't avail himself of the privilege. Old Wade got very fond of the child and insisted that she should be called by his name."

"I see," said Bundle. "That explains it."

"Explains what?"

"Something that puzzled me about that letter."

"She's rather a pretty girl, I believe," said Lord Caterham. "Or so I've heard."

Bundle went upstairs thoughtfully. She had several

objects in view. First she must find this Jimmy Thesiger. Bill, perhaps, would be helpful there. Ronny Devereux had been a friend of Bill's. If Jimmy Thesiger was a friend of Ronny's, the chances were that Bill would know him too. Then there was the girl, Loraine Wade. It was possible that she could throw some light on the problem of Seven Dials. Evidently Gerry Wade had said something to her about it. His anxiety that she should forget the fact had a sinister suggestion.

CHAPTER VII

Bundle Pays a Call

GETTING hold of Bill presented few difficulties. Bundle motored up to town on the following morning—this time without adventures by the way—and rang him up. Bill responded with alacrity, and made various suggestions as to lunch, tea, dinner and dancing. All of which suggestions Bundle turned down as made.

"But in a day or two, I'll come and frivol with you, Bill. But for the moment I'm up on business."

"Oh," said Bill. "What a beastly bore."

"It's not that kind," said Bundle. "It's anything but boring. Bill, do you know anyone called Jimmy Thesiger?"

"Of course. So do you."

"No, I don't," said Bundle.

"Yes, you do. You must. Everyone knows old Jimmy."

"Sorry," said Bundle. "Just for once I don't seem to be everyone."

"Oh! but you must know Jimmy—pink-faced chap. Looks a bit of an ass. But really he's got as many brains as I have."

"You don't say so," said Bundle. "He must feel a bit top heavy when he walks about."

"Was that meant for sarcasm?"

"It was a feeble effort at it. What does Jimmy Thesiger do?"

"How do you mean, what does he do?"

"Does being at the Foreign Office prevent you from understanding your native language?"

"Oh! I see, you mean, has he got a job? No, he just tools around. Why should he do anything?"

"In fact, more money than brains?"

"Oh! I wouldn't say that. I told you just now that he had more brains than you'd think."

Bundle was silent. She was feeling more and more doubtful. This gilded youth did not sound a very promising ally. And yet it was his name that had come first to the dying man's lips. Bill's voice chimed in suddenly with singular appropriateness.

"Ronny always thought a lot of his brains. You know, Ronny Devereux. Thesiger was his greatest pal."

"Ronny—"

Bundle stopped, undecided. Clearly Bill knew nothing of the other's death. It occurred to Bundle for the first time that it was odd the morning papers had contained nothing of the tragedy. Surely it was the kind of spicy item of news that would never be passed over. There could be one explanation, and one explanation only. The police, for reasons of their own, were keeping the matter quiet.

Bill's voice was continuing.

"I haven't seen Ronny for an age—not since that weekend down at your place. You know, when poor old Gerry Wade passed out."

He paused and then went on.

"Rather a foul business that altogether. I expect you've heard about it. I say, Bundle—are you there still?"

"Of course I'm here."

"Well, you haven't said anything for an age. I began to think that you had gone away."

"No, I was just thinking over something."

Should she tell Bill of Ronny's death? She decided against it—it was not the sort of thing to be said over the telephone. But soon, very soon, she must have a meeting with Bill. In the meantime—

"Bill?"

"Hullo."

"I might dine with you to-morrow night."

"Good, and we'll dance afterwards. I've got a lot to talk to you about. As a matter of fact I've been rather hard hit—the foulest luck—"

"Well, tell me about it to-morrow," said Bundle, cutting him short rather unkindly. "In the meantime, what is Jimmy Thesiger's address?"

"Jimmy Thesiger?"

"That's what I said."

"He's got rooms in Jermyn Street—do I mean Jermyn Street or the other one?"

"Bring that class A brain to bear upon it."

"Yes, Jermyn Street. Wait a bit and I'll give you the number."

There was a pause.

"Are you there still?"

"I'm always there."

"Well, one never knows with these dashed telephones. The number is 103. Got it?"

"103. Thank you, Bill."

"Yes, but I say—what do you want it for? You said you didn't know him."

"I don't, but I shall in half an hour."

"You're going round to his rooms?"

"Quite right, Sherlock."

"Yes, but I say—well, for one thing he won't be up."

"Won't be up?"

"I shouldn't think so. I mean, who would if they hadn't got to? Look at it that way. You've no idea what an effort it is for me to get here at eleven every morning, and the fuss Codders makes if I'm behind time is simply appalling. You haven't the least idea, Bundle, what a dog's life this is—"

"You shall tell me all about it to-morrow night," said Bundle hastily.

She slammed down the receiver and took stock of the situation. First she glanced at the clock. It was five and twenty minutes to twelve. Despite Bill's knowledge of his friend's habits, she inclined to the belief that Mr. Thesiger would by now be in a fit state to receive visitors. She took a taxi to 103 Jermyn Street.

The door was opened by a perfect example of the retired gentleman's gentleman. His face, expressionless and polite, was such a face as may be found by the score in that particular district of London.

"Will you come this way, madam?"

He ushered her upstairs into an extremely comfortable sitting-room containing leather covered arm-chairs of immense dimensions. Sunk in one of those monstrosities was another girl, rather younger than Bundle. A small, fair girl, dressed in black.

"What name shall I say, madam?"

"I won't give any name," said Bundle. "I just want to see Mr. Thesiger on important business."

The grave gentleman bowed and withdrew, shutting the door noiselessly behind him.

There was a pause.

"It's a nice morning," said the fair girl timidly.

"It's an awfully nice morning," agreed Bundle.

There was another pause.

"I motored up from the country this morning," said Bundle, plunging once more into speech. "And I thought it was going to be one of those foul fogs. But it wasn't."

"No," said the other girl. "It wasn't." And she added: "I've come up from the country too."

Bundle eyed her more attentively. She had been slightly annoyed at finding the other there. Bundle belonged to the energetic order of people who like "to get on with it," and she foresaw that the second visitor would have to be disposed of and got rid of before she could broach her own business. It was not a topic she could introduce before a stranger.

Now, as she looked more closely, an extraordinary idea rose in her brain. Could it be? Yes, the girl was in deep mourning; her black, silk-clad ankles showed that. It was a long shot, but Bundle was convinced that her idea was right. She drew a long breath.

"Look here," she said. "Are you by any chance Loraine Wade?"

Loraine's eyes opened wide.

"Yes, I am. How clever of you to know. We've never met, have we?"

Bundle shook her head.

"I wrote to you yesterday, though. I'm Bundle Brent."

"It was so very kind of you to send me Gerry's letter," said Loraine. "I've written to thank you. I never expected to see you here."

"I'll tell you why I'm here," said Bundle. "Did you know Ronny Devereux?"

Loraine nodded.

"He came over the day that Gerry—you know. And he's been to see me two or three times since. He was one of Gerry's greatest friends."

"I know. Well—he's dead."

Loraine's lips parted in surprise.

"Dead! But he always seemed so fit."

Bundle narrated the events of the preceding day as briefly as possible. A look of fear and horror came into Loraine's face.

"Then it *is* true. It *is* true."

"What's true?"

"What I've thought—what I've been thinking all these weeks. Gerald didn't die a natural death. He was killed."

"You've thought that, have you?"

"Yes. Gerry would never have taken things to make him sleep." She gave the little ghost of a laugh. "He slept much too well to need them. I always thought it queer. And *he* thought so too—I know he did."

"Who?"

"Ronny. And now this happens. Now he's killed too." She paused and then went on: "That's what I came for to-day. That letter of Gerry's you sent me— as soon as I read it, I tried to get hold of Ronny, but they said he was away. So I thought I'd come and see Jimmy—he was Ronny's other great friend. I thought perhaps he'd tell me what I ought to do."

"You mean—" Bundle paused. "About—Seven Dials."

Loraine nodded.

"You see—" she began.

But at that moment Jimmy Thesiger entered the room.

CHAPTER VIII

Visitors for Jimmy

WE must at this point go back to some twenty minutes earlier. To a moment when Jimmy Thesiger, emerging from the mists of sleep, was conscious of a familiar voice speaking unfamiliar words.

His sleep-ridden brain tried for a moment to cope with the situation, but failed. He yawned and rolled over again.

"A young lady, sir, has called to see you."

The voice was implacable. So prepared was it to go on repeating the statement indefinitely that Jimmy resigned himself to the inevitable. He opened his eyes and blinked.

"Eh, Stevens?" he said. "Say that again."

"A young lady, sir, has called to see you."

"Oh!" Jimmy strove to grasp the situation. "Why?"

"I couldn't say, sir."

"No, I suppose not. No," he thought it over. "I suppose you couldn't."

Stevens swooped down upon a tray by the bedside.

"I will bring you some fresh tea, sir. This is cold."

"You think that I ought to get up and—er—see the lady?"

Stevens made no reply, but he held his back very stiff and Jimmy read the signs correctly.

"Oh! very well," he said. "I suppose I'd better. She didn't give her name?"

"No, sir."

"H'm. She couldn't be by any possible chance my

Aunt Jemima, could she? Because if so, I'm damned if I'm going to get up."

"The lady, sir, could not possibly be anyone's aunt, I should say, unless the youngest of a large family."

"Aha," said Jimmy. "Young and lovely. Is she—what kind is she?"

"The young lady, sir, is most undoubtedly strictly *comme il faut,* if I may use the expression."

"You may use it," said Jimmy graciously. "Your French pronunciation, Stevens, if I may say so, is very good. Much better than mine."

"I am gratified to hear it, sir. I have lately been taking a correspondence course in French."

"Have you really? You're a wonderful chap, Stevens."

Stevens smiled in a superior fashion and left the room. Jimmy lay trying to recall the names of any young and lovely girls strictly *comme il faut* who might be likely to come and call upon him.

Stevens re-entered with fresh tea, and as Jimmy sipped it he felt a pleasurable curiosity.

"You've given her the paper and all that, I hope, Stevens," he said.

"I supplied her with the *Morning Post* and *Punch,* sir."

A ring at the bell took him away. In a few minutes he returned.

"Another young lady, sir."

"What?"

Jimmy clutched his head.

"Another young lady; she declines to give her name, sir, but says her business is important."

Jimmy stared at him.

"This is damned odd, Stevens. Damned odd. Look here, what time did I come home last night?"

"Just upon five o'clock, sir."

"And was I—er—how was I?"

"Just a little cheerful, sir—nothing more. Inclined to sing 'Rule Britannia.' "

"What an extraordinary thing," said Jimmy. " 'Rule Britannia,' eh? I cannot imagine myself in a sober state ever singing 'Rule Britannia.' Some latent patriotism must have emerged under the stimulus of—er—just a couple too many. I was celebrating at the 'Mustard and Cress,' I remember. Not nearly such an innocent spot as it sounds, Stevens." He paused. "I was wondering—"

"Yes, sir?"

"I was wondering whether under the aforementioned stimulus I had put an advertisement in a newspaper asking for a nursery governess or something of that sort."

Stevens coughed.

"*Two* girls turning up. It looks odd. I shall eschew the 'Mustard and Cress' in future. That's a good word, Stevens—*eschew*—I met it in a cross word the other day and took a fancy to it."

Whilst he was talking Jimmy was rapidly apparelling himself. At the end of ten minutes he was ready to face his unknown guests. As he opened the door of his sitting-room the first person he saw was a dark, slim girl who was totally unknown to him. She was standing by the mantelpiece, leaning against it. Then his glance went on to the big leather covered arm-chair, and his heart missed a beat. Loraine!

It was she who rose and spoke first a little nervously.

"You must be very surprised to see me. But I had to come. I'll explain in a minute. This is Lady Eileen Brent."

"Bundle—that's what I'm usually known as. You've probably heard of me from Bill Eversleigh."

"Oh! rather, of course I have," said Jimmy, endeavouring to cope with the situation. "I say, do sit down and let's have a cocktail or something."

But both girls declined.

"As a matter of fact," continued Jimmy, "I'm only just out of bed."

"That's what Bill said," remarked Bundle. "I told him I was coming round to see you, and he said you wouldn't be up."

"Well, I'm up now," said Jimmy encouragingly.

"It's about Gerry," said Loraine. "And now about Ronny—"

"What do you mean by 'and now about Ronny'?"

"He was shot yesterday."

"What?" cried Jimmy.

Bundle told her story for the second time. Jimmy listened like a man in a dream.

"Old Ronny—shot," he murmured. "What *is* this damned business?"

He sat down on the edge of a chair, thinking for a minute or two, and then spoke in a quiet, level voice.

"There's something I think I ought to tell you."

"Yes," said Bundle encouragingly.

"It was on the day Gerry Wade died. On the way over to break the news to *you*"—he nodded at Loraine —"in the car Ronny said something to me. That is to say, he started to tell me something. There was something he wanted to tell me, and he began about it, and then he said he was bound by a promise and couldn't go on."

"Bound by a promise," said Loraine thoughtfully.

"That's what he said. Naturally I didn't press him after that. But he was odd—darned odd—all through. I got the impression then that he suspected—well, foul play. I thought he'd tell the doctor so. But no, not even a hint. So I thought I'd been mistaken. And afterwards, with the evidence and all—well, it seemed such a very clear case. I thought my suspicions had been all bosh."

"But you think Ronny still suspected?" asked Bundle.

Jimmy nodded.

"That's what I think now. Why, none of us have seen anything of him since. I believe he was playing a lone hand—trying to find out the truth about Gerry's death, and what's more, I believe he *did* find out. That's why the devils shot him. And then he tried to send word to me, but could only get out those two words."

"Seven Dials," said Bundle, and shivered a little.

"Seven Dials," said Jimmy gravely. "At any rate we've got that to go on with."

Bundle turned to Loraine.

"You were just going to tell me——"

"Oh! yes. First, about the letter." She spoke to Jimmy.

"Gerry left a letter. Lady Eileen——"

"Bundle."

"Bundle found it." She explained the circumstances in a few words.

Jimmy listened, keenly interested. This was the first he had heard of the letter. Loraine took it from her bag and handed it to him. He read it, then looked across at her.

"This is where you can help us. What was it Gerry wanted you to forget?"

Loraine's brows wrinkled a little in perplexity.

"It's so hard to remember exactly now. I opened a letter of Gerry's by mistake. It was written on cheap sort of paper, I remember, and very illiterate handwriting. It had some address in Seven Dials at the head of it. I realized it wasn't for me, so I put it back in the envelope without reading it."

"Sure?" asked Jimmy very gently.

Loraine laughed for the first time.

"I know what you think, and I admit that women *are* curious. But, you see, this didn't even look interesting. It was a kind of list of names and dates."

"Names and dates," said Jimmy thoughtfully.

"Gerry didn't seem to mind much," continued Loraine. "He laughed. He asked me if I had ever heard of the Mafia, and then said it would be queer if a society like the Mafia started in England—but that that kind of secret society didn't take on much with English people. 'Our criminals,' he said, 'haven't got a picturesque imagination.' "

Jimmy pursed up his lips into a whistle.

"I'm beginning to see," he said. "Seven Dials must be the headquarters of some secret society. As he says in his letter to you, he thought it rather a joke to start with. But evidently it wasn't a joke—he says as much. And there's something else: his anxiety that you should forget what he'd told you. There can be only one reason for that—if that society suspected that you had any knowledge of its activity, you too would be in danger. Gerald realized the peril, and he was terribly anxious— for you."

He stopped, then he went on quietly:

"I rather fancy that we're all going to be in danger— if we go on with this."

"If—?" cried Bundle indignantly.

"I'm talking to you two. It's different for me. I was poor old Ronny's pal." He looked at Bundle. "You've done your bit. You've delivered the message he sent me. No; for God's sake keep out of it, you and Loraine."

Bundle looked questioningly at the other girl. Her own mind was definitely made up, but she gave no indication of it just then. She had no wish to push Loraine Wade into a dangerous undertaking. But Loraine's small face was alight at once with indignation.

"You say that! Do you think for one minute I'd be contented to keep out of it—when they killed Gerry —my own dear Gerry, the best and dearest and kindest brother any girl ever had. The only person belonging to me I had in the whole world!"

Jimmy cleared his throat uncomfortably. Loraine, he thought, was wonderful; simply wonderful.

"Look here," he said awkwardly, "you mustn't say that. About being alone in the world—all that rot. You've got lots of friends—only too glad to do what they can. See what I mean?"

It is possible that Loraine did, for she suddenly blushed, and to cover her confusion began to talk nervously.

"That's settled," she said. "I'm going to help. Nobody's going to stop me."

"And so am I, of course," said Bundle.

They both looked at Jimmy.

"Yes," he said slowly. "Yes, quite so."

They looked at him inquiringly.

"I was just wondering," said Jimmy, "how we were going to begin."

CHAPTER IX

Plans

JIMMY's words lifted the discussion at once into a more practical sphere.

"All things considered," he said, "we haven't got much to go on. In fact, just the words Seven Dials. As a matter of fact I don't even know exactly where Seven Dials is. But, anyway, we can't very well comb out the whole of that district, house by house."

"We could," said Bundle.

"Well, perhaps we could eventually—though I'm not so sure. I imagine it's a well-populated area. But it wouldn't be very subtle."

The word reminded him of the girl Socks and he smiled.

"Then, of course, there's the part of the country where Ronny was shot. We could nose around there. But the police are probably doing everything we could do, and doing it much better."

"What I like about you," said Bundle sarcastically, "is your cheerful and optimistic disposition."

"Never mind her, Jimmy," said Loraine softly. "Go on."

"Don't be so impatient," said Jimmy to Bundle. "All the best sleuths approach a case this way, by eliminating unnecessary and unprofitable investigation. I'm coming now to the third alternative—Gerald's death. Now that we know it was murder—by the way, you do both believe that, don't you?"

"Yes," said Loraine.

"Yes," said Bundle.

"Good. So do I. Well, it seems to me that there we do stand some faint chance. After all, if Gerry didn't take the chloral himself, someone must have got into his room and put it there—dissolved it in the glass of water, so that when he woke up he drank it off. And of

54

course left the empty box or bottle or whatever it was. You agree with that?"

"Ye-es," said Bundle slowly. "But—"

"Wait. And that someone must have been in the house at the time. It couldn't very well have been some-one from outside."

"No," agreed Bundle, more readily this time.

"Very well. Now, that narrows down things consider-ably. To begin with, I suppose a good many of the servants are family ones—they're your lot, I mean."

"Yes," said Bundle. "Practically all the staff stayed when we let it. All the principal ones are there still—of course there have been changes among the under ser-vants."

"Exactly—that's what I am getting at. *You*,"—he addressed Bundle—"must go into all that. Find out when new servants were engaged—what about footmen, for instance?"

"One of the footmen is new. John, his name is."

"Well, make inquiries about John. And about any others who have only come recently."

"I suppose," said Bundle slowly, "it must have been a servant. It couldn't have been one of the guests?"

"I don't see how that's possible."

"Who were there exactly?"

"Well, there were three girls—Nancy and Helen and Socks—"

"Socks Daventry? I know her."

"May have been. Girl who was always saying things were subtle."

"That's Socks all right. Subtle is one of her words."

"And then there were Gerry Wade and me and Bill Eversleigh and Ronny. And, of course, Sir Oswald and Lady Coote. Oh! and Pongo."

"Who's Pongo?"

"Chap called Bateman—secretary to old Coote. Solemn sort of cove but very conscientious. I was at school with him."

"There doesn't seem anything very suspicious there," remarked Loraine.

"No, there doesn't," said Bundle. "As you say, we'll

have to look amongst the servants. By the way, you
don't suppose that clock being thrown out of the window had anything to do with it."

"A clock thrown out of the window," said Jimmy,
staring. It was the first he had heard of it.

"I can't see how it can have anything to do with it,"
said Bundle. "But it's odd somehow. There seems no
sense in it."

"I remember," said Jimmy slowly. "I went in to—to
see poor old Gerry, and there were the clocks ranged
along the mantelpiece. I remember noticing there were
only seven—not eight."

He gave a sudden shiver and explained himself apologetically.

"Sorry. But somehow those clocks have always given
me the shivers. I dream of them sometimes. I'd hate
to go into that room in the dark and see them there in a
row."

"You wouldn't be able to see them if it was dark,"
said Bundle practically. "Not unless they had luminous
dials—Oh!" She gave a sudden gasp and the colour
rushed into her cheeks. "Don't you see? *Seven Dials!*"

The others looked at her doubtfully, but she insisted
with increasing vehemence.

"It must be. It can't be a coincidence."

There was a pause.

"You may be right," said Jimmy Thesiger at last.
"It's—it's dashed odd."

Bundle started questioning him eagerly.

"Who bought the clocks?"

"All of us."

"Who thought of them?"

"All of us."

"Nonsense, somebody must have thought of them
first."

"It didn't happen that way. We were discussing what
we could do to get Gerry up, and Pongo said an alarum
clock, and somebody said one would be no good, and
somebody else—Bill Eversleigh, I think—said why not
get a dozen. And we all said good egg and hoofed off
to get them. We got one each and an extra one for

Pongo and one for Lady Coote—just out of the generosity of our hearts. There was nothing premeditated about it—it just happened."

Bundle was silenced, but not convinced.

Jimmy proceeded to sum up methodically.

"I think we can say we're sure of certain facts. There's a secret society, with points of resemblance to the Mafia, in existence. Gerry Wade came to know about it. At first he treated it as rather a joke—as an absurdity, shall we say. He couldn't believe in its being really dangerous. But later something happened to convince him, and then he got the wind up in earnest. I rather fancy he must have said something to Ronny Devereux about it. Anyway, when he was put out of the way, Ronny suspected, and he must have known enough to get on the same track himself. The unfortunate thing is that we've got to start quite from the outer darkness. We haven't got the knowledge the other two had."

"Perhaps that's an advantage," said Loraine coolly. "They won't suspect us and therefore they won't be trying to put us out of the way."

"I wish I felt sure about that," said Jimmy in a worried voice. "You know, Loraine, old Gerry himself wanted you to keep out of it. Don't you think you could—"

"No, I couldn't," said Loraine. "Don't let's start discussing that again. It's only a waste of time."

At the mention of the word time, Jimmy's eyes rose to the clock and he uttered an exclamation of astonishment. He rose and opened the door.

"Stevens."

"Yes, sir?"

"What about a spot of lunch, Stevens? Could it be managed?"

"I anticipated that it would be required, sir. Mrs. Stevens has made preparations accordingly."

"That's a wonderful man," said Jimmy, as he returned, heaving a sigh of relief. "Brain, you know. Sheer brain. He takes correspondence courses. I sometimes wonder if they'd do any good to me."

"Don't be silly," said Loraine.

Stevens opened the door and proceeded to bring in a most recherché meal. An omelette was followed by quails and the very lightest things in soufflés.

"Why are men so happy when they're single," said Loraine tragically. "Why are they so much better looked after by other people than by us?"

"Oh! but that's rot, you know," said Jimmy. "I mean, they're not. How could they be. I often think——"

He stammered and stopped. Loraine blushed again.

Suddenly Bundle let out a whoop and both the others started violently.

"Idiot," said Bundle. "Imbecile. Me, I mean. I knew there was something I'd forgotten."

"What?"

"You know Codders—George Lomax, I mean?"

"I've heard of him a good deal," said Jimmy. "From Bill and Ronny, you know."

"Well, Codders is giving some sort of a dry party next week—and he's had a warning letter from Seven Dials."

"What?" cried Jimmy excitedly, leaning forward. "You can't mean it?"

"Yes, I do. He told Father about it. Now what do you think that points to?"

Jimmy leant back in his chair. He thought rapidly and carefully. At last he spoke. His speech was brief and to the point.

"Something's going to happen at that party," he said.

"That's what I think," said Bundle.

"It all fits in," said Jimmy almost dreamily.

He turned to Loraine.

"How old were you when the war was on?" he asked unexpectedly.

"Nine—no, eight."

"And Gerry, I suppose, was about twenty. Most lads of twenty fought in the war. Gerry didn't."

"No," said Loraine, after thinking a minute or two. "No, Gerry wasn't a soldier. I don't know why."

"I can tell you why," said Jimmy. "Or at least I can make a very shrewd guess. He was out of England from 1915 to 1918. I've taken the trouble to find that out. And nobody seems to know exactly where he was. I think he was in Germany."

The colour rose in Loraine's cheeks. She looked at Jimmy with admiration.

"How clever of you."

"He spoke German well, didn't he?"

"Oh! yes, like a native."

"I'm sure I'm right. Listen, you two. Gerry Wade was at the Foreign Office. He appeared to be the same sort of amiable idiot—excuse the term, but you know what I mean—as Bill Eversleigh and Ronny Devereux. A purely ornamental excrescence. But in reality he was something quite different. I think Gerry Wade was the real thing. Our secret service is suppose to be the best in the world. I think Gerry Wade was pretty high up in that service. And that explains everything! I remember saying idly that last evening at Chimneys that Gerry couldn't be quite such an ass as he made himself out to be."

"And if you're right?" said Bundle, practical as ever.

"Then the thing's bigger than we thought. This Seven Dials business isn't merely criminal—it's international. One thing's certain, somebody has got to be at this house-party of Lomax's."

Bundle made a slight grimace.

"I know George well—but he doesn't like me. He'd never think of asking me to a serious gathering. All the same, I might—"

She remained a moment lost in thought.

"Do you think *I* could work it through Bill?" asked Jimmy. "He's bound to be there as Codders's right hand man. He might bring me along somehow or other."

"I don't see why not," said Bundle. "You'll have to prime Bill and make him say the right things. He's incapable of thinking of them for himself."

"What do you suggest?" asked Jimmy humbly.

"Oh! it's quite easy. Bill describes you as a rich young man—interested in politics, anxious to stand for Parliament. George will fall at once. You know what these political parties are: always looking for new, rich young men. The richer Bill says you are, the easier it will be to manage."

"Short of being described as Rothschild, I don't mind," said Jimmy.

"Then I think that's practically settled. I'm dining with Bill to-morrow night, and I'll get a list of who is to be there. That will be useful."

"I'm sorry you can't be there," said Jimmy. "But on the whole I think it's all for the best."

"I'm not so sure I shan't be there," said Bundle. "Codders hates me like poison—but there are other ways."

She became meditative.

"And what about me?" asked Loraine in a small, meek voice.

"You're not on in this act," said Jimmy instantly. "See? After all, we've got to have someone outside to—er—"

"To what?" said Loraine.

Jimmy decided not to pursue this tack. He appealed to Bundle.

"Look here," he said. "Loraine must keep out of this, mustn't she?"

"I certainly think she'd better."

"Next time," said Jimmy kindly.

"And suppose there isn't a next time," said Loraine.

"Oh! there probably will be. Not a doubt of it."

"I see. I'm just to go home and—wait."

"That's it," said Jimmy, with every appearance of relief. "I thought you'd understand."

"You see," explained Bundle, "three of us forcing our way in might look rather suspicious. And you would be particularly difficult. You do see that, don't you?"

"Oh! yes," said Loraine.

"Then it's settled—you do nothing," said Jimmy.

"I do nothing," said Loraine meekly.

Bundle looked at her in sudden suspicion. The tameness with which Loraine was taking it seemed hardly natural. Loraine looked at her. Her eyes were blue and guileless. They met Bundle's without a quiver even of

the lashes. Bundle was only partly satisfied. She found
the meekness of Loraine Wade's highly suspicious.

CHAPTER X

Bundle Visits Scotland Yard

Now it may be said at once that in the foregoing conversation each one of the three participants had, as it
were, held something in reserve. That "Nobody tells
everything" is a very true motto.

It may be questioned, for instance, if Loraine Wade
was perfectly sincere in her account of the motives
which had led her to seek out Jimmy Thesiger.

In the same way, Jimmy Thesiger himself had various ideas and plans connected with the forthcoming
party at George Lomax's which he had no intention of
revealing to—say, Bundle.

And Bundle herself had a fully-fledged plan which
she proposed to put into immediate execution and
which she had said nothing whatever about.

On leaving Jimmy Thesiger's rooms, she drove to
Scotland Yard, where she asked to see Superintendent
Battle.

Superintendent Battle was rather a big man. He
worked almost entirely on cases of a delicate political
nature. On such a case he had come to Chimneys four
years ago, and Bundle was frankly trading on his remembering this fact.

After a short delay, she was taken along several
corridors and into the Superintendent's private room.
Battle was a stolid-looking man with a wooden face. He
looked supremely unintelligent and more like a commissionaire than a detective.

He was standing by the window when she entered,
gazing in an expressionless manner at some sparrows.

"Good-afternoon, Lady Eileen," he said. "Sit down,
won't you?"

"Thank you," said Bundle. "I was afraid you mightn't remember me."

"Always remember people," said Battle. He added: "Got to in my job."

"Oh!" said Bundle, rather damped.

"And what can I do for you?" inquired the Superintendent.

Bundle came straight to the point.

"I've always heard that you people at Scotland Yard have lists of all secret societies and things like that that are formed in London."

"We try to keep up to date," said Superintendent Battle cautiously.

"I suppose a great many of them aren't really dangerous."

"We've got a very good rule to go by," said Battle. "The more they talk, the less they'll do. You'd be surprised how well that works out."

"And I've heard that very often you let them go on?"

Battle nodded.

"That's so. Why shouldn't a man call himself a Brother of Liberty and meet twice a week in a cellar and talk about rivers of blood—it won't hurt either him or us. And if there *is* trouble any time, we know where to lay our hands on him."

"But sometimes, I suppose," said Bundle slowly, "a society may be more dangerous than anyone imagines?"

"Very unlikely," said Battle.

"But it *might* happen," persisted Bundle.

"Oh! it *might*," admitted the Superintendent.

There was a moment or two's silence. Then Bundle said quietly.

"Superintendent Battle, could you give me a list of secret societies that have their headquarters in Seven Dials?"

It was Superintendent Battle's boast that he had never been seen to display emotion. But Bundle could have sworn that just for a moment his eyelids flickered and he looked taken aback. Only for a moment, however. He was his usual wooden self as he said:

"Strictly speaking, Lady Eileen, there's no such place as Seven Dials nowadays."

"No?"

"No. Most of it is pulled down and rebuilt. It was rather a low quarter once, but it's very respectable and high class nowadays. Not at all a romantic spot to poke about in for mysterious secret societies."

"Oh!" said Bundle, rather nonplussed.

"But all the same I should very much like to know what put that neighborhood into your head, Lady Eileen?"

"Have I got to tell you?"

"Well, it saves trouble, doesn't it? We know where we are, so to speak?"

Bundle hesitated for a minute.

"There was a man shot yesterday," she said slowly. "I thought I had run over him—"

"Mr. Ronald Devereux?"

"You know about it, of course. Why has there been nothing in the papers?"

"Do you really want to know that, Lady Eileen?"

"Yes, please."

"Well, we just thought we should like to have a clear twenty-four hours—see? It will be in the papers to-morrow."

"Oh!" Bundle studied him, puzzled.

What was hidden behind that immovable face. Did he regard the shooting of Ronald Devereux as an ordinary crime or as an extraordinary one.

"He mentioned Seven Dials when he was dying," said Bundle slowly.

"Thank you," said Battle. "I'll make a note of that."

He wrote a few words on the blotting pad in front of him.

Bundle started on another tack.

"Mr. Lomax, I understand, came to see you yesterday about a threatening letter he had had."

"He did."

"And that was written from Seven Dials?"

"It had Seven Dials written at the top of it, I believe."

Bundle felt as though she was battering hopelessly on a locked door.

"If you'll let me advise you, Lady Eileen—"

"I know what you're going to say."

"I should go home and—well, think no more about these matters."

"Leave it to you, in fact?"

"Well," said Superintendent Battle, "after all, we *are* the professionals."

"And I'm only an amateur? Yes, but you forget one thing—I mayn't have your knowledge and skill—but I have one advantage over you. I can work in the dark."

She thought that the Superintendent seemed a little taken aback, as though the force of her words struck home.

"Of course," said Bundle, "if you won't give me a list of secret societies—"

"Oh! I never said that. You shall have a list of the whole lot."

He went to the door, put his head through and called out something, then came back to his chair. Bundle, rather unreasonably, felt baffled. The ease with which he acceded to her request seemed to her suspicious. He was looking at her now in a placid fashion.

"Do you remember the death of Mr. Gerald Wade?" she asked abruptly.

"Down at your place, wasn't it? Took an overdraught of sleeping mixture."

"His sister says he never took things to make him sleep."

"Ah!" said the Superintendent. "You'd be surprised what a lot of things there are that sisters don't know."

Bundle again felt baffled. She sat in silence till a man came in with a typewritten sheet of paper, which he handed to the Superintendent.

"Here you are," said the latter when the other had left the room. "The Blood Brothers of St. Sebastian. The Wolf Hounds. The Comrades of Peace. The Comrades Club. The Friends of Oppression. The Children of Moscow. The Red Standard Bearers. The Herrings.

The Comrades of the Fallen—and half a dozen more."

He handed it to her with a distinct twinkle in his eye.

"You give it to me," said Bundle, "because you know it's not going to be the slightest use to me. Do you want me to leave the whole thing alone?"

"I should prefer it," said Battle. "You see—if you go messing round all these places—well, it's going to give us a lot of trouble."

"Looking after me, you mean?"

"Looking after you, Lady Eileen."

Bundle had risen to her feet. Now she stood undecided. So far the honours lay with Superintendent Battle. Then she remembered one slight incident, and she based a last appeal upon it.

"I said just now that an amateur could do some things which a professional couldn't. You didn't contradict me. That's because you're an honest man, Superintendent Battle. You knew I was right."

"Go on," said Battle quietly.

"At Chimneys you let me help. Won't you let me help now?"

Battle seemed to be turning the thing over in his mind. Emboldened by his silence, Bundle continued.

"You know pretty well what I'm like, Superintendent Battle. I butt into things. I'm a Nosey Parker. I don't want to get in your way or to try and do things that you're doing and can do a great deal better. But if there's a chance for an amateur, let me have it."

Again there was a pause, and then Superintendent Battle said quietly:

"You couldn't have spoken fairer than you have done, Lady Eileen. But I'm just going to say this to you. What you propose is dangerous. And when I say dangerous, I *mean* dangerous."

"I've grasped that," said Bundle. "I'm not a fool."

"No," said Superintendent Battle. "Never knew a young lady who was less so. What I'll do for you, Lady Eileen, is this. I'll just give you one little hint. And I'm doing it because I never have thought much of the motto 'Safety First.' In my opinion half the people

who spend their lives avoiding being run over by buses
had much better be run over and put safely out of the
way. They're no good."

This remarkable utterance issuing from the conventional lips of Superintendent Battle quite took Bundle's
breath away.

"What was the hint you were going to give me,"
she asked at last.

"You know Mr. Eversleigh, don't you?"

"Know Bill? Why, of course. But what——"

"I think Mr. Bill Eversleigh will be able to tell you
all you want to know about Seven Dials."

"Bill knows about it? *Bill?*"

"I didn't say that. Not at all. But I think, being a
quick-witted young lady, you'll get what you want from
him.

"And now," said Superintendent Battle firmly, "I'm
not going to say another word."

CHAPTER XI

Dinner with Bill

BUNDLE set out to keep her appointment with Bill on
the following evening full of expectation.

Bill greeted her with every sign of elation.

"Bill really *is* rather nice," thought Bundle to herself. "Just like a large, clumsy dog that wags its tail
when it's pleased to see you."

The large dog was uttering short staccato yelps of
comment and information.

"You look tremendously fit, Bundle. I can't tell you
how pleased I am to see you. I've ordered oysters—you
do like oysters, don't you? And how's everything?
What did you want to go mouldering about abroad so
long? Were you having a very gay time?"

"No, deadly," said Bundle. "Perfectly foul. Old dis-
eased colonels creeping about in the sun, and active,
wizened spinsters running libraries and churches."

"Give me England," said Bill. "I bar this foreign business—except Switzerland. Switzerland's all right. I'm thinking of going this Christmas. Why don't you come along?"

"I'll think of it," said Bundle. "What have you been doing with yourself lately, Bill?"

It was an incautious query. Bundle had merely made it out of politeness and as a preliminary to introducing her own topics of conversation. It was, however, the opening for which Bill had been waiting.

"That's just what I've been wanting to tell you about. You're brainy, Bundle, and I want your advice. You know that musical show, 'Damn Your Eyes'?"

"Yes."

"Well, I'm going to tell you about one of the dirtiest pieces of work imaginable. My God! the theatrical crowd. There's a girl—a Yankee girl—a perfect stunner—"

Bundle's heart sank. The grievances of Bill's lady friends were always interminable—they went on and on and there was no stemming them.

"This girl, Babe St. Maur her name is—"

"I wonder how she got that name?" said Bundle sarcastically.

Bill replied literally.

"She got it out of *Who's Who*. Opened it and jabbed her finger down on a page without looking. Pretty nifty, eh? Her real name's Goldschmidt or Abrameier—something quite impossible."

"Oh! quite," agreed Bundle.

"Well, Babe St. Maur is pretty smart. And she's got muscles. She was one of the eight girls who made the living bridge—"

"Bill," said Bundle desperately, "I went to see Jimmy Thesiger yesterday morning."

"Good old Jimmy," said Bill. "Well, as I was telling you, Babe's pretty smart. You've got to be nowadays. She can put it over on most theatrical people. If you want to live, be high-handed, that's what Babe says. And mind you, she's the goods all right. She can act—it's marvellous how that girl can act. She'd not much chance in 'Damn Your Eyes'—just swamped in a pack of good-looking girls. I said why not try the legitimate stage—you know, Mrs. Tanqueray—that sort of stuff —but Babe just laughed—"

"Have you seen Jimmy at all?"

"Saw him this morning. Let me see, where was I? Oh, yes, I hadn't got to the rumpus yet. And mind you it was jealousy—sheer, spiteful jealousy. The other girl wasn't a patch on Babe for looks and she knew it. So she went behind her back—"

Bundle resigned herself to the inevitable and heard the whole story of the unfortunate circumstances which had led up to Babe St. Maur's summary disappearance from the cast of "Damn Your Eyes." It took a long time. When Bill finally paused for breath and sympathy, Bundle said:

"You're quite right, Bill, it's a rotten shame. There must be a lot of jealousy about—"

"The whole theatrical world's rotten with it."

"It must be. Did Jimmy say anything to you about coming down to the Abbey next week?"

For the first time, Bill gave his attention to what Bundle was saying.

"He was full of a long rigmarole he wanted me to stuff Codders with. About wanting to stand in the Conservative interest. But you know, Bundle, it's too damned risky."

"Stuff," said Bundle. "If George *does* find him out, he won't blame you. You'll just have been taken in, that's all."

"That's not it at all," said Bill. "I mean it's too damned risky for Jimmy. Before he knows where he is, he'll be parked down somewhere like Tooting West, pledged to kiss babies and make speeches. You don't know how thorough Codders is and how frightfully energetic."

"Well, we'll have to risk that," said Bundle. "Jimmy can take care of himself all right."

"You don't know Codders," repeated Bill.

"Who's coming to this party, Bill? Is it anything very special?"

"Only the usual sort of muck. Mrs. Macatta for one."

"The M.P.?"

"Yes, you know, always going off the deep end about Welfare and Pure Milk and Save the Children. Think of poor Jimmy being talked to by her."

"Never mind Jimmy. Go on telling me."

"Then there's a Hungarian, what they call a Young Hungarian. Countess something unpronounceable. She's all right."

He swallowed as though embarrassed and Bundle observed that he was crumbling his bread nervously.

"Young and beautiful?" she inquired delicately.

"Oh! rather."

"I didn't know George went in for female beauty much."

"Oh! he doesn't. She runs baby feeding in Buda Pesth—something like that. Naturally she and Mrs. Macatta want to get together."

"Who else?"

"Sir Stanley Digby—"

"The Air Minister?"

"Yes. And his secretary, Terence O'Rourke. He's rather a lad, by the way—or used to be in his flying days. Then there's a perfectly poisonous German chap called Herr Eberhard. I don't know who he is, but we're all making the hell of a fuss about him. I've been twice told off to take him out to lunch, and I can tell you, Bundle, it was no joke. He's not like the Embassy chaps, who are all very decent. This man sucks in soup and eats peas with a knife. Not only that, but the brute is always biting his finger-nails—positively gnaws at them."

"Pretty foul."

"Isn't it? I believe he invents things—something of the kind. Well, that's all. Oh! yes, Sir Oswald Coote."

"And Lady Coote?"

"Yes, I believe she's coming too."

Bundle sat lost in thought for some minutes. Bill's list was suggestive, but she hadn't time to think out various possibilities just now. She must get on to the next point.

"Bill?" she said. "What's all this about Seven Dials?"

Bill at once looked horribly embarrassed. He blinked and avoided her glance.

"I don't know what you mean," he said.

"Nonsense," said Bundle. "I was told you know all about it."

"About what?"

This was rather a poser. Bundle shifted her ground.

"I don't see what you want to be so secretive for," she complained.

"Nothing to be secretive about. Nobody goes there much now. It was only a craze."

This sounded puzzling.

"One gets so out of things when one is away," said Bundle in a sad voice.

"Oh! you haven't missed much," said Bill. "Everyone went there just to say they had been. It was boring really, and, my God, you *can* get tired of fried fish."

"Where did everyone go?"

"To the Seven Dials Club, of course," said Bill, staring. "Wasn't that what you were asking about?"

"I didn't know it by that name," said Bundle.

"Used to be a slummy sort of district round about Tottenham Court Road way. It's all pulled down and cleaned up now. But the Seven Dials Club keeps to the old atmosphere. Fried fish and chips. General squalor. Kind of East End stunt, but awfully handy to get at after a show."

"It's a night club, I suppose," said Bundle. "Dancing and all that?"

"That's it. Awfully mixed crowd. Not a posh affair. Artists, you know, and all sorts of odd women and a sprinkling of our lot. They say quite a lot of things, but I think that that's all bunkum myself, just said to make the place go."

"Good," said Bundle. "We'll go there to-night."

"Oh! I shouldn't do that," said Bill. His embarrassment had returned. "I tell you it's played out. Nobody goes there now."

"Well, we're going."

"You wouldn't care for it, Bundle. You wouldn't really."

"You're going to take me to the Seven Dials Club and nowhere else, Bill. And I should like to know why you are so unwilling?"

"I? Unwilling?"

"Painfully so. What's the guilty secret?"

"Guilty secret?"

"Don't keep repeating what I say. You do it to give yourself time."

"I don't," said Bill indignantly. "It's only—"

"Well? I know there's something. You never can conceal anything."

"I've got nothing to conceal. It's only—"

"Well?"

"It's a long story— You see, I took Babe St. Maur there one night—"

"Oh! Babe St. Maur again."

"Why not?"

"I didn't know it was about her—" said Bundle, stifling a yawn.

"As I say, I took Babe there. She rather fancied a lobster. I had a lobster under my arm—"

The story went on— When the lobster had been finally dismembered in a struggle between Bill and a fellow who was a rank outsider, Bundle brought her attention back to him.

"I see," she said. "And there was a row?"

"Yes, but it was *my* lobster. I'd bought it and paid for it. I had a perfect right—"

"Oh! you had, you had," said Bundle hastily. "But I'm sure that's all forgotten now. And I don't care for lobsters anyway. So let's go."

"We may be raided by the police. There's a room upstairs where they play baccarat."

"Father will have to come out and bail me out, that's all. Come on, Bill."

Bill still seemed rather reluctant, but Bundle was adamant, and they were soon speeding to their destination in a taxi.

The place, when they got to it, was much as she

imagined it would be. It was a tall house in a narrow
street, 14 Hunstanton Street; she noted the number.

A man whose face was strangely familiar opened the
door. She thought he started slightly when he saw her,
but he greeted Bill with respectful recognition. He was
a tall man, with fair hair, a rather weak, anaemic face
and slightly shifty eyes. Bundle puzzled to herself where
she could have seen him before.

Bill had recovered his equilibrium now and quite
enjoyed doing showman. They danced in the cellar,
which was very full of smoke—so much so that you
saw everyone through a blue haze. The smell of fried
fish was almost overpowering.

On the wall, were rough charcoal sketches, some of
them executed with real talent. The company was extremely mixed. There were portly foreigners, opulent
Jewesses, a sprinkling of the really smart, and several
ladies belonging to the oldest profession in the world.

Soon Bill led Bundle upstairs. There the weak-faced
man was on guard, watching all those admitted to the
gambling room with a lynx eye. Suddenly recognition
came to Bundle.

"Of course," she said. "How stupid of me. It's Alfred, who used to be second footman at Chimneys.
How are you, Alfred?"

"Nicely, thank you, your ladyship."

"When did you leave Chimneys, Alfred? Was it long
before we got back?"

"It was about a month ago, m'lady. I got a chance of
bettering myself, and it seemed a pity not to take it."

"I suppose they pay you very well here," remarked
Bundle.

"Very fair, m'lady."

Bundle passed in. It seemed to her that in this room
the real life of the club was exposed. The stakes were
high, she saw that at once, and the people gathered
round the two tables were of the true type—hawk-
eyed, haggard, with the gambling fever in their blood.

She and Bill stayed there for about half an hour.
Then Bill grew restive.

"Let's get out of this place, Bundle, and go on dancing."

Bundle agreed. There was nothing to be seen here. They went down again. They danced for another half hour, had fish and chips, and then Bundle declared herself ready to go home.

"But it's so early," Bill protested.

"No, it isn't. Not really. And, anyway, I've got a long day in front of me to-morrow."

"What are you going to do?"

"That depends," said Bundle mysteriously. "But I can tell you this, Bill, the grass is not going to grow under my feet."

"It never does," said Mr. Eversleigh.

CHAPTER XII

Inquiries at Chimneys

BUNDLE'S temperament was certainly not inherited from her father, whose prevailing characteristic was a wholly amiable inertia. As Bill Eversleigh had very justly remarked, the grass never did grow under Bundle's feet.

On the morning following her dinner with Bill, Bundle woke full of energy. She had three distinct plans which she meant to put into operation that day, and she realized that she was going to be slightly hampered by the limits of time and space.

Fortunately she did not suffer from the affliction of Gerry Wade, Ronny Devereux and Jimmy Thesiger— that of not being able to get up in the morning. Sir Oswald Coote himself would have had no fault to find with her on the score of early rising. At half-past eight Bundle had breakfasted and was on her way to Chimneys in the Hispano.

Her father seemed mildly pleased to see her.

"I never know when you're going to turn up," he

said. "But this will save me ringing up, which I hate. Colonel Melrose was here yesterday about the inquest."

Colonel Melrose was Chief Constable of the county, and an old friend of Lord Caterham.

"You mean the inquest on Ronny Devereux? When is it to be?"

"To-morrow. Twelve o'clock. Melrose will call for you. Having found the body, you'll have to give evidence, but he said you needn't be at all alarmed."

"Why on earth should I be alarmed?"

"Well, you know," said Lord Caterham apologetically, "Melrose is a bit old-fashioned."

"Twelve o'clock," said Bundle. "Good. I shall be here, if I'm still alive."

"Have you any reason to anticipate not being alive?"

"One never knows," said Bundle. "The strain of modern life—as the newspapers say."

"Which reminds me that George Lomax asked me to come over to the Abbey next week. I refused, of course."

"Quite right," said Bundle. "We don't want you mixed up in any funny business."

"Is there going to be any funny business?" asked Lord Caterham with a sudden awakening of interest.

"Well—warning letters and all that, you know," said Bundle.

"Perhaps George is going to be assassinated," said Lord Caterham hopefully. "What do you think, Bundle —perhaps I'd better go after all."

"You curb your bloodthirsty instincts and stay quietly at home," said Bundle. "I'm going to talk to Mrs. Howell."

Mrs. Howell was the housekeeper, that dignified, creaking lady who had struck such terror to the heart of Lady Coote. She had no terrors for Bundle, whom, indeed, she always called Miss Bundle, a relic of the days when Bundle had stayed at Chimneys, a long-legged, impish child, before her father had succeeded to the title.

"Now, Howelly," said Bundle, "let's have a cup of

rich cocoa together, and let me hear all the household news."

She gleaned what she wanted without much difficulty, making mental notes as follows:

"Two new scullery maids—village girls—doesn't seem much there. New third housemaid—head housemaid's niece. That sounds all right. Howelly seems to have bullied poor Lady Coote a good deal. She would."

"I never thought the day would come when I should see Chimneys inhabited by strangers, Miss Bundle."

"Oh! one must go with the times," said Bundle. "You'll be lucky, Howelly, if you never see it converted into desirable flats with use of superb pleasure grounds."

Mrs. Howell shivered all down her reactionary aristocratic spine.

"I've never seen Sir Oswald Coote," remarked Bundle.

"Sir Oswald is no doubt a very clever gentleman," said Mrs. Howell distantly.

Bundle gathered that Sir Oswald had not been liked by his staff.

"Of course, it was Mr. Bateman who saw to everything," continued the housekeeper. "A very efficient gentleman. A very efficient gentleman indeed, and one who knew the way things ought to be done."

Bundle led the talk on to the topic of Gerald Wade's death. Mrs. Howell was only too willing to talk about it, and was full of pitying ejaculations about the poor young gentleman, but Bundle gleaned nothing new. Presently she took leave of Mrs. Howell and came downstairs again, where she promptly rang for Tredwell.

"Tredwell, when did Alfred leave?"

"It would be about a month ago now, my lady."

"Why did he leave?"

"It was by his own wish, my lady. I believe he has gone to London. I was not dissatisfied with him in any way. I think you will find the new footman, John, very satisfactory. He seems to know his work and to be most anxious to give satisfaction."

"Where did he come from?"

"He had excellent references, my lady. He had lived last with Lord Mount Vernon."

"I see," said Bundle thoughtfully.

She was remembering that Lord Mount Vernon was at present on a shooting trip in East Africa.

"What's his last name, Tredwell?"

"Bower, my lady."

Tredwell paused for a minute or two and then, seeing that Bundle had finished, he quietly left the room. Bundle remained lost in thought.

John had opened the door to her on her arrival that day, and she had taken particular notice of him without seeming to do so. Apparently, he was the perfect servant, well trained, with an expressionless face. He had, perhaps, a more soldierly bearing than most footmen and there was something a little odd about the shape of the back of his head.

But these details, as Bundle realized, were hardly relevant to the situation. She sat frowning down at the blotting paper in front of her. She had a pencil in her hand and was idly tracing the name Bower over and over again.

Suddenly an idea struck her and she stopped dead, staring at the word. Then she summoned Tredwell once more.

"Tredwell, how is the name Bower spelt?"

"B-A-U-E-R, my lady."

"That's not an English name."

"I believe he is of Swiss extraction, my lady."

"Oh! That's all, Tredwell, thank you."

Swiss extraction? No. German! That martial carriage, that flat back to the head. And he had come to Chimneys a fortnight before Gerry Wade's death.

Bundle rose to her feet. She had done all she could here. Now to get on with things! She went in search of her father.

"I'm off again," she said. "I've got to go and see Aunt Marcia."

"Got to see Marcia?" Lord Caterham's voice was full

of astonishment. "Poor child, how did you get let in for that?"

"Just for once," said Bundle, "I happen to be going of my own free will."

Lord Caterham looked at her in amazement. That anyone could have a genuine desire to face his redoubtable sister-in-law was quite incomprehensible to him. Marcia, Marchioness of Caterham, the widow of his late brother Henry, was a very prominent personality. Lord Caterham admitted that she had made Henry an admirable wife and that but for her in all probability he would never have held the office of Secretary of State for Foreign Affairs. On the other hand, he had always looked upon Henry's early death as a merciful release.

It seemed to him that Bundle was foolishly putting her head into the lion's mouth.

"Oh! I say," he said. "You know, I shouldn't do that. You don't know what it may lead to."

"I know what I hope it's going to lead to," said Bundle. "I'm all right, Father, don't you worry about me."

Lord Caterham sighed and settled himself more comfortably in his chair. He went back to his perusal of the *Field*. But in a minute or two Bundle suddenly put her head in again.

"Sorry," she said. "But there's one other thing I wanted to ask you. What is Sir Oswald Coote?"

"I told you—a steam-roller."

"I don't mean your personal impression of him. How did he make his money—trouser buttons or brass beds or what?"

"Oh! I see. He's steel. Steel and iron. He's got the biggest steel works, or whatever you call it, in England. He doesn't, of course, run the show personally now. It's a company or companies. He got me in as a director of something or other. Very good business for me—nothing to do except go down to the city once or twice a year to one of those hotel places—Cannon Street or Liverpool Street—and sit round a table where they have very nice new blotting paper. Then Coote

or some clever Johnny makes a speech simply bristling
with figures, but fortunately you needn't listen to it—
and I can tell you, you often get a jolly good lunch
out of it."

Uninterested in Lord Caterham's lunches, Bundle
had departed again before he had finished speaking.
On the way back to London, she tried to piece together things to her satisfaction.

As far as she could see, steel and infant welfare did
not go together. One of the two, then, was just padding
—presumably the latter. Mrs. Macatta and the Hungarian countess could be ruled out of court. They were
camouflage. No, the pivot of the whole thing seemed to
be the unattractive Herr Eberhard. He did not seem
to be the type of man whom George Lomax would
normally invite. Bill had said vaguely that he invented.
Then there was the Air Minister and Sir Oswald Coote,
who was steel. Somehow that seemed to hang together.

Since it was useless speculating further, Bundle
abandoned the attempt and concentrated on her forthcoming interview with Lady Caterham.

The lady lived in a large gloomy house in one of
London's higher class squares. Inside it smelt of sealing
wax, bird seed and slightly decayed flowers. Lady Caterham was a large woman—large in every way. Her
proportions were majestic, rather than ample. She had
a large beaked nose, wore gold rimmed pince-nez and
her upper lip bore just the faintest suspicion of a moustache.

She was somewhat surprised to see her niece, but
accorded her a frigid cheek, which Bundle duly
kissed.

"This is quite an unexpected pleasure, Eileen," she
observed coldly.

"We've only just got back, Aunt Marcia."

"I know. How is your father? Much as usual?"

Her tone conveyed disparagement. She had a poor
opinion of Alastair Edward Brent, ninth Marquis of
Caterham. She would have called him, had she known
the term, a "poor fish."

"Father is very well. He's down at Chimneys."

"Indeed. You know, Eileen, I never approved of the letting of Chimneys. The place is, in many ways, a historical monument. It should not be cheapened."

"It must have been wonderful in Uncle Henry's day," said Bundle with a slight sigh.

"Henry realized his responsibilities," said Henry's widow.

"Think of the people who stayed there," went on Bundle ecstatically. "All the principal statesmen of Europe."

Lady Caterham sighed.

"I can truly say that history has been made there more than once," she observed. "If only your father—"

She shook her head sadly.

"Politics bore Father," said Bundle, "and yet they are about the most fascinating study there is, I should say. Especially if one knew about them from the inside."

She made this extravagantly untruthful statement of her feelings without even a blush. Her aunt looked at her with some surprise.

"I am pleased to hear you say so," she said. "I always imagined, Eileen, that you cared for nothing but this modern pursuit of pleasure."

"I used to," said Bundle.

"It is true that you are still very young," said Lady Caterham thoughtfully. "But with your advantages, and if you were to marry suitably, you might be one of the leading political hostesses of the day."

Bundle felt slightly alarmed. For a moment she feared that her aunt might produce a suitable husband straight away.

"But I feel such a fool," said Bundle. "I mean I know so little."

"That can easily be remedied," said Lady Caterham briskly. "I have any amount of literature I can lend you."

"Thank you, Aunt Marcia," said Bundle, and proceeded hastily to her second line of attack.

"I wondered if you knew Mrs. Macatta, Aunt Marcia?"

"Certainly I know her. A most estimable woman with a brilliant brain. I may say that as a general rule I do not hold with women standing for Parliament. They can make their influence felt in a more womanly fashion." She paused, doubtless to recall the womanly way in which she had forced a reluctant husband into the political arena and the marvellous success which had crowned his and her efforts. "But still, times change. And the work Mrs. Macatta is doing is of truly national importance, and of the utmost value to all women. It is, I think I may say, true womanly work. You must certainly meet Mrs. Macatta."

Bundle gave a rather dismal sigh.

"She's going to be at a house-party at George Lomax's next week. He asked Father, who, of course, won't go, but he never thought of asking me. Thinks I'm too much of an idiot, I suppose."

It occurred to Lady Caterham that her niece was really wonderfully improved. Had she, perhaps, had an unfortunate love affair? An unfortunate love affair, in Lady Caterham's opinion, was often highly beneficial to young girls. It made them take life seriously.

"I don't suppose George Lomax realizes for a moment that you have—shall we say, grown up? Eileen, dear," she said, "I must have a few words with him."

"He doesn't like me," said Bundle. "I know he won't ask me."

"Nonsense," said Lady Caterham. "I shall make a point of it. I knew George Lomax when he was so high." She indicated a quite impossible height. "He will be only too pleased to do me a favour. And he will be sure to see for himself that it is vitally important that the present day young girls of our own class should take an intelligent interest in the welfare of their country."

Bundle nearly said: "Hear, hear," but checked herself.

"I will find you some literature now," said Lady Caterham, rising.

She called in a piercing voice, "Miss Connor."

A very neat secretary with a frightened expression

came running. Lady Caterham gave her various directions. Presently Bundle was driving back to Brook Street with an armful of the driest looking literature imaginable.

Her next proceeding was to ring up Jimmy Thesiger. His first words were full of triumph.

"I've managed it," he said. "Had a lot of trouble with Bill, though. He'd got it into his thick head that I should be a lamb among the wolves. But I made him see sense at last. I've got a lot of thingummybobs now and I'm studying them. You know, blue books and white papers. Deadly dull—but one must do the thing properly. Have you ever heard of the Santa Fé boundary dispute?"

"Never," said Bundle.

"Well, I'm taking special pains with that. It went on for years and was very complicated. I'm making it my subject. Nowadays one has to specialize."

"I've got a lot of the same sort of things," said Bundle. "Aunt Marcia gave them to me."

"Aunt who?"

"Aunt Marcia—Father's sister-in-law. She's very political. In fact, she's going to get me invited to George's party."

"No? Oh, I say, that will be splendid." There was a pause and then Jimmy said:

"I say, I don't think we'd better tell Loraine that—eh?"

"Perhaps not."

"You see, she mayn't like being out of it. And she really must be kept out of it."

"Yes."

"I mean you can't let a girl like that run into danger!"

Bundle reflected that Mr. Thesiger was slightly deficient in tact. The prospect of *her* running into danger did not seem to give him any qualms whatever.

"Have you gone away?" asked Jimmy.

"No, I was only thinking."

"I see. I say, are you going to the inquest to-morrow?"

"Yes; are you?"

"Yes. By the way, it's in the evening papers. But tucked away in a corner. Funny—I should have thought they'd have made rather a splash about it."

"Yes—so should I."

"Well, said Jimmy, "I must be getting on with my task. I've just got to where Bolivia sent us a Note."

"I suppose I must get on with my little lot," said Bundle. "Are you going to swot at it all the evening?"

"I think so. Are you?"

"Oh, probably. Good-night."

They were both liars of the most unblushing order. Jimmy Thesiger knew perfectly well that he was taking Loraine Wade out to dinner.

As for Bundle, no sooner had she rung off than she attired herself in various nondescript garments belonging, as a matter of fact, to her maid. And having donned them, she sallied out on foot deliberating whether bus or tube would be the best route by which to reach the Seven Dials Club.

CHAPTER XIII

The Seven Dials Club

BUNDLE reached 14 Hunstanton Street about 6 P.M. At that hour, as she rightly judged, the Seven Dials Club was a dead spot. Bundle's aim was a simple one. She intended to get hold of the ex-footman Alfred. She was convinced that once she had got hold of him the rest would be easy. Bundle had a simple autocratic method of dealing with retainers. It seldom failed, and she saw no reason why it should fail now.

The only thing of which she was not certain was how many people inhabited the club premises. Naturally she wished to disclose her presence to as few people as possible.

Whilst she was hesitating as to her best line of attack, the problem was solved for her in a singularly easy fashion. The door of No. 14 opened and Alfred himself came out.

"Good afternoon, Alfred," said Bundle pleasantly.

Alfred jumped.

"Oh! good afternoon, your ladyship. I—I didn't recognize your ladyship just for a moment."

Paying a tribute in her own mind to her maid's clothing, Bundle proceeded to business.

"I want a few words with you, Alfred? Where shall we go?"

"Well—really, my lady—I don't know—it's not what you might call a nice part round here—I don't know, I'm sure—"

Bundle cut him short.

"Who's in the club?"

"No one at present, my lady."

"Then we'll go in there."

Alfred produced a key and opened the door. Bundle passed in. Alfred, troubled and sheepish, followed her. Bundle sat down and looked straight at the uncomfortable Alfred.

"I suppose you know," she said crisply, "that what you're doing here is dead against the law?"

Alfred shifted uncomfortably from one foot to the other.

"It's true as we've been raided twice," he admitted. "But nothing compromising was found, owing to the neatness of Mr. Mosgorovsky's arrangements."

"I'm not talking of the gambling only," said Bundle. "There's more than that—probably a great deal more than you know. I'm going to ask you a direct question, Alfred, and I should like the truth, please. *How much were you paid for leaving Chimneys?*"

Alfred looked twice round the cornice as though seeking for inspirations, swallowed three or four times, and then took the inevitable course of a weak will opposed to a strong one.

"It was this way, your ladyship. Mr. Mosgorovsky, he come with a party to visit Chimneys on one of the show days. Mr. Tredwell, he was indisposed like—an ingrowing toe-nail as a matter of fact—so it fell to me to show the parties over. At the end of the tour, Mr. Mosgorovsky, he stays behind the rest, and after giving me something handsome, he falls into conversation."

"Yes," said Bundle encouragingly.

"And the long and the short of it was," said Alfred, with a sudden acceleration of his narrative, "that he offers me a hundred pound down to leave that instant minute and to look after this here club. He wanted someone as was used to the best families—to give the place a tone, as he put it. And, well, it seemed flying in the face of providence to refuse—let alone that the wages I get here are just three times what they were as second footman."

"A hundred pounds," said Bundle. "That's a very large sum, Alfred. Did they say anything about who was to fill your place at Chimneys?"

"I demurred a bit, my lady, about leaving at once. As I pointed out, it wasn't usual and might cause inconvenience. But Mr. Mosgorovsky he knew of a young chap—been in good service and ready to come any minute. So I mentioned his name to Mr. Tredwell and everything was settled pleasant like."

Bundle nodded. Her own suspicions had been correct and the *modus operandi* was much as she had thought it to be. She essayed a further inquiry.

"Who is Mr. Mosgorovsky?"

"Gentleman as runs this club. Russian gentleman. A very clever gentleman too."

Bundle abandoned the getting of information for the moment and proceeded to other matters.

"A hundred pounds is a very large sum of money, Alfred."

"Larger than I ever handled, my lady," said Alfred with simple candour.

"Did you never suspect that there was something wrong?"

"Wrong, my lady?"

"Yes. I'm not talking about the gambling. I mean something far more serious. You don't want to be sent to penal servitude, do you, Alfred?"

"Oh, Lord, my lady, you don't mean it?"

"I was at Scotland Yard the day before yesterday," said Bundle impressively. "I heard some very curious things. I want you to help me, Alfred, and if you do, well—if things go wrong, I'll put in a good word for you."

"Anything I can do, I shall be only too pleased, my lady. I mean, I would anyway."

"Well, first," said Bundle, "I want to go all over this place—from top to bottom."

Accompanied by a mystified and scared Alfred, she made a very thorough tour of inspection. Nothing struck her eye till she came to the gaming room. There she noticed an inconspicuous door in a corner, and the door was locked.

Alfred explained readily.

"That's used as a getaway, your ladyship. There's a room and a door on to a staircase what comes out in the next street. That's the way the gentry goes when there's a raid."

"But don't the police know about it?"

"It's a cunning door, you see, my lady. Looks like a cupboard, that's all."

Bundle felt a rising excitement.

"I must get in here," she said.

Alfred shook his head.

"You can't, my lady; Mr. Mosgorovsky, he has the key."

"Well," said Bundle, "there are other keys."

She perceived that the lock was a perfectly ordinary one which probably could be easily unlocked by the key of one of the other doors. Alfred, rather troubled, was sent to collect likely specimens. The fourth that Bundle tried fitted. She turned it, opened the door and passed through.

She found herself in a small, dingy apartment. A long table occupied the centre of the room with chairs ranged round it. There was no other furniture in the room. Two built-in cupboards stood on either side of the fireplace. Alfred indicated the nearer one with a nod.

"That's it," he explained.

Bundle tried the cupboard door, but it was locked, and she saw at once that this lock was a very different affair. It was of the patent kind that would only yield to its own key.

" 'Ighly ingenious, it is," explained Alfred. "It looks all right when opened. Shelves, you know, with a few ledgers and that on 'em. Nobody'd ever suspect, but you touch the right spot and the whole thing swings open."

Bundle had turned round and was surveying the room thoughtfully. The first thing she noticed was that the door by which they had entered was carefully fitted round with baize. It must be completely soundproof. Then her eyes wandered to the chairs. There were seven of them, three each side and one rather more imposing in design at the head of the table.

Bundle's eyes brightened. She had found what she was looking for. This, she felt sure, was the meeting place of the secret organization. The place was almost perfectly planned. It looked so innocent—you could reach it just by stepping through from the gaming room, or you could arrive there by the secret entrance—and any secrecy, any precautions were easily explained by the gaming going on in the next room.

Idly, as these thoughts passed through her mind, she drew a finger across the marble of the mantelpiece. Alfred saw and misinterpreted the action.

"You won't find no dirt, not to speak of," he said. "Mr. Mosgorovsky, he ordered the place to be swept out this morning, and I did it while he waited."

"Oh!" said Bundle, thinking very hard. "This morning, eh?"

"Has to be done sometimes," said Alfred. "Though the room's never what you might call used."

Next minute he received a shock.

"Alfred," said Bundle, "you've got to find me a place in this room where I can hide."

Alfred looked at her in dismay.

"But it's impossible, my lady. You'll get me into trouble and I'll lose my job."

"You'll lose it anyway when you go to prison," said

Bundle unkindly. "But as a matter of fact, you needn't worry, nobody will know anything about it."

"And there ain't no place," wailed Alfred. "Look round for yourself, your ladyship, if you don't believe me."

Bundle was forced to admit that there was something in this argument. But she had the true spirit of one undertaking adventures.

"Nonsense," she said with determination. "There has *got* to be a place."

"But there ain't one," wailed Alfred.

Never had a room shown itself more unpropitious for concealment. Dingy blinds were drawn down over the dirty window panes, and there were no curtains. The window sill outside, which Bundle examined, was about four inches wide! Inside the room there were the table, the chairs and the cupboards.

The second cupboard had a key in the lock. Bundle went across and pulled it open. Inside were shelves covered with an odd assortment of glasses and crockery.

"Surplus stuff as we don't use," explained Alfred. "You can see for yourself, my lady, there's no place here as a cat could hide."

But Bundle was examining the shelves.

"Flimsy work," she said. "Now then, Alfred, have you got a cupboard downstairs where you could shove all this glass? You have? Good. Then get a tray and start to carry it down at once. Hurry—there's no time to lose."

"You can't, my lady. And it's getting late, too. The cooks will be here any minute now."

"Mr. Mosgo-what-not doesn't come till later, I suppose?"

"He's never here much before midnight. But, oh, my lady—"

"Don't talk so much, Alfred," said Bundle. "Get that tray. If you stay here arguing, you *will* get into trouble."

Doing what is familiarly known as "wringing his hands," Alfred departed. Presently he returned with a tray, and having by now realized that his protests were

useless, he worked with a nervous energy quite surprising.

As Bundle had seen, the shelves were easily detach-
able. She took them down, ranged them upright against
the wall, and then stepped in.

"H'm," she remarked. "Pretty narrow. It's going to
be a tight fit. Shut the door on me carefully, Alfred—
that's right. Yes, it can be done. Now I want a gimlet."

"A gimlet, my lady?"

"That's what I said."

"I don't know—"

"Nonsense, you must have a gimlet—perhaps you've
got an auger as well. If you haven't got what I want,
you'll have to go out and buy it, so you'd better try
hard to find the right thing."

Alfred departed and returned presently with quite a
creditable assortment of tools. Bundle seized what she
wanted and proceeded swiftly and efficiently to bore a
small hole at the level of her right eye. She did this
from the outside so that it should be less noticeable,
and she dared not make it too large lest it should attract attention.

"There, that'll do," she remarked at last.

"Oh! but, my lady, my lady—"

"Yes?"

"But they'll find you—if they should open the door."

"They won't open the door," said Bundle, "because
you are going to lock it and take the key away."

"And if by chance Mr. Mosgorovsky should ask for
the key?"

"Tell him it's lost," said Bundle briskly. "But nobody's going to worry about this cupboard—it's only
here to attract attention from the other one and make a
pair. Go on, Alfred, someone might come at any time.
Lock me in and take the key and come and let me out
when everyone's gone."

"You'll be taken bad, my lady. You'll faint—"

"I never faint," said Bundle. "But you might as well
get me a cocktail. I shall certainly need it. Then lock
the door of the room again—don't forget—and take all
the door keys back to their proper doors. And, Alfred

—don't be too much of a rabbit. Remember, if anything goes wrong, I'll see you through."

"And that's that," said Bundle to herself when, having served the cocktail, Alfred had finally departed.

She was not nervous lest Alfred's nerve should fail and he should give her away. She knew that his sense of self-preservation was far too strong for that. His training alone helped him to conceal private emotions beneath the mask of the well trained servant.

Only one thing worried Bundle. The interpretation she had chosen to put upon the cleaning of the room that morning might be all wrong. And if so—Bundle sighed in the narrow confines of the cupboard. The prospect of spending long hours in it for nothing was not attractive.

CHAPTER XIV

The Meeting of the Seven Dials

IT would be as well to pass over the sufferings of the next four hours as quickly as possible. Bundle found her position extremely cramped. She had judged that the meeting, if meeting there was to be, would take place at a time when the club was in full swing—somewhere probably between the hours of midnight and 2 A.M.

She was just deciding that it must be at least six o'clock in the morning when a welcome sound came to her ears, the sound of the unlocking of a door.

In another minute the electric light was switched on. The hum of voices, which had come to her for a minute or two rather like the far-off roar of sea waves, ceased as suddenly as it had begun, and Bundle heard the sound of a bolt being shot. Clearly someone had come in from the gaming room next door, and she paid tribute to the thoroughness with which the communicating door had been rendered sound proof.

In another minute the intruder came into her line of

vision—a line of vision that was necessarily somewhat incomplete but which yet answered its purpose. A tall man, broad shouldered and powerful looking, with a long black beard. Bundle remembered having seen him sitting at one of the baccarat tables on the preceding night.

This, then, was Alfred's mysterious Russian gentleman, the proprietor of the club, the sinister Mr. Mosgorovsky. Bundle's heart beat faster with excitement. So little did she resemble her father that at this minute she fairly gloried in the extreme discomfort of her position.

The Russian remained for some minutes standing by the table, stroking his beard. Then he drew a watch from his pocket and glanced at the time. Nodding his head as though satisfied, he again thrust his hand into his pocket, and, pulling out something that Bundle could not see, he moved out of her line of vision.

When he reappeared again, she could hardly help giving a gasp of surprise.

His face was now covered by a mask—but hardly a mask in the conventional sense. It was not shaped to the face. It was a mere piece of material hanging in front of the features like a curtain in which two slits were pierced for the eyes. In shape it was round and on it was the representation of a clock face, with the hands pointing to six o'clock.

"The Seven Dials!" said Bundle to herself.

And at that minute there came a new sound—seven muffled taps.

Mosgorovsky strode across to where Bundle knew was the other cupboard door. She heard a sharp click, and then the sound of greetings in a foreign tongue.

Presently she had a view of the newcomers.

They also wore clock masks, but in their case the hands were in a different position—four o'clock and five o'clock respectively. Both men were in evening dress—but with a difference. One was an elegant, slender young man wearing evening clothes of exquisite cut. The grace with which he moved was foreign rather than English. The other man could be better described as wiry and lean. His clothes fitted him sufficiently well, but no more, and Bundle guessed at his nationality even before she heard his voice.

"I reckon we're the first to arrive at this little meeting."

A full pleasant voice with a slight American drawl, and an inflection of Irish behind it.

The elegant young man said in good, but slightly stilted, English:

"I had much difficulty in getting away to-night. These things do not always arrange themselves fortunately. I am not, like No. 4 here, my own master."

Bundle tried to guess at his nationality. Until he spoke, she had thought he might be French, but the accent was not a French one. He might possibly, she thought, be an Australian, or a Hungarian, or even a Russian.

The American moved to the other side of the table, and Bundle heard a chair being pulled out.

"One o'clock's being a great success," he said. "I congratulate you on taking the risk."

Five o'clock shrugged his shoulders.

"Unless one takes risks—" He left the sentence unfinished.

Again seven taps sounded, and Mosgorovsky moved across to the secret door.

She failed to catch anything definite for some moments since the whole company were out of sight, but presently she heard the bearded Russian's voice upraised.

"Shall we begin proceedings?"

He himself came round the table and took the seat next to the armchair at the top. Sitting thus, he was directly facing Bundle's cupboard. The elegant five o'clock took the place next to him. The third chair that side was out of Bundle's sight, but the American, No. 4, moved into her line of vision for a moment or two before he sat down.

On the near side of the table also, only two chairs were visible, and as she watched a hand turned the second—really the middle chair—down. And then with a swift movement, one of the newcomers brushed past the cupboard and took the chair opposite Mosgorovsky. Whoever sat there had, of course, their back directly turned to Bundle—and it was at that back that Bundle was staring with a good deal of interest, for it was the back of a singularly beautiful woman very much *décolleté*.

It was she who spoke first. Her voice was musical, foreign—with a deep seductive note in it. She was glancing towards the empty chair at the head of the table.

"So we are not to see No. 7 to-night?" she said. "Tell me, my friends, shall we ever see him?"

"That's darned good," said the American. "Darned good! As for seven o'clock—*I'm* beginning to believe there is no such person."

"I should not advise you to think that, my friend," said the Russian pleasantly.

There was a silence—rather an uncomfortable silence, Bundle felt.

She was still staring as though fascinated at the beautiful back in front of her. There was a tiny black mole just below the right shoulder blade that enhanced the whiteness of the skin. Bundle felt that at last the term "beautiful adventuress," so often read, had a real meaning for her. She was quite certain that this woman had a beautiful face—a dark Slavonic face with passionate eyes.

She was recalled from her imaginings by the voice of the Russian, who seemed to act as master of ceremonies.

"Shall we get on with our business? First to our absent comrade! No. 2!"

He made a curious gesture with his hand towards the turned down chair next to the woman, which every one present imitated, turning to the chair as they did so.

"I wish No. 2 were with us to-night," he continued. "There are many things to be done. Unsuspected difficulties have arisen."

"Have you had his report?" It was the American who spoke.

"As yet—I have nothing from him." There was a pause. "I cannot understand it."

"You think it may have—gone astray?"

"That is—a possibility."

"In other words," said five o'clock softly, "there is —danger."

He spoke the word delicately—and yet with relish.

The Russian nodded emphatically.

"Yes—there's danger. Too much is getting known about us—about this place. I know of several people who suspect." He added coldly: "They must be silenced."

Bundle felt a little cold shiver pass down her spine. If she were to be found, would she be silenced? She was recalled suddenly to attention by a word.

"So nothing has come to light about Chimneys?"

Mosgorovsky shook his head.

"Nothing."

Suddenly No. 5 leant forward.

"I agree with Anna; where is our president—No. 7? He who called us into being. Why do we never see him?"

"No. 7," said the Russian, "has his own ways of working."

"So you always say."

"I will say more," said Mosgorovsky. "I pity the man —or woman—who comes up against him."

There was an awkward silence.

"We must get on with our business," said Mosgorovsky quietly. "No. 3, you have the plans of Wyvern Abbey?"

Bundle strained her ears. So far she had neither caught a glimpse of No. 3, nor had she heard his voice. She heard it now and recognized it as unmistakable. Low, pleasant, indistinct—the voice of a well-bred Englishman.

"I've got them here, sir."

Some papers were shoved across the table. Everyone bent forward. Presently Mosgorovsky raised his head again.

"And the list of guests?"

"Here."

The Russian read them.

"Sir Stanley Digby. Mr. Terence O'Rourke. Sir Os-

wald and Lady Coote. Mr. Bateman. Countess Anna
Radzky. Mrs. Macatta. Mr. James Thesiger—" he
paused and then asked sharply:

"Who is Mr. James Thesiger?"

The American laughed.

"I guess you needn't worry any about him. The usual
complete young ass."

The Russian continued reading.

"Herr Eberhard and Mr. Eversleigh. That completes
the list."

"Does it?" said Bundle silently. "What about that
sweet girl, Lady Eileen Brent?"

"Yes, there seems nothing to worry about there," said
Mosgorovsky. He looked across the table. "I suppose
there's no doubt whatever about the value of Eberhard's invention?"

Three o'clock made a laconic British reply.

"None whatever."

"Commercially it should be worth millions," said the
Russian. "And internationally—well, one knows only
too well the greed of nations."

Bundle had an idea that behind his mask he was
smiling unpleasantly.

"Yes," he went on, "a gold mine."

"Well worth a few lives," said No. 5, cynically, and
laughed.

"But you know what inventions are," said the American. "Sometimes these darned things won't work."

"A man like Sir Oswald Coote will have made no
mistake," said Mosgorovsky.

"Speaking as an aviator myself," said No. 5, "the
thing is perfectly feasible. It has been discussed for
years—but it needed the genius of Eberhard to bring
it to fruition."

"Well," said Mosgorovsky, "I don't think we need
discuss matters any further. You have all seen the
plans. I do not think our original scheme can be bet-
tered. By the way, I hear something about a letter of
Gerald Wade's that has been found—a letter that men-
tions this organization. Who found it?"

"Lord Caterham's daughter—Lady Eileen Brent."

"Bauer should have been on to that," said Mosgo-rovsky. "It was careless of him. Who was the letter written to?"

"His sister, I believe," said No. 3.

"Unfortunate," said Mosgorovsky. "But it cannot be helped. The inquest on Ronald Devereux is to-morrow. I suppose that has been arranged for?"

"Reports as to local lads having been practising with rifles have been spread everywhere," said the Ameri-can.

"That should be all right then. I think there is noth-ing further to be said. I think we must all congratulate our dear one o'clock and wish her luck in the part she has to play."

"Hurrah!" cried No. 5. "To Anna!"

All hands flew out in the same gesture which Bundle had noticed before.

"To Anna!"

One o'clock acknowledged the salutation with a typically foreign gesture. Then she rose to her feet and the others followed suit. For the first time, Bundle caught a glimpse of No. 3 as he came to put Anna's cloak round her—a tall, heavily built man.

Then the party filed out through the secret door. Mosgorovsky secured it after them. He waited a few moments and then Bundle heard him unbolt the other door and pass through, after extinguishing the electric light.

It was not until two hours later that a white and anxious Alfred came to release Bundle. She almost fell into his arms and he had to hold her up.

"Nothing," said Bundle. "Just stiff, that's all. Here, let me sit down."

"Oh, Gord, my lady, it's been awful."

"Nonsense," said Bundle. "It all went off spendidly. Don't get the wind up now it's all over. It might have gone wrong, but thank goodness it didn't."

"Thank goodness, as you say, my lady. I've been in a twitter all the evening. They're a funny crowd, you know."

"A damned funny crowd," said Bundle, vigorously

massaging her arms and legs. "As a matter of fact, they're the sort of crowd I always imagined until to-night only existed in books. In this life, Alfred, one never stops learning."

CHAPTER XV

The Inquest

BUNDLE reached home about 6 A.M. She was up and dressed by half-past nine, and rang up Jimmy Thesiger on the telephone.

The promptitude of his reply somewhat surprised her, till he explained that he was going down to attend the inquest.

"So am I," said Bundle. "And I've got a lot to tell you."

"Well, suppose you let me drive you down and we can talk on the way. How about that?"

"All right. But allow a bit extra because you'll have to take me to Chimneys. The Chief Constable's picking me up there."

"Why?"

"Because he's a kind man," said Bundle.

"So am I," said Jimmy. "Very kind."

"Oh! you—you're an ass," said Bundle. "I heard somebody say so last night."

"Who?"

"To be strictly accurate—a Russian Jew. No, it wasn't. It was—"

But an indignant protest drowned her words.

"I may be an ass," said Jimmy. "I daresay I am— but I won't have Russian Jews saying so. What were you doing last night, Bundle?"

"That's what I'm going to talk about," said Bundle. "Goodbye for the moment."

She rang off in a tantalizing manner which left Jimmy pleasantly puzzled. He had the highest respect for

Bundle's capabilities, though there was not the slightest trace of sentiment in his feeling towards her.

"She's been up to something," he opined, as he took a last hasty drink of coffee. "Depend upon it, she's been up to something."

Twenty minutes later, his little two-seater drew up before the Brook Street house and Bundle, who had been waiting, came tripping down the steps. Jimmy was not ordinarily an observant young man, but he noticed that there were black rings around Bundle's eyes and that she had all the appearance of having had a late night the night before.

"Now then," he said, as the car began to nose her way through the suburbs, "What dark deeds have you been up to?"

"I'll tell you," said Bundle. "But don't interrupt until I've finished."

It was a somewhat long story, and Jimmy had all he could do to keep sufficient attention on the car to prevent an accident. When Bundle had finished he sighed—then looked at her searchingly.

"Bundle?"

"Yes?"

"Look here, you're not pulling my leg?"

"What do you mean?"

"I'm sorry," apologized Jimmy, "but it seems to me as though I'd heard it all before—in a dream, you know."

"I know," said Bundle sympathetically.

"It's impossible," said Jimmy, following out his own train of thought. "The beautiful foreign adventuress, the international gang, the mysterious No. 7, whose identity nobody knows—I've read it all a hundred times in books."

"Of course you have. So have I. But it's no reason why it shouldn't really happen."

"I suppose not," admitted Jimmy.

"After all—I suppose fiction is founded on the truth. I mean unless things did happen, people couldn't think of them."

"There is something in what you say," agreed Jimmy. "But all the same I can't help pinching myself to see if I'm awake."

"That's how I felt."

Jimmy gave a deep sigh.

"Well, I suppose we are awake. Let me see, a Russian, an American, an Englishman—a possible Austrian or Hungarian—and the lady who may be any nationality—for choice Russian or Polish—that's a pretty representative gathering."

"And a German," said Bundle. "You've forgotten the German."

"Oh!" said Jimmy slowly. "You think—"

"The absent No. 2 is Bauer—our footman. That seems to me quite clear from what they said about expecting a report which hadn't come in—though what there can be to report about Chimneys, I can't think."

"It must be something to do with Gerry Wade's death," said Jimmy. "There's something there we haven't fathomed yet. You say they actually mentioned Bauer by name?"

Bundle nodded.

"They blamed him for not having found that letter."

"Well, I don't see what you could have clearer than that. There's no going against it. You'll have to forgive my first incredulity, Bundle—but you know, it was rather a tall story. You say they knew about my going down to Wyvern Abbey next week?"

"Yes, that's when the American—it was him, not the Russian—said they needn't worry—you were only the usual kind of ass."

"Ah!" said Jimmy. He pressed his foot down on the accelerator viciously and the car shot forward. "I'm very glad you told me that. It gives me what you might call a personal interest in the case."

He was silent for a minute or two and then he said:

"Did you say that German inventor's name was Eberhard?"

"Yes. Why?"

"Wait a minute. Something's coming back to me.

Eberhard, Eberhard—yes, I'm sure that was the name."

"Tell me."

"Eberhard was a Johnny who'd got some patent process he applied to steel. I can't put the thing properly because I haven't got the scientific knowledge—but I know the result was that it became so toughened that a wire was as strong as a steel bar had previously been. Eberhard had to do with aeroplanes and his idea was that the weight would be so enormously reduced that flying would be practically revolutionized—the cost of it, I mean. I believe he offered his invention to the German Government, and they turned it down, pointed out some undeniable flaw in it—but they did it rather nastily. He set to work and circumvented the difficulty, whatever it was, but he'd been offended by their attitude and swore they shouldn't have his ewe lamb. I always thought the whole thing was probably bunkum, but now—it looks differently."

"That's it," said Bundle eagerly. "You must be right, Jimmy. Eberhard must have offered his invention to our Government. They've been taking, or are going to take, Sir Oswald Coote's expert opinion on it. There's going to be an unofficial conference at the Abbey. Sir Oswald, George, the Air Minister and Eberhard. Eberhard will have the plans or the process or whatever you call it—"

"Formula," suggested Jimmy. "I think 'formula' is a good word myself."

"He'll have the formula with him, and the Seven Dials are out to steal the formula. I remember the Russian saying it was worth millions."

"I suppose it would be," said Jimmy.

"And well worth a few lives—that's what the other man said."

"Well, it seems to have been," said Jimmy, his face clouding over. "Look at this damned inquest to-day. Bundle, are you sure Ronny said nothing else?"

"No," said Bundle. "Just that. *Seven Dials. Tell Jimmy Thesiger*. That's all he could get out, poor lad."

"I wish we knew what he knew," said Jimmy. "But

we've found out one thing. I take it that the footman, Bauer, must almost certainly have been responsible for Gerry's death. You know, Bundle—"

"Yes?"

"Well, I'm a bit worried sometimes. Who's going to be the next one! It really isn't the sort of business for a girl to be mixed up in."

Bundle smiled in spite of herself. It occurred to her that it had taken Jimmy a long time to put her in the same category as Loraine Wade.

"It's far more likely to be you than me," she remarked cheerfully.

"Hear, hear," said Jimmy. "But what about a few casualties on the other side for a change? I'm feeling rather bloodthirsty this morning. Tell me, Bundle, would you recognize any of these people if you saw them?"

Bundle hesitated.

"I think I should recognize No. 5," she said at last. "He's got a queer way of speaking—a kind of venomous, lisping way—that I think I'd know again."

"What about the Englishman?"

Bundle shook her head.

"I saw him least—only a glimpse—and he's got a very ordinary voice. Except that he's a big man, there's nothing much to go by."

"There's the woman, of course," continued Jimmy. "She ought to be easier. But then, you're not likely to run across her. She's probably putting in the dirty work being taken out to dinner by amorous Cabinet Ministers and getting State secrets out of them when they've had a couple. At least, that's how it's done in books. As a matter of fact, the only Cabinet Minister I know drinks hot water with a dash of lemon in it."

"Take George Lomax, for instance, can you imagine him being amorous with beautiful foreign women?" said Bundle with a laugh.

Jimmy agreed with her criticism.

"And now about the man of mystery—No. 7," went on Jimmy. "You've no idea who he could be?"

"None whatever."

"Again—by book standard, that is—he ought to be someone we all know. What about George Lomax himself?"

Bundle reluctantly shook her head.

"In a book, it would be perfect," she agreed. "But knowing Codders—" And she gave herself up to a sudden uncontrollable mirth. "Codders, the great criminal organizer," she gasped. "Wouldn't it be marvellous?"

Jimmy agreed that it would. Their discussion had taken some time and his driving had slowed down involuntarily once or twice. They arrived at Chimneys, to find Colonel Melrose already there waiting. Jimmy was introduced to him and they all three proceeded to the inquest together.

As Colonel Melrose had predicted, the whole affair was very simple. Bundle gave her evidence. The doctor gave his. Evidence was given of rifle practice in the neighbourhood. A verdict of death by misadventure was brought in.

After the proceedings were over, Colonel Melrose volunteered to drive Bundle back to Chimneys, and Jimmy Thesiger returned to London. For all his lighthearted manner, Bundle's story had impressed him profoundly. He set his lips closely together.

"Ronny, old boy," he murmured, "I'm going to be up against it. And you're not here to join in the game."

Another thought flashed into his mind. Loraine! Was she in danger?

After a minute or two's hesitation, he went over to the telephone and rang her up.

"It's me—Jimmy. I thought you'd like to know the result of the inquest. Death by misadventure."

"Oh, but—"

"Yes, but I think there's something behind that. The coroner had had a hint. Someone's at work to hush it up. I say, Loraine—"

"Yes?"

"Look here. There's—there's some funny business going about. You'll be very careful, won't you? For my sake."

He heard the quick note of alarm that sprang into her voice.

"Jimmy—but then it's dangerous—for *you.*"

He laughed.

"Oh, *that's* all right. I'm the cat that had nine lives. Bye-bye, old thing."

He rang off and remained a minute or two lost in thought. Then he summoned Stevens.

"Do you think you could go out and buy me a pistol, Stevens?"

"A pistol, sir?"

True to his training, Stevens betrayed no hint of surprise.

"What kind of a pistol would you be requiring?"

"The kind where you put your finger on the trigger and the thing goes on shooting until you take it off again."

"An automatic, sir."

"That's it," said Jimmy. "An automatic. And I should like it to be a blue-nosed one—if you and the shopman know what that is. In American stories, the hero always takes his blue-nosed automatic from his hip pocket."

Stevens permitted himself a faint, discreet smile.

"Most American gentlemen that I have known, sir, carry something very different in their hip pockets," he observed.

Jimmy Thesiger laughed.

CHAPTER XVI

The House Party at the Abbey

BUNDLE drove over to Wyvern Abbey just in time for tea on Friday afternoon. George Lomax came forward to welcome her with considerable *empressement.*

"My dear Eileen," he said, "I can't tell you how pleased I am to see you here. You must forgive my not having invited you when I asked your father, but to tell the truth I never dreamed that a party of this kind would appeal to you. I was both—er—surprised and—er—delighted when Lady Caterham told me of your—er—interest in—er—politics."

"I wanted to come so much," said Bundle in a simple, ingenuous manner.

"Mrs. Macatta will not arrive till the later train," explained George. "She was speaking at a meeting in Manchester last night. Do you know Thesiger? Quite a young fellow, but a remarkable grasp of foreign politics. One would hardly suspect it from his appearance."

"I know Mr. Thesiger," said Bundle, and she shook hands solemnly with Jimmy, whom she observed had parted his hair in the middle in the endeavour to add earnestness to his expression.

"Look here," said Jimmy in a low hurried voice, as George temporarily withdrew. "You mustn't be angry, but I've told Bill about our little stunt."

"Bill?" said Bundle, annoyed.

"Well, after all," said Jimmy, "Bill is one of the lads, you know. Ronny was a pal of his and so was Gerry."

"Oh! I know," said Bundle.

"But you think it's a pity? Sorry."

"Bill's all right, of course. It isn't that," said Bundle. "But he's—well, Bill's a born blunderer."

"Not mentally very agile?" suggested Jimmy. "But you forget one thing—Bill's got a very hefty fist. And I've an idea that a hefty fist is going to come in handy."

"Well, perhaps you're right. How did he take it?"

"Well, he clutched his head a good bit, but—I mean the facts took some driving home. But by repeating the thing patiently in words of one syllable I at last got it into his thick head. And, naturally, he's with us to the death, as you might say."

George reappeared suddenly.

"I must make some introductions, Eileen. This is Sir Stanley Digby—Lady Eileen Brent. Mr. O'Rourke." The Air Minister was a little round man with a cheerful smile. Mr. O'Rourke, a tall young man with laughing blue eyes and a typical Irish face, greeted Bundle with enthusiasm.

"And I thinking it was going to be a dull political party entirely," he murmured in an adroit whisper.

"Hush," said Bundle. "I'm political—very political."

"Sir Oswald and Lady Coote you know," continued George.

"We've never actually met," said Bundle, smiling.

She was mentally applauding her father's descriptive powers.

Sir Oswald took her hand in an iron grip and she winced slightly.

Lady Coote, after a somewhat mournful greeting, had turned to Jimmy Thesiger, and appeared to be registering something closely akin to pleasure. Despite his reprehensible habit of being late for breakfast, Lady Coote had a fondness for this amiable, pink-faced young man. His air of irrepressible good nature fascinated her. She had a motherly wish to cure him of his bad habits and form him into one of the world's workers. Whether, once formed, he would be as attractive was a question she had never asked herself. She began now to tell him of a very painful motor accident which had happened to one of her friends.

"Mr. Bateman," said George briefly, as one who would pass on to better things.

A serious, pale-faced young man bowed.

"And now," continued George, "I must introduce you to Countess Radzky."

Countess Radzky had been conversing with Mr. Bateman. Leaning very far back on a sofa, with her legs crossed in a daring manner, she was smoking a cigarette in an incredibly long turquoise studded holder.

Bundle thought she was one of the most beautiful women she had ever seen. Her eyes were very large and blue, her hair was coal black, she had a matte skin, the slightly flattened nose of the Slav, and a sinuous, slender body. Her lips were reddened to a degree with which Bundle was sure Wyvern Abbey was totally unacquainted.

She said eagerly: "This is Mrs. Macatta—yes?"

On George's replying in the negative and introducing Bundle, the Countess gave her a careless nod, and at once resumed her conversation with the serious Mr. Bateman.

Bundle heard Jimmy's voice in her ear:

"Pongo is absolutely fascinated by the lovely Slav," he said. "Pathetic, isn't it? Come and have some tea."

They drifted once more into the neighbourhood of Sir Oswald Coote.

"That's a fine place of yours, Chimneys," remarked the great man.

"I'm glad you liked it," said Bundle meekly.

"Wants new plumbing," said Sir Oswald. "Bring it up to date, you know."

He ruminated for a minute or two.

"I'm taking the Duke of Alton's place. Three years. Just while I'm looking round for a place of my own. Your father couldn't sell if he wanted to, I suppose."

Bundle felt her breath taken away. She had a nightmare vision of England with innumerable Cootes in innumerable counterparts of Chimneys—all, be it understood, with an entirely new system of plumbing installed.

She felt a sudden violent resentment which, she told herself, was absurd. After all, contrasting Lord Caterham with Sir Oswald Coote, there was no doubt as to who would go to the wall. Sir Oswald had one of those powerful personalities which make all those with whom they come in contact appear faded. He was, as Lord Caterham had said, a human steam-roller. And yet, undoubtedly, in many ways, Sir Oswald was a stupid man. Apart from his special line of knowledge and his terrific driving force, he was probably intensely ignorant. A hundred delicate appreciations of life which Lord Caterham could and did enjoy were a sealed book to Sir Oswald.

Whilst indulging in these reflections Bundle continued to chat pleasantly. Herr Eberhard, she heard, had arrived, but was lying down with a nervous headache. This was told her by Mr. O'Rourke, who managed to find a place by her side and keep it.

Altogether, Bundle went up to dress in a pleasant mood of expectation, with a slight nervous dread hovering in the background whenever she thought of the imminent arrival of Mrs. Macatta. Bundle felt that dalliance with Mrs. Macatta was going to prove no primrose path.

Her first shock was when she came down, demurely attired in a black lace frock, and passed along the hall. A footman was standing there—at least a man dressed as a footman. But that square, burly figure lent itself badly to the deception. Bundle stopped and stared.

"Superintendent Battle," she breathed.

"That's right, Lady Eileen."

"Oh!" said Bundle uncertainly. "Are you here to—to—"

"Keep an eye on things."

"I see."

"That warning letter, you know," said the Superintendent, "fairly put the wind up Mr. Lomax. Nothing would do for him but that I should come down myself."

"But don't you think——" began Bundle, and stopped. She hardly liked to suggest to the Superintendent that his disguise was not a particularly efficient one. He seemed to have "police officer" written all over him, and Bundle could hardly imagine the most unsuspecting criminal failing to be put on his guard.

"You think," said the Superintendent stolidly, "that I might be recognized?"

He gave the final word a distinct capital letter.

"I did think so—yes—" admitted Bundle.

Something that might conceivably have been intended for a smile crossed the woodenness of Superintendent Battle's features.

"Put them on their guard, eh? Well, Lady Eileen, why not?"

"Why not?" echoed Bundle, rather stupidly, she felt.

Superintendent Battle was nodding his head slowly.

"We don't want any unpleasantness, do we?" he said. "Don't want to be too clever—just show any light-fingered gentry that may be about—well, just show them that there's somebody on the spot, so to speak."

Introducing the first and only complete hardcover collection of Agatha Christie's mysteries

Now you can enjoy the
greatest mysteries ever written
in a magnificent
Home Library Edition.

Discover Agatha Christie's world of mystery, adventure and intrigue

Agatha Christie's timeless tales of mystery and suspense offer something for every reader—mystery fan or not—young and old alike. And now, you can build a complete hardcover library of her world-famous mysteries by subscribing to The Agatha Christie Mystery Collection.

This exciting Collection is your passport to a world where mystery reigns supreme. Volume after volume, you and your family will enjoy mystery reading at its very best.

You'll meet Agatha Christie's world-famous detectives like Hercule Poirot, Jane Marple, and the likeable Tommy and Tuppence Beresford.

In your readings, you'll visit Egypt, Paris, England and other exciting destinations where murder is always on the itinerary. And wherever you travel, you'll become deeply involved in some of the most ingenious and diabolical plots ever invented . . . "cliff-hangers" that only Dame Agatha could create!

It all adds up to mystery reading that's so good . . . it's almost criminal. And it's yours every month with The Agatha Christie Mystery Collection.

Solve the greatest mysteries of all time. The Collection contains all of Agatha Christie's classic works including *Murder on the Orient Express, Death on the Nile, And Then There Were None, The ABC Murders* and her ever-popular whodunit, *The Murder of Roger Ackroyd.*

Each handsome hardcover volume is Smythe sewn and printed on high quality acid-free paper so it can withstand even the most murderous treatment. Bound in Sussex-blue simulated leather with gold titling, The Agatha Christie Mystery Collection will make a tasteful addition to your living room, or den.

Ride the Orient Express for 10 days without obligation. To introduce you to the Collection, we're inviting you to examine the classic mystery, *Murder on the Orient Express*, without risk or obligation. If you're not completely satisfied, just return it within 10 days and owe nothing.

However, if you're like the millions of other readers who love Agatha Christie's thrilling tales of mystery and suspense, keep *Murder on the Orient Express* and pay just $9.95 plus postage and handling.

You will then automatically receive future volumes once a month as they are published on a fully returnable, 10-day free-examination basis. No minimum purchase is required, and you may cancel your subscription at any time.

This unique collection is not sold in stores. It's available only through this special offer. So don't miss out, begin your subscription now. Just mail this card today.

BUSINESS REPLY CARD

FIRST CLASS   PERMIT NO. 2154   HICKSVILLE, N.Y.

Postage will be paid by addressee:

The Agatha Christie
Mystery Collection
Bantam Books
P.O. Box 956
Hicksville, N.Y. 11802

Bundle gazed at him in some admiration. She could imagine that the sudden appearance of so renowned a personage as Superintendent Battle might have a depressing effect on any scheme and the hatchers of it.

"It's a great mistake to be too clever," Superintendent Battle was repeating. "The great thing is not to have any unpleasantness this week-end."

Bundle passed on, wondering how many of her fellow guests had recognized or would recognize the Scotland Yard detective. In the drawing-room George was standing with a puckered brow and an orange envelope in his hand.

"Most vexatious," he said. "A telegram from Mrs. Macatta to say she will be unable to be with us. Her children are suffering from mumps."

Bundle's heart gave a throb of relief.

"I especially feel this on your account, Eileen," said George kindly. "I know how anxious you were to meet her. The Countess too will be sadly disappointed."

"Oh, never mind," said Bundle. "I should hate it if she'd come and given me mumps."

"A very distressing complaint," agreed George. "But I do not think that infection could be carried that way. Indeed, I am sure that Mrs. Macatta would have run no risk of that kind. She is a most highly principled woman, with a very real sense of her responsibilities to the community. In these days of national stress, we must all take into account—"

On the brink of embarking on a speech, George pulled himself up short.

"But it must be for another time," he said. "Fortunately there is no hurry in your case. But the Countess, alas, is only a visitor to our shores."

"She's a Hungarian, isn't she?" said Bundle, who was curious about the Countess.

"Yes. You have heard, no doubt, of the Young Hungarian party? The Countess is a leader in that party. A woman of great wealth, left a widow at an early age, she has devoted her money and her talents to the public service. She has especially devoted herself to the problem of infant mortality—a terrible one under present conditions in Hungary. I—Ah! here is Herr Eberhard."

The German inventor was younger than Bundle had imagined him. He was probably not more than thirty-three or four. He was boorish and ill at ease, and yet his personality was not an unpleasing one. His blue eyes were more shy than furtive, and his more unpleasant mannerisms, such as the one that Bill had described of gnawing his finger nails, arose, she thought, more from nervousness than from any other cause. He was thin and weedy in appearance and looked anaemic and delicate.

He conversed rather awkwardly with Bundle in stilted English and they both welcomed the interruption of the joyous Mr. O'Rourke. Presently Bill bustled in—there is no other word for it. In the same such way does a favoured Newfoundland make his entrance, and at once came over to Bundle. He was looking perplexed and harassed.

"Hullo, Bundle. Heard you'd got here. Been kept with my nose to the grindstone all the blessed afternoon or I'd have seen you before."

"Cares of State heavy to-night?" suggested O'Rourke sympathetically.

Bill groaned.

"I don't know what your fellow's like," he complained. "Looks a good-natured, tubby little chap. But Codders is absolutely impossible. Drive, drive, drive, from morning to night. Everything you do is wrong, and everything you haven't done you ought to have done."

"Quite like a quotation from the prayer book," remarked Jimmy, who had just strolled up.

Bill glanced at them reproachfully.

"Nobody knows," he said pathetically, "what I have to put up with."

"Entertaining the Countess, eh?" suggested Jimmy. "Poor Bill, that must have been a sad strain—to a woman hater like yourself."

"What's this?" asked Bundle.

"After tea," said Jimmy with a grin, "the Countess asked Bill to show her round the interesting old place."

"Well, I couldn't refuse, could I?" said Bill, his countenance assuming a brick-red tint.

Bundle felt faintly uneasy. She knew, only too well, the susceptibility of Mr. William Eversleigh to female charms. In the hands of a woman like the Countess, Bill would be as wax. She wondered once more whether Jimmy Thesiger had been wise to take Bill into their confidence.

"The Countess," said Bill, "is a very charming woman. And no end intelligent. You should have seen her going round the house. All sorts of questions she asked."

"What kind of questions?" asked Bundle suddenly. Bill was vague.

"Oh! I don't know. About the history of it. And old furniture. And—oh! all sorts of things."

At that moment the Countess swept into the room. She seemed a shade breathless. She was looking magnificent in a close-fitting black velvet gown. Bundle noticed how Bill gravitated at once into her immediate neighbourhood. The serious, spectacled young man joined him.

"Bill and Pongo have both got it badly," observed Jimmy Thesiger with a laugh.

Bundle was by no means so sure that it was a laughing matter.

CHAPTER XVII

After Dinner

GEORGE was not a believer in modern innovations. The Abbey was innocent of anything so up to date as central heating. Consequently, when the ladies entered the drawing-room after dinner, the temperature of the room was woefully inadequate to the needs of modern evening clothes. The fire that burnt in the well burnished steel grate became as a magnet. The three women huddled round it.

"Brrrrrrrrrrr!" said the Countess, a fine, exotic, foreign sound.

"The days are drawing in," said Lady Coote, and drew a flowered atrocity of a scarf closer about her ample shoulders.

"Why on earth doesn't George have the house properly heated?" said Bundle.

"You English, you never heat your houses," said the Countess.

She took out her long cigarette holder and began to smoke.

"That grate is old-fashioned," said Lady Coote. "The heat goes up the chimney instead of into the room."

"Oh!" said the Countess.

There was a pause. The Countess was so plainly bored by her company that conversation became difficult.

"It's funny," said Lady Coote, breaking the silence, "that Mrs. Macatta's children should have mumps. At least, I don't mean exactly funny—"

"What," said the Countess, "are mumps?"

Bundle and Lady Coote started simultaneously to explain. Finally, between them, they managed it.

"I suppose Hungarian children have it?" asked Lady Coote.

"Eh?" said the Countess.

"Hungarian children. They suffer from it?"

"I do not know," said the Countess. "How should I?"

Lady Coote looked at her in some surprise.

"But I understood that you worked—"

"Oh, that!" The Countess uncrossed her legs, took her cigarette holder from her mouth and began to talk rapidly.

"I will tell you some horrors," she said. "Horrors that I have seen. Incredible! You would not believe!"

And she was as good as her word. She talked fluently and with a graphic power of description. Incredible scenes of starvation and misery were painted by her for the benefit of her audience. She spoke of Buda Pesth shortly after the war and traced its vicissitudes to the present day. She was dramatic, but she was also, to Bundle's mind, a little like a gramophone record. You turned her on, and there you were. Presently, just as suddenly, she would stop.

Lady Coote was thrilled to the marrow—that much was clear. She sat with her mouth slightly open and her large, sad, dark eyes fixed on the Countess. Occasionally, she interpolated a comment of her own.

"One of my cousins had three children burned to death. Awful, wasn't it?"

The Countess paid no attention. She went on and on. And she finally stopped as suddenly as she had begun.

"There!" she said. "I have told you! We have money —but no organization. It is organization we need."

Lady Coote sighed.

"I've heard my husband say that nothing can be done without regular methods. He attributes his own success entirely to that. He declares he would have never got on without them."

She sighed again. A sudden fleeting vision passed before her eyes of a Sir Oswald who had not got on in the world. A Sir Oswald who retained, in all essentials, the attributes of that cheery young man in the bicycle shop. Just for a second it occurred to her how much pleasanter life might have been for her if Sir Oswald had *not* had regular methods.

By a quite understandable association of ideas she turned to Bundle.

"Tell me, Lady Eileen," she said, "do you like that head gardener of yours?"

"MacDonald? Well—" Bundle hesitated. "One couldn't exactly *like* MacDonald," she explained apologetically. "But he's a first class gardener."

"Oh! I know he is," said Lady Coote.

"He's all right if he's kept in his place," said Bundle.

"I suppose so," said Lady Coote.

She looked enviously at Bundle, who appeared to approach the task of keeping MacDonald in his place so light heartedly.

"I'd just adore a high-toned garden," said the Countess dreamily.

Bundle stared, but at that moment a diversion occurred. Jimmy Thesiger entered the room and spoke directly to her in a strange, hurried voice.

"I say, will you come and see those etchings now? They're waiting for you."

Bundle left the room hurriedly, Jimmy close behind her.

"What etchings?" she asked, as the drawing-room door closed behind her.

"No etchings," said Jimmy. "I'd got to say something to get hold of you. Come on, Bill is waiting for us in the library. There's nobody there."

Bill was striding up and down the library, clearly in a very perturbed state of mind.

"Look here," he burst out, "I don't like this."

"Don't like what?"

"You being mixed up in this. Ten to one there's going to be a rough house and then——"

He looked at her with a kind of pathetic dismay that gave Bundle a warm and comfortable feeling.

"She ought to be kept out of it, oughtn't she, Jimmy?"

He appealed to the other.

"I've told her so," said Jimmy.

"Dash it all, Bundle, I mean—someone might get hurt."

Bundle turned round to Jimmy.

"How much have you told him?"

"Oh! everything."

"I haven't got the hang of it all yet," confessed Bill. "You in that place in Seven Dials and all that." He looked at her unhappily. "I say, Bundle, I wish you wouldn't."

"Wouldn't what?"

"Get mixed up in these sorts of things."

"Why not?" said Bundle. "They're exciting."

"Oh, yes—exciting. But they may be damnably dangerous. Look at poor old Ronny."

"Yes," said Bundle. "If it hadn't been for your friend Ronny, I don't suppose I should ever have got what you call 'mixed up' in this thing. But I am. And it's no earthly use your bleating about it."

"I know you're the most frightful sport, Bundle, but—"

"Cut out the compliments. Let's make plans."

To her relief, Bill reacted favourably to the suggestion.

"You're right about the formula," he said. "Eberhard's got some sort of formula with him, or rather Sir Oswald has. The stuff has been tested out at his works —very secretly and all that. Eberhard has been down there with him. They're all in the study now—what you might call coming down to brass tacks."

"How long is Sir Stanley Digby staying?" asked Jimmy.

"Going back to town to-morrow."

"H'm," said Jimmy. "Then one thing's quite clear. If, as I suppose, Sir Stanley will be taking the formula with him, any funny business there's going to be will be to-night."

"I suppose it will."

"Not a doubt of it. That narrows the thing down very comfortably. But the bright lads will have to be their very brightest. We must come down to details. First of all, where will the sacred formula be to-night? Will Eberhard have it, or Sir Oswald Coote?"

"Neither. I understand it's to be handed over to the Air Minister this evening, for him to take to town to-morrow. In that case O'Rourke will have it. Sure to."

"Well, there's only one thing for it. If we believe someone's going to have a shot at pinching that paper, we've got to keep watch to-night, Bill, my boy."

Bundle opened her mouth as though to protest, but shut it again without speaking.

"By the way," continued Jimmy, "did I recognize the commissionaire from Harrods in the hall this evening, or was it our old friend Lestrade from Scotland Yard?"

"Scintillating, Watson," said Bill.

"I suppose," said Jimmy, "that we are rather butting in on his preserves."

"Can't be helped," said Bill. "Not if we mean to see this thing through."

"Then it's agreed," said Jimmy. "We divide the night into two watches?"

Again Bundle opened her mouth, and again shut it without speaking.

"Right you are," agreed Bill. "Who'll take first duty?"

"Shall we spin for it?"

"Might as well."

"All right. Here goes. Heads you first and I second. Tails, vice versa."

Bill nodded. The coin spun in the air. Jimmy bent to look at it.

"Tails," he said.

"Damn," said Bill. "You get first half and probably any fun that's going."

"Oh, you never know," said Jimmy. "Criminals are very uncertain. What time shall I wake you? Three thirty?"

"That's about fair, I think."

And now, at last, Bundle spoke:

"What about *me?*" she asked.

"Nothing doing. You go to bed and sleep."

"Oh!" said Bundle. "That's not very exciting."

"You never know," said Jimmy kindly. "You may be murdered in your sleep whilst Bill and I escape scot-free."

"Well, there's always that possibility. Do you know, Jimmy, I don't half like the look of that Countess. I suspect her."

"Nonsense," cried Bill hotly. "She's absolutely above suspicion."

"How do you know?" retorted Bundle.

"Because I do. Why, one of the fellows at the Hungarian Embassy vouched for her."

"Oh!" said Bundle, momentarily taken aback by his fervour.

"You girls are all the same," grumbled Bill. "Just because she's a jolly good-looking woman——"

Bundle was only too well acquainted with this unfair masculine line of argument.

"Well, don't you go and pour confidences into her shell-pink ear," she remarked. "I'm going to bed. I was bored stiff in that drawing-room and I'm not going back."

She left the room. Bill looked at Jimmy.

"Good old Bundle," he said. "I was afraid we might have trouble with her. You know how keen she is to be in everything. I think the way she took it was just wonderful."

"So did I," said Jimmy. "It staggered me."

"She's got some sense, Bundle has. She knows when a thing's plumb impossible. I say, oughtn't we to have some lethal weapons? Chaps usually do when they're going on this sort of stunt."

"I have a blue-nosed automatic," said Jimmy with gentle pride. "It weighs several pounds and looks most murderous. I'll lend it to you when the time comes."

Bill looked at him with respect and envy.

"What made you think of getting that?" he said.

"I don't know," said Jimmy carelessly. "It just came to me."

"I hope we shan't go and shoot the wrong person," said Bill with some anxiety.

"That would be unfortunate," said Mr. Thesiger gravely.

CHAPTER XVIII

Jimmy's Adventures

OUR chronicle must here split into three separate and distinct portions. The night was to prove an eventful one and each of the three persons involved saw it from his or her own individual angle.

We will begin with that pleasant and engaging youth,

Mr. Jimmy Thesiger, at a moment when he has at last exchanged final good-nights with his fellow conspirator, Bill Eversleigh.

"Don't forget," said Bill, "3 A.M. If you're still alive, that is," he added kindly.

"I may be an ass," said Jimmy, with rancorous remembrance of the remark Bundle had repeated to him, "but I'm not nearly so much of an ass as I look."

"That's what you said about Gerry Wade," said Bill slowly. "Do you remember? And that very night he—"

"Shut up, you damned fool," said Jimmy. "Haven't you got *any* tact?"

"Of course I've got tact," said Bill. "I'm a budding diplomatist. All diplomatists have tact."

"Ah!" said Jimmy. "You must be still in what they call the larval stage."

"I can't get over Bundle," said Bill, reverting abruptly to a former topic. "I should certainly have said that she'd be—well, difficult. Bundle's improved. She's improved very much."

"That's what your Chief was saying," said Jimmy. "He said he was agreeably surprised."

"I thought Bundle was laying it on a bit thick myself," said Bill. "But Codders is such an ass he'd swallow anything. Well, night-night. I expect you'll have a bit of a job waking me when the time comes—but stick to it."

"It won't be much good if you've taken a leaf out of Gerry Wade's book," said Jimmy maliciously.

Bill looked at him reproachfully.

"What the hell do you want to go and make a chap uncomfortable for?" he demanded.

"You're only getting your own back," said Jimmy. "Toddle along."

But Bill lingered. He stood uncomfortably, first on one foot and then on the other.

"Look here," he said.

"Yes?"

"What I mean to say is—well, I mean you'll be all right and all that, won't you? It's all very well ragging, but when I think of poor old Gerry—and then poor old Ronny—"

Jimmy gazed at him in exasperation. Bill was one of those who undoubtedly meant well, but the result of his efforts would not be described as heartening.

"I see," he remarked, "that I shall have to show you Leopold."

He slipped his hand into the pocket of the dark blue suit into which he had just changed and held out something for Bill's inspection.

"A real, genuine, blue-nosed automatic," he said with modest pride.

"No, I say," Bill said. "Is it really?"

He was undoubtedly impressed.

"Stevens, my man, got him for me. Warranted clean and methodical in his habits. You press the button and Leopold does the rest."

"Oh!" said Bill. "I say, Jimmy?"

"Yes?"

"Be careful, won't you? I mean, don't go loosing that thing off at anybody. Pretty awkward if you shot old Digby walking in his sleep."

"That's all right," said Jimmy. "Naturally, I want to get value out of Leopold now I've bought him, but I'll curb my bloodthirsty instincts as far as possible."

"Well, night-night," said Bill for the fourteenth time, and this time really did depart.

Jimmy was left alone to take up his vigil.

Sir Stanley Digby occupied a room at the extremity of the west wing. A bathroom adjoined it on one side, and on the other a communicating door led into a smaller room, which was tenanted by Mr. Terence O'Rourke. The doors of these three rooms gave on to a short corridor. The watcher had a simple task. A chair placed inconspicuously in the shadow of an oak press just where the corridor ran into the main gallery formed a perfect vantage ground. There was no other way into the west wing, and anyone going to or from it could not fail to be seen. One electric light was still on.

Jimmy ensconced himself comfortably, crossed his

legs and waited. Leopold lay in readiness across his knee.

He glanced at his watch. It was twenty minutes to one—just an hour since the household had retired to rest. Not a sound broke the stillness, except for the far-off ticking of a clock somewhere.

Somehow or other, Jimmy did not much care for that sound. It recalled things. Gerald Wade—and those seven ticking clocks on the mantelpiece. . . . Whose hand had placed them there, and why? He shivered.

It was a creepy business, this waiting. He didn't wonder that things happened at spiritualistic séances. Sitting in the gloom, one got all worked up—ready to start at the least sound. And unpleasant thoughts came crowding in on a fellow.

Ronny Devereux! Ronny Devereux and Gerry Wade! Both young, both full of life and energy; ordinary, jolly, healthy young men. And now, where were they? Dank earth . . . worms getting them. . . . Ugh! why couldn't he put these horrible thoughts out of his mind?

He looked again at his watch. Twenty minutes past one only. How the time crawled.

Extraordinary girl, Bundle! Fancy having the nerve and the daring actually to get into the midst of that Seven Dials place. Why hadn't he had the nerve and the initiative to think of that? He supposed because the thing *was* so fantastic.

No. 7. Who the hell could No. 7 be? Was he, perhaps, in the house at this minute? Disguised as a servant. He couldn't, surely, be one of the guests. No, that was impossible. But then, the whole thing was impossible. If he hadn't believed Bundle to be essentially truthful—well, he would have thought she had invented the whole thing.

He yawned. Queer, to feel sleepy, and yet at the same time strung up. He looked again at his watch. Ten minutes to two. Time was getting on.

And then, suddenly, he held his breath and leaned forward, listening. He had heard something.

The minutes went past. . . . There it was again.

The creak of a board. . . . But it came from downstairs somewhere. There it was again! A slight, ominous creak. Somebody was moving stealthily about the house.

Jimmy sprang noiselessly to his feet. He crept silently to the head of the staircase. Everything seemed perfectly quiet. Yet he was quite certain he had really heard that stealthy sound. It was not imagination.

Very quietly and cautiously he crept down the staircase, Leopold clasped tightly in his right hand. Not a sound in the big hall. If he had been correct in assuming that the muffled sound came from directly beneath him, then it must have come from the library.

Jimmy stole to the door of it, listened, but heard nothing; then, suddenly flinging open the door, he switched on the lights.

Nothing! The big room was flooded with light. But it was empty.

Jimmy frowned.

"I could have sworn—" he murmured to himself.

The library was a large room with three windows which opened on to the terrace. Jimmy strode across the room. The middle window was unlatched.

He opened it and stepped out on the terrace, looking from end to end of it. Nothing!

"Looks all right," he murmured to himself. "And yet—"

He remained for a minute lost in thought. Then he stepped back into the library. Crossing to the door, he locked it and put the key in his pocket. Then he switched off the light. He stood for a minute listening, then crossed softly to the open window and stood there, Leopold ready in his hand.

Was there, or was there not, a soft patter of feet along the terrace? No—his imagination. He grasped Leopold tightly and stood listening. . . .

In the distance a stable clock chimed two.

CHAPTER XIX

Bundle's Adventures

BUNDLE BRENT was a resourceful girl—she was also a girl of imagination. She had foreseen that Bill, if not Jimmy, would make objections to her participation in the possible dangers of the night. It was not Bundle's idea to waste time in argument. She had laid her own plans and made her own arrangements. A glance from her bedroom window shortly before dinner had been highly satisfactory. She had known that the gray walls of the Abbey were plentifully adorned with ivy, but the ivy outside her window was particularly solid looking and would present no difficulties to one of her athletic propensities.

She had no fault to find with Bill's and Jimmy's arrangements as far as they went. But in her opinion they did not go far enough. She offered no criticism, because she intended to see to that side of things herself. Briefly, while Jimmy and Bill were devoting themselves to the inside of the Abbey, Bundle intended to devote her attentions to the outside.

Her own meek acquiescence in the tame rôle assigned to her gave her an infinity of pleasure, though she wondered scornfully how either of the two men could be so easily deceived. Bill, of course, had never been famous for scintillating brain power. On the other hand, he knew, or should know, his Bundle. And she considered that Jimmy Thesiger, though only slightly acquainted with her, ought to have known better than to imagine that she could be so easily and summarily disposed of.

Once in the privacy of her own room, Bundle set rapidly to work. First she discarded her evening dress and the negligible trifle which she wore beneath it, and started again, so to speak, from the foundations. Bundle had not brought her maid with her, and she herself had packed. Otherwise, the puzzled Frenchwoman might have wondered why her lady took a pair of riding breeches and no further equine equipment.

Arrayed in riding breeches, rubber-soled shoes, and a dark-coloured pullover, Bundle was ready for the fray. She glanced at the time. As yet, it was only half-past twelve. Too early by far. Whatever was going to happen would not happen for some time yet. The occupants of the house must all be given time to get off to sleep. Half past one was the time fixed by Bundle for the start of operations.

She switched off her light and sat down by the window to wait. Punctually at the appointed moment, she rose, pushed up the sash and swung her leg over the sill. The night was a fine one, cold and still. There was starlight but no moon.

She found the descent very easy. Bundle and her two sisters had run wild in the park at Chimneys as small children, and they could all climb like cats. Bundle arrived on a flower-bed, rather breathless, but quite unscathed.

She paused a minute to take stock of her plans. She knew that the rooms occupied by the Air Minister and his secretary were in the west wing; that was the opposite side of the house from where Bundle was now standing. A terrace ran along the south and west side of the house, ending abruptly against a walled fruit garden.

Bundle stepped out of her flower-bed and turned the corner of the house to where the terrace began on the south side. She crept very quietly along it, keeping close to the shadow of the house. But, as she reached the second corner, she got a shock, for a man was standing there, with the clear intention of barring her way.

The next instant she had recognized him.

"Superintendent Battle! You did give me a fright!"

"That's what I'm here for," said the Superintendent pleasantly.

Bundle looked at him. It struck her now, as so often before, how remarkably little camouflage there was about him. He was large and solid and noticeable. He was, somehow, very English. But of one thing Bundle was quite sure. Superintendent Battle was no fool.

"What are you really doing here?" she asked, still in a whisper.

"Just seeing," said Battle, "that nobody's about who shouldn't be."

"Oh!" said Bundle, rather taken aback.

"You, for instance, Lady Eileen. I don't suppose you usually take a walk at this time of night."

"Do you mean," said Bundle slowly, "that you want me to go back?"

Superintendent Battle nodded approvingly.

"You're very quick, Lady Eileen. That's just what I do mean. Did you—er—come out of a door, or the window?"

"The window. It's easy as anything climbing down this ivy."

Superintendent Battle looked up at it thoughtfully.

"Yes," he said. "I should say it would be."

"And you want me to go back?" said Bundle. "I'm rather sick about that. I wanted to go round on to the west terrace."

"Perhaps you won't be the only one who'll want to do that," said Battle.

"Nobody could miss seeing you," said Bundle rather spitefully.

The Superintendent seemed rather pleased than otherwise.

"I hope they won't," he said. *"No unpleasantness.* That's my motto. And if you'll excuse me, Lady Eileen, I think it's time you were going back to bed."

The firmness of his tone admitted of no parley. Rather crestfallen, Bundle retraced her steps. She was halfway up the ivy when a sudden idea occurred to her, and she nearly relaxed her grip and fell.

Supposing Superintendent Battle suspected *her*.

There had been something—yes, surely there had been something in his manner that vaguely suggested the idea. She couldn't help laughing as she crawled over the sill into her bedroom. Fancy the solid Superintendent suspecting *her!*

Though she had so far obeyed Battle's orders as to return to her room, Bundle had no intention of going to bed and sleeping. Nor did she think that Battle had really intended her to do so. He was not a man to expect impossibilities. And to remain quiescent when something daring and exciting might be going on was a sheer impossibility to Bundle.

She glanced at her watch. It was ten minutes to two. After a moment or two of irresolution, she cautiously opened her door. Not a sound. Everything was still and peaceful. She stole cautiously along the passage.

Once she halted, thinking she heard a board creak somewhere, but then convinced that she was mistaken, she went on again. She was now in the main corridor, making her way to the west wing. She reached the angle of intersection and peered cautiously round—then she stared in blank surprise.

The watcher's post was empty. Jimmy Thesiger was not there.

Bundle stared in complete amazement. What had happened? Why had Jimmy left his post? What did it mean?

And at that moment she heard a clock strike two.

She was still standing there, debating what to do next, when suddenly her heart gave a leap and then seemed to stand still.

The door handle of Terence O'Rourke's room was slowly turning.

Bundle watched, fascinated. But the door did not open. Instead the knob returned slowly to its original position. What did it mean?

Suddenly Bundle came to a resolution. Jimmy, for some unknown reason, had deserted his post. She must get hold of Bill.

Quickly and noiselessly, Bundle fled along the way she had come. She burst unceremoniously into Bill's room.

"Bill, wake up! Oh, do wake up!"

It was an urgent whisper she sent forth, but there came no response to it.

"Bill," breathed Bundle.

Impatiently she switched on the lights, and then stood dumfounded.

The room was empty, and the bed had not even been slept in.

Where then was Bill?

Suddenly she caught her breath. *This was not Bill's room.* The dainty négligé thrown over a chair, the feminine knick-knacks on the dressing-table, the black velvet evening dress thrown carelessly over a chair— Of course, in her haste she had mistaken the doors. This was the Countess Radzky's room.

But where, oh, where, was the Countess?

And just as Bundle was asking herself this question, the silence of the night was suddenly broken, and in no uncertain manner.

The clamour came from below. In an instant Bundle had sped out of the Countess's room and downstairs. The sounds came from the library—a violent crashing of chairs being overturned.

Bundle rattled vainly at the library door. It was locked. But she could clearly hear the struggle that was going on within—the panting and scuffling, curses in manly tones, the occasional crash as some light piece of furniture came into the line of battle.

And then, sinister and distinct, breaking the peace of the night for good and all, two shots in rapid succession.

CHAPTER XX

Loraine's Adventures

LORAINE WADE sat up in bed and switched on the light. It was exactly ten minutes to one. She had gone to bed early—at half-past nine. She possessed the useful art of being able to wake herself up at the required time, so she had been able to enjoy some hours of refreshing sleep.

Two dogs slept in the room with her, and one of these now raised his head and looked at her inquiringly.

"Quiet, Lurcher," said Loraine, and the big animal put his head down again obediently, watching her from between his shaggy eyelashes.

It is true that Bundle had once doubted the meekness of Loraine Wade, but that brief moment of suspicion had passed. Loraine had seemed so entirely reasonable, so willing to be kept out of everything.

And yet, if you studied the girl's face, you saw that there was strength of purpose in the small, resolute jaw and the lips that closed together so firmly.

Loraine rose and dressed herself in a tweed coat and skirt. Into one pocket of the coat she dropped an electric torch. Then she opened the drawer of her dressing table and took out a small ivory-handled pistol—almost a toy in appearance. She had bought it the day before at Harrods and she was very pleased with it.

She gave a final glance round the room to see if she had forgotten anything, and at that moment the big dog rose and came over to her, looking up at her with pleading eyes and wagging his tail.

Loraine shook her head.

"No, Lurcher. Can't go. Missus can't take you. Got to stay here and be a good boy."

She dropped a kiss on the dog's head, made him lie down on his rug again, and then slipped noiselessly out of the room, closing the door behind her.

She let herself out of the house by a side door and made her way round to the garage, where her little two-seater car was in readiness. There was a gentle slope, and she let the car run silently down it, not starting the engine till she was some way from the house. Then she glanced at the watch on her arm and pressed her foot down on the accelerator.

She left the car at a spot she had previously marked down. There was a gap there in the fencing that she could easily get through. A few minutes later, slightly muddy, Loraine stood inside the grounds of Wyvern Abbey.

As noiselessly as possible, she made her way towards the venerable ivy-covered building. In the distance a stable clock chimed two.

Loraine's heart beat faster as she drew near to the terrace. There was no one about—no sign of life anywhere. Everything seemed peaceful and undisturbed. She reached the terrace and stood there, looking about her.

Suddenly, without the least warning, something from above fell with a flop almost at her feet. Loraine stooped to pick it up. It was a brown paper packet, loosely wrapped. Holding it, Loraine looked up.

There was an open window just above her head, and even as she looked a leg swung over it and a man began to climb down the ivy.

Loraine waited for no more. She took to her heels and ran, still clasping the brown paper packet.

Behind her, the noise of a struggle suddenly broke out. A hoarse voice: "Lemme go"; another that she knew well: "Not if I know it—ah, you would, would you?"

Still Loraine ran—blindly, as though panic stricken—right round the corner of the terrace—and slap into the arms of a large, solidly built man.

"There, there," said Superintendent Battle kindly.

Loraine was struggling to speak.

"Oh, quick—oh, quick! They're killing each other. Oh, do be quick!"

There was a sharp crack of a revolver shot—and then another.

Superintendent Battle started to run. Loraine followed. Back round the corner of the terrace and along to the library window. The window was open.

Battle stooped and switched on an electric torch. Loraine was close beside him, peering over his shoulder. She gave a little sobbing gasp.

On the threshold of the window lay Jimmy Thesiger in what looked like a pool of blood. His right arm lay dangling in a curious position.

Loraine gave a sharp cry.

"He's dead," she wailed. "Oh, Jimmy—Jimmy—he's dead!"

"Now, now," said Superintendent Battle soothingly, "don't you take on so. The young gentleman isn't dead, I'll be bound. See if you can find the lights and turn them on."

Loraine obeyed. She stumbled across the room, found the switch by the door and pressed it down. The room was flooded with light. Superintendent Battle uttered a sigh of relief.

"It's all right—he's only shot in the right arm. He's fainted through loss of blood. Come and give me a hand with him."

There was a pounding on the library door. Voices were heard, asking, expostulating, demanding.

Loraine looked doubtfully at it.

"Shall I—"

"No hurry," said Battle. "We'll let them in presently. You come and give me a hand."

Loraine came obediently. The Superintendent had produced a large, clean pocket-handkerchief and was neatly bandaging the wounded man's arm. Loraine helped him.

"He'll be all right," said the Superintendent. "Don't you worry. As many lives as cats, these young fellows. It wasn't the loss of blood knocked him out either. He must have caught his head a crack on the floor as he fell."

Outside the knocking on the door had become tremendous. The voice of George Lomax, furiously upraised, came loud and distinct:

"Who is in there? Open the door at once."

Superintendent Battle sighed.

"I suppose we shall have to," he said. "A pity."

His eyes darted round, taking in the scene. An automatic lay by Jimmy's side. The Superintendent picked it up gingerly, holding it very delicately and examined it. He grunted and laid it on the table. Then he stepped across and unlocked the door.

Several people almost fell into the room. Nearly everybody said something at the same minute. George Lomax, spluttering with obdurate words which refused to come with sufficient fluency, exclaimed:

"The—the—the meaning of this? Ah! It's you, Superintendent. What's happened? I say—what has—happened?"

Bill Eversleigh said: "My God! Old Jimmy!" and stared at the limp figure on the ground.

Lady Coote, clad in a resplendent purple dressing gown, cried out: "The poor boy!" and swept past Superintendent Battle to bend over the prostrate Jimmy in a motherly fashion.

Bundle said: "Loraine!"

Herr Eberhard said: "Gott im Himmel!" and other words of that nature.

Sir Stanley Digby said: "My God, what's all this?"

A housemaid said: "Look at the blood," and screamed with pleasurable excitement.

A footman said: "Lor!"

The butler said, with a good deal more bravery in his manner than had been noticeable a few minutes earlier: "Now then, this won't do!" and waved away underservants.

The efficient Mr. Rupert Bateman said to George: "Shall we get rid of some of these people, sir?"

Then they all took fresh breath.

"Incredible!" said George Lomax. "Battle, what has *happened?*"

Battle gave him a look, and George's discreet habits assumed their usual sway.

"Now then," he said, moving to the door, "everyone go back to bed, please. There's been a—er—"

"A little accident," said Superintendent Battle easily.

"A—er—an accident. I shall be much obliged if everyone will go back to bed."

Everyone was clearly reluctant to do so.

"Lady Coote—please—"

"The poor boy," said Lady Coote in a motherly fashion.

She rose from a kneeling position with great reluctance. And as she did so, Jimmy stirred and sat up.

"Hallo!" he said thickly. "What's the matter?"

He looked round him vacantly for a minute or two and then intelligence returned to his eye.

"Have you got him?" he demanded eagerly.

"Got who?"

"The man. Climbed down the ivy. I was by the window there. Grabbed him and we had no end of a set-to—"

"One of those nasty, murderous cat burglars," said Lady Coote. "Poor boy."

Jimmy was looking round him.

"I say—I'm afraid we—er—have made rather a mess of things. Fellow was as strong as an ox and we went fairly waltzing around."

The condition of the room was clear proof of this statement. Everything light and breakable within a range of twelve feet that could be broken *had* been broken.

"And what happened then?"

But Jimmy was looking round for something.

"Where's Leopold? The pride of the blue-nosed automatics."

Battle indicated the pistol on the table.

"Is this yours, Mr. Thesiger?"

"That's right. That's little Leopold. How many shots have been fired?"

"One shot."

Jimmy looked chagrined.

"I'm disappointed in Leopold," he murmured. "I can't have pressed the button properly, or he'd have gone on shooting."

"Who shot first?"

"I did, I'm afraid," said Jimmy. "You see, the man twisted himself out of my grasp suddenly. I saw him making for the window and I closed my finger down on Leopold and let him have it. He turned in the window and fired at me and—well, I suppose after that I took the count."

He rubbed his head rather ruefully.

But Sir Stanley Digby was suddenly alert.

"Climbing down the ivy, you said? My God, Lomax, you don't think they've got away with it?"

He rushed from the room. For some curious reason nobody spoke during his absence. In a few minutes Sir Stanley returned. His round, chubby face was white as death.

"My God Battle," he said, "they've got it. O'Rourke's fast asleep—drugged, I think. I can't wake him. And the papers have vanished."

CHAPTER XXI

The Recovery of the Formula

"DER liebe Gott!" said Herr Eberhard in a whisper.

His face had gone chalky white.

George turned a face of dignified reproach on Battle.

"Is this true, Battle? I left all arrangements in your hands."

The rock-like quality of the Superintendent showed out well. Not a muscle of his face moved.

"The best of us are defeated sometimes, sir," he said quietly.

"Then you mean—you really mean—that the document is gone?"

But to everyone's intense surprise Superintendent Battle shook his head.

"No, no, Mr. Lomax, it's not so bad as you think. Everything's all right. But you can't lay the credit for it at my door. You've got to thank this young lady."

He indicated Loraine, who stared at him in surprise. Battle stepped across to her and gently took the brown paper parcel which she was still clutching mechanically.

"I think, Mr. Lomax," he said, "that you will find what you want here."

Sir Stanley Digby, quicker in action than George, snatched at the package and tore it open, investigating its contents eagerly. A sigh of relief escaped him and he mopped his brow. Herr Eberhard fell upon the child of his brain and clasped it to his heart, whilst a torrent of German burst from him.

Sir Stanley turned to Loraine, shaking her warmly by the hand.

"My dear young lady," he said, "we are infinitely obliged to you, I am sure."

"Yes, indeed," said George. "Though I—er—"

He paused in some perplexity, staring at a young lady who was a total stranger to him. Loraine looked appealingly at Jimmy, who came to the rescue.

"Er—this is Miss Wade," said Jimmy. "Gerald Wade's sister."

"Indeed," said George, shaking her warmly by the hand. "My dear Miss Wade, I must express my deep gratitude to you for what you have done. I must confess that I do not quite see—"

He paused delicately and four of the persons present felt that explanations were going to be fraught with much difficulty. Superintendent Battle came to the rescue.

"Perhaps we'd better not go into that just now, sir," he suggested tactfully.

The efficient Mr. Bateman created a further diversion.

"Wouldn't it be wise for someone to see to O'Rourke? Don't you think, sir, that a doctor had better be sent for?"

"Of course," said George. "Of course. Most remiss of us not to have thought of it before." He looked towards Bill. "Get Dr. Cartwright on the telephone. Ask him to come. Just hint, if you can, that—er—discretion should be observed."

Bill went off on his errand.

"I will come up with you, Digby," said George. "Something, possibly, could be done—measures should, perhaps, be taken—whilst awaiting the arrival of the doctor."

He looked rather helplessly at Rupert Bateman. Efficiency always makes itself felt. It was Pongo who was really in charge of the situation.

"Shall I come up with you, sir?"

George accepted the offer with relief. Here, he felt, was someone on whom he could lean. He experienced that sense of complete trust in Mr. Bateman's efficiency which came to all those who encountered that excellent young man.

The three men left the room together. Lady Coote, murmuring in deep rich tones: "The poor young fellow. Perhaps I could do something—" hurried after them.

"That's a very motherly woman," observed the Superintendent thoughtfully. "A very motherly woman. I wonder—"

Three pairs of eyes looked at him inquiringly.

"I was wondering," said Superintendent Battle slowly, "where Sir Oswald Coote may be."

"Oh!" gasped Loraine. "Do you think he's been murdered?"

Battle shook his head at her reproachfully.

"No need for anything so melodramatic," he said. "No—I rather think—"

He paused, his head on one side, listening—one large hand raised to enjoin silence.

In another minute they all heard what his sharper ears had been the first to notice—footsteps coming along the terrace outside. They rang out clearly with no kind of subterfuge about them. In another minute the window was blocked by a bulky figure which stood there regarding them and who conveyed, in an odd way, a sense of dominating the situation.

Sir Oswald, for it was he, looked slowly from one face to another. His keen eyes took in the details of the situation. Jimmy, with his roughly bandaged arm; Bundle, in her somewhat anomalous attire; Loraine, a perfect stranger to him. His eyes came last to Superintendent Battle. He spoke sharply and crisply:

"What's been happening here, officer?"

"Attempted robbery, sir."

"*Attempted*—eh?"

"Thanks to this young lady, Miss Wade, the thieves failed to get away with it."

"Ah!" he said again, his scrutiny ended. "And now, officer, what about *this?*"

He held out a small Mauser pistol which he carried delicately by the butt.

"Where did you find that, Sir Oswald?"

"On the lawn outside. I presume it must have been thrown down by one of the thieves as he took to his heels. I've held it carefully, as I thought you might wish to examine it for finger-prints."

"You think of everything, Sir Oswald," said Battle.

He took the pistol from the other, handling it with equal care, and laid it down on the table beside Jimmy's Colt.

"And now, if you please," said Sir Oswald, "I should like to hear exactly what occurred."

Superintendent Battle gave a brief résumé of the events of the night. Sir Oswald frowned thoughtfully.

"I understand," he said sharply. "After wounding and disabling Mr. Thesiger, the man took to his heels and ran, throwing away the pistol as he did so. What I cannot understand is why no one pursued him."

"It wasn't till we heard Mr. Thesiger's story that we knew there was anyone to pursue," remarked Superintendent Battle dryly.

"You didn't—er—catch sight of him making off as you turned the corner of the terrace?"

"No, I missed him by just about forty seconds, I should say. There's no moon and he'd be invisible as soon as he'd left the terrace. He must have leapt for it as soon as he'd fired the shot."

"H'm," said Sir Oswald. "I still think that a search should have been organized. Someone else should have been posted—"

"There are three of my men in the grounds," said the Superintendent quietly.

"Oh!" Sir Oswald seemed rather taken aback.

"They were to hold and detain any one attempting to leave the grounds."

"And yet—they haven't done so?"

"And yet they haven't done so," agreed Battle gravely.

Sir Oswald looked at him as though something in the words puzzled him. He said sharply:

"Are you telling me all that you know, Superintendent Battle?"

"All that I *know*—yes, Sir Oswald. What I think is a different matter. Maybe I think some rather curious things—but until thinking's got you somewhere it's no use talking about it."

"And yet," said Sir Oswald slowly, "I should like to know what you think, Superintendent Battle."

"For one thing, sir, I think there's a lot too much ivy about this place—excuse me, sir, you've got a bit on your coat—yes, a great deal too much ivy. It complicates things."

Sir Oswald stared at him, but any reply he might have contemplated making was arrested by the entrance of Rupert Bateman.

"Oh, there you are, Sir Oswald. I'm so glad. Lady Coote has just discovered that you were missing—and she has been insisting upon it that you had been murdered by the thieves. I really think, Sir Oswald, that you had better come to her at once. She is terribly upset."

"Maria is an incredibly foolish woman," said Sir Oswald. "Why should I be murdered? I'll come with you, Bateman."

He left the room with his secretary.

"That's a very efficient young man," said Battle, looking after them. "What's his name—Bateman?"

Jimmy nodded.

"Bateman—Rupert," he said. "Commonly known as Pongo. I was at school with him."

"Were you? Now, that's interesting, Mr. Thesiger. What was your opinion of him in those days?"

"Oh, he was always the same sort of ass."

"I shouldn't have thought," said Battle mildly, "that he was an ass."

"Oh, you know what I mean. Of course he wasn't really an ass. Tons of brains and always swotting at things. But deadly serious. No sense of humour."

"Ah!" said Superintendent Battle. "That's a pity. Gentlemen who have no sense of humour get to taking themselves too seriously—and that leads to mischief."

"I can't imagine Pongo getting into mischief," said

Jimmy. "He's done extremely well for himself so far—dug himself in with old Coote and looks like being a permanency in the job."

"Superintendent Battle," said Bundle.

"Yes, Lady Eileen?"

"Don't you think it very odd that Sir Oswald didn't say what he was doing wandering about in the garden in the middle of the night?"

"Ah!" said Battle. "Sir Oswald's a great man—and a great man always knows better than to explain unless an explanation is demanded. To rush into explanations and excuses is always a sign of weakness. Sir Oswald knows that as well as I do. He's not going to come in explaining and apologizing—not he. He just stalks in and hauls *me* over the coals. He's a big man, Sir Oswald."

Such a warm admiration sounded in the Superintendent's tones that Bundle pursued the subject no further.

"And now," said Superintendent Battle, looking round with a slight twinkle in his eye, "now that we're together and friendly like—I *should* like to hear just how Miss Wade happened to arrive on the scene so pat."

"She ought to be ashamed of herself," said Jimmy. "Hoodwinking us all as she did."

"Why should I be kept out of it all?" cried Loraine passionately. "I never meant to be—no, not the very first day in your rooms when you both explained how the best thing for me to do was to stay quietly at home and keep out of danger. I didn't say anything, but I made up my mind then."

"I half suspected it," said Bundle. "You were so surprisingly meek about it. I might have known you were up to something."

"I thought you were remarkably sensible," said Jimmy Thesiger.

"You would, Jimmy dear," said Loraine. "It was easy enough to deceive you."

"Thank you for these kind words," said Jimmy. "Go on, and don't mind me."

"When you rang up and said there might be danger,

I was more determined than ever," went on Loraine. "I went to Harrods and I bought a pistol. Here it is."

She produced the dainty weapon, and Superintendent Battle took it from her and examined it.

"Quite a deadly little toy, Miss Wade," he said. "Have you had much—er—practice with it?"

"None at all," said Loraine. "But I thought if I took it with me—well, that it would give me a comforting feeling."

"Quite so," said Battle gravely.

"My idea was to come over here and see what was going on. I left the car in the road and climbed through the hedge and came up to the terrace. I was just looking about me when—plop—something fell right at my feet. I picked it up and then looked to see where it could have come from. And then I saw the man climbing down the ivy and I ran."

"Just so," said Battle. "Now, Miss Wade, can you describe that man at all?"

The girl shook her head.

"It was too dark to see much. I think he was a big man—but that's about all."

"And now you, Mr. Thesiger." Battle turned to him. "You struggled with the man—can you tell me anything about him?"

"He was a pretty hefty individual—that's all I can say. He gave a few hoarse whispers—that's when I had him by the throat. He said, 'Lemme go, guvnor,' something like that."

"An uneducated man, then?"

"Yes, I suppose he was. He spoke like one."

"I still don't quite understand about the packet," said Loraine. "Why should he throw it down as he did? Was it because it hampered him climbing?"

"No," said Battle. "I've got an entirely different theory about that. That packet, Miss Wade, was deliberately thrown down to you—or so I believe."

"To *me?*"

"Shall we say—to the person the thief thought you were."

"This is getting very involved," said Jimmy.

"Mr. Thesiger, when you came into this room, did you switch on the light at all?"

"Yes."

"And there was no one in the room?"

"No one at all."

"But previously you thought you heard someone moving about down here?"

"Yes."

"And then, after trying the window, you switched off the light again and locked the door?"

Jimmy nodded.

Superintendent Battle looked slowly round him. His glance was arrested by a big screen of Spanish leather which stood near one of the bookcases.

Brusquely he strode across the room and looked behind it.

He uttered a sharp ejaculation, which brought the three young people quickly to his side.

Huddled on the floor, in a dead faint, lay the Countess Radzky.

CHAPTER XXII

The Countess Radzky's Story

THE Countess's return to consciousness was very different from that of Jimmy Thesiger. It was more prolonged and infinitely more artistic.

Artistic was Bundle's word. She had been zealous in her ministrations—largely consisting of the application of cold water—and the Countess had instantly responded, passing a white, bewildered hand across her brow and murmuring faintly.

It was at this point that Bill, at last relieved from his duties with telephone and doctors, had come bustling into the room and had instantly proceeded to make (in Bundle's opinion) a most regrettable idiot of himself.

He had hung over the Countess with a concerned and anxious face and had addressed a series of singularly idiotic remarks to her:

"I say, Countess. It's all right. It's really all right. Don't try to talk. It's bad for you. Just lie still. You'll be all right in a minute. It'll all come back to you. Don't say anything till you're quite all right. Take your time. Just lie still and close your eyes. You'll remember everything in a minute. Have another sip of water. Have some brandy. That's the stuff. Don't you think, Bundle, that some brandy . . . ?"

"For God's sake, Bill, leave her alone," said Bundle crossly. "She'll be all right."

And with an expert hand she flipped a good deal of cold water on to the exquisite make-up of the Countess's face.

The Countess flinched and sat up. She looked considerably more wide awake.

"Ah!" she murmured. "I am here. Yes, I am here."

"Take your time," said Bill. "Don't talk till you feel quite all right again."

The Countess drew the folds of a very transparent négligé closer around her.

"It is coming back to me," she murmured. "Yes, it is coming back."

She looked at the little crowd grouped around her. Perhaps something in the attentive faces struck her as unsympathetic. In any case she smiled deliberately up at the one face which clearly displayed a very opposite emotion.

"Ah, my big Englishman," she said very softly, "do not distress yourself. All is well with me."

"Oh! I say, but are you sure?" demanded Bill anxiously.

"Quite sure." She smiled at him reassuringly. "We Hungarians, we have nerves of steel."

A look of intense relief passed over Bill's face. A fatuous look settled down there instead—a look which made Bundle earnestly long to kick him.

"Have some water," she said coldly.

The Countess refused water. Jimmy, kindlier to

beauty in distress, suggested a cocktail. The Countess reacted favourably to this suggestion. When she had swallowed it, she looked round once more, this time with a livelier eye.

"Tell me, what has happened?" she demanded briskly.

"We were hoping you might be able to tell us that," said Superintendent Battle.

The Countess looked at him sharply. She seemed to become aware of the big, quiet man for the first time.

"I went to your room," said Bundle. "The bed hadn't been slept in and you weren't there."

She paused—looking accusingly at the Countess. The latter closed her eyes and nodded her head slowly.

"Yes, yes, I remember it all now. Oh, it was horrible!" She shuddered. "Do you want me to tell you?"

Superintendent Battle said, "If you please" at the same moment that Bill said, "Not if you don't feel up to it."

The Countess looked from one to the other, but the quiet, masterful eye of Superintendent Battle won the game.

"I could not sleep," began the Countess. "The house —it oppressed me. I was all, as you say, on wires, the cat on the hot bricks. I knew that in the state I was in it was useless to think of going to bed. I walked about my room. I read. But the books placed there did not interest me greatly. I thought I would come down here and find something more absorbing."

"Very natural," said Bill.

"Very often done, I believe," said Battle.

"So as soon as the idea occurred to me, I left my room and came down. The house was very still—"

"Excuse me," interrupted the Superintendent, "but can you give me an idea of the time when this occurred?"

"I never know the time," said the Countess superbly, and swept on with her story.

"The house was very quiet. One could even hear the little mouse run, if there had been one. I come down the stairs—very quietly—"

"Very quietly?"

"Naturally, I do not want to disturb the household," said the Countess reproachfully. "I come in here. I go into this corner and I search the shelves for a suitable book."

"Having, of course, switched on the light?"

"No, I did not switch on the light. I had, you see, my little electric torch with me. With that, I scanned the shelves."

"Ah!" said the Superintendent.

"Suddenly," continued the Countess dramatically, "I hear something. A stealthy sound. A muffled footstep. I switch out my torch and listen. The footsteps draw nearer—stealthy, horrible footsteps. I shrink behind the screen. In another minute the door opens and the light is switched on. The man—the burglar is in the room."

"Yes, but I say—" began Mr. Thesiger.

A large-sized foot pressed his, and realizing that Superintendent Battle was giving him a hint, Jimmy shut up.

"I nearly died of fear," continued the Countess. "I tried not to breathe. The man waited for a minute, listening. Then, still with that horrible, stealthy tread—"

Again Jimmy opened his mouth in protest, and again shut it.

"—he crossed to the window and peered out. He remained there for a minute or two, then he recrossed the room and turned out the lights again, locking the door. I am terrified. He is in the room, moving stealthily about in the dark. Ah, it is horrible. Suppose he should come upon me in the dark! In another minute I hear him again by the window. Then silence. I hope that perhaps he may have gone out that way. As the minutes pass and I hear no further sound, I am almost sure that he has done so. Indeed I am in the very act of switching on my torch and investigating when—*prestissimo!*—it all begins."

"Yes?"

"Ah! But it was terrible—never—never shall I forget it! Two men trying to murder each other. Oh, it was horrible! They reeled about the room, and furniture crashed in every direction. I thought, too, that I heard a woman scream—but that was not in the room. It was outside somewhere. The criminal had a hoarse voice. He croaked rather than spoke. He kept saying, 'Lemme go—lemme go.' The other man was a gentleman. He had a cultured, English voice."

Jimmy looked gratified.

"He swore—mostly," continued the Countess.

"Clearly a gentleman," said Superintendent Battle.

"And then," continued the Countess, "a flash and a shot. The bullet hit the bookcase beside me. I—I suppose I must have fainted."

She looked up at Bill. He took her hand and patted it.

"You poor dear," he said. "How rotten for you."

"Silly idiot," thought Bundle.

Superintendent Battle had moved on swift, noiseless feet over to the bookcase a little to the right of the screen. He bent down, searching. Presently he stooped and picked something up.

"It wasn't a bullet, Countess," he said. "It's the shell of the cartridge. Where were you standing when you fired, Mr. Thesiger?"

Jimmy took up a position by the window.

"As nearly as I can say, about here."

Superintendent Battle placed himself in the same spot.

"That's right," he agreed. "The empty shell would throw right rear. It's a .455. I don't wonder the Countess thought it was a bullet in the dark. It hit the bookcase about a foot from her. The bullet itself grazed the window frame and we'll find it outside to-morrow—unless your assailant happens to be carrying it about in him."

Jimmy shook his head regretfully.

"Leopold, I fear, did not cover himself with glory," he remarked sadly.

The Countess was looking at him with most flattering attention.

"Your arm!" she exclaimed. "It is all tied up! Was it you then——"

Jimmy made her a mock bow.

"I'm so glad I've got a cultured English voice," he said. "And I can assure you that I wouldn't have dreamed of using the language I did if I had had any suspicion that a lady was present."

"I did not understand all of it," the Countess hastened to explain. "Although I had an English governess when I was young——"

"It isn't the sort of thing she'd be likely to teach you," agreed Jimmy. "Kept you busy with your uncle's pen, and the umbrella of the gardener's niece. I know the sort of stuff."

"But what has happened?" asked the Countess. "That is what I want to know. I demand to know what has happened."

There was a moment's silence whilst everybody looked at Superintendent Battle.

"It's very simple," said Battle mildly. "Attempted robbery. Some political papers stolen from Sir Stanley Digby. The thieves nearly got away with them, but thanks to this young lady"——he indicated Loraine——"they didn't."

The Countess flashed a glance at the girl——rather an odd glance.

"Indeed," she said coldly.

"A very fortunate coincidence that she happened to be there," said Superintendent Battle, smiling.

The Countess gave a little sigh and half closed her eyes again.

"It is absurd, but I still feel extremely faint," she murmured.

"Of course you do," cried Bill. "Let me help you up to your room. Bundle will come with you."

"It is very kind of Lady Eileen," said the Countess, "but I should prefer to be alone. I am really quite all right. Perhaps you will just help me up the stairs?"

She rose to her feet, accepted Bill's arm and, leaning heavily on it, went out of the room. Bundle followed as far as the hall but, the Countess reiterating her assurance—with some tartness—that she was quite all right, she did not accompany them upstairs.

But as she stood watching the Countess's graceful form, supported by Bill, slowly mounting the stairway, she stiffened suddenly to acute attention. The Countess's négligé, as previously mentioned, was thin—a mere veil of orange chiffon. Through it Bundle saw distinctly below the right shoulder blade *a small black mole*.

With a gasp, Bundle swung impetuously round to where Superintendent Battle was just emerging from the library. Jimmy and Loraine had preceded him.

"There," said Battle. "I've fastened the window and there will be a man on duty outside. And I'll lock this door and take the key. In the morning we'll do what the French call reconstruct the crime—Yes, Lady Eileen, what is it?"

"Superintendent Battle, I must speak to you—at once."

"Why, certainly, I—"

George Lomax suddenly appeared, Dr. Cartwright by his side.

"Ah, there you are, Battle. You'll be relieved to hear that there's nothing seriously wrong with O'Rourke."

"I never thought there would be much wrong with Mr. O'Rourke," said Battle.

"He's had a strong hypnotic administered to him," said the doctor. "He'll wake perfectly all right in the morning. Perhaps a bit of a head, perhaps not. Now then, young man, let's look at this bullet wound of yours."

"Come on, nurse," said Jimmy to Loraine. "Come and hold the basin or my hand. Witness a strong man's agony. You know the stunt."

Jimmy, Loraine and the doctor went off together. Bundle continued to throw agonized glances in the direction of Superintendent Battle, who had been buttonholed by George.

The Superintendent waited patiently till a pause occurred in George's loquacity. He then swiftly took advantage of it.

"I wonder, sir, if I might have a word privately with Sir Stanley? In the little study at the end there."

"Certainly," said George. "Certainly. I'll go and fetch him at once."

He hurried off upstairs again. Battle drew Bundle swiftly into the drawing-room and shut the door.

"Now, Lady Eileen, what is it?"

"I'll tell you as quickly as I can—but it's rather long and complicated."

As concisely as she could, Bundle related her introduction to the Seven Dials Club and her subsequent adventures there. When she had finished, Superintendent Battle drew a long breath. For once, his facial woodenness was laid aside.

"Remarkable," he said. "Remarkable. I wouldn't have believed it possible—even for you, Lady Eileen. I ought to have known better."

"But you did give me a hint, Superintendent Battle. You told me to ask Bill Eversleigh."

"It's dangerous to give people like you a hint, Lady Eileen. I never dreamt of your going to the lengths you have."

"Well, it's all right, Superintendent Battle. My death doesn't lie at your door."

"Not yet, it doesn't," said Battle grimly.

He stood as though in thought, turning things over in his mind.

"What Mr. Thesiger was about, letting you run into danger like that, I can't think," he said presently.

"He didn't know till afterwards," said Bundle. "I'm not a complete mug, Superintendent Battle. And anyway, he's got his hands full looking after Miss Wade."

"Is that so?" said the Superintendent. "Ah!"

He twinkled a little.

"I shall have to detail Mr. Eversleigh to look after you, Lady Eileen."

"Bill!" said Bundle contemptuously. "But Superintendent Battle, you haven't heard the end of my story. The woman I saw there—Anna—No. 1. Yes, No. 1 is the Countess Radzky."

And rapidly she went on to describe her recognition of the mole.

To her surprise the Superintendent hemmed and hawed.

"A mole isn't much to go upon, Lady Eileen. Two women might have an identical mole very easily. You must remember that the Countess Radzky is a very well-known figure in Hungary."

"Then this isn't the real Countess Radzky. I tell you I'm sure this is the same woman I saw there. And look at her to-night—the way we found her. I don't believe she ever fainted at all."

"Oh, I shouldn't say that, Lady Eileen. That empty shell striking the bookcase beside her might have frightened any woman half out of her wits."

"But what was she doing there anyway? One doesn't come down to look for a book with an electric torch."

Battle scratched his cheek. He seemed unwilling to speak. He began to pace up and down the room, as though making up his mind. At last he turned to the girl.

"See here, Lady Eileen, I'm going to trust you. The Countess's conduct *is* suspicious. I know that as well as you do. It's very suspicious—but we've got to go carefully. There mustn't be any unpleasantness with the Embassies. One has got to be *sure*."

"I see. If you were *sure* . . ."

"There's something else. During the war, Lady Eileen, there was a great outcry about German spies being left at large. Busybodies wrote letters to the papers about it. We paid no attention. Hard words didn't hurt us. The small fry were left alone. Why? Because through them, sooner or later, *we got the big fellow—the man at the top*."

"You mean?"

"Don't bother about what I mean, Lady Eileen. But remember this. *I know all about the Countess.* And I want her let alone.

"And now," added Superintendent Battle ruefully, "I've got to think of something to say to Sir Stanley Digby!"

CHAPTER XXIII

Superintendent Battle in Charge

It was ten o'clock on the following morning. The sun poured in through the windows of the library, where Superintendent Battle had been at work since six. On a summons from him, George Lomax, Sir Oswald Coote and Jimmy Thesiger had just joined him, having repaired the fatigues of the night with a substantial breakfast. Jimmy's arm was in a sling, but he bore little other trace of the night's affray.

The Superintendent eyed all three of them benevolently, somewhat with the air of a kindly curator explaining a museum to little boys. On the table beside him were various objects, neatly labelled. Amongst them Jimmy recognized Leopold.

"Ah, Superintendent," said George, "I have been anxious to know how you have progressed. Have you caught the man?"

"He'll take a lot of catching, he will," said the Superintendent easily.

His failure in that respect did not appear to rankle with him.

George Lomax did not look particularly well pleased. He detested levity of any kind.

"I've got everything taped out pretty clearly," went on the detective.

He took up two objects from the table.

"Here we've got the two bullets. The largest is a .455, fired from Mr. Thesiger's Colt automatic. Grazed the window sash and I found it embedded in the trunk of that cedar tree. This little fellow was fired from the Mauser .25. After passing through Mr. Thesiger's arm, it embedded itself in this arm chair here. As for the pistol itself—"

"Well?" said Sir Oswald eagerly. "Any fingerprints?"

Battle shook his head.

"The man who handled it wore gloves," he said slowly.

"A pity," said Sir Oswald.

"A man who knew his business would wear gloves. Am I right in thinking, Sir Oswald, that you found this pistol just about twenty yards from the bottom of the steps leading up to the terrace?"

Sir Oswald stepped to the window.

"Yes, almost exactly, I should say."

"I don't want to find fault, but it would have been wiser on your part, sir, to leave it exactly as you found it."

"I am sorry," said Sir Oswald stiffly.

"Oh, it doesn't matter. I've been able to reconstruct things. There were your footprints, you see, leading up from the bottom of the garden, and a place where you had obviously stopped and stooped down, and a kind of dent in the grass which was highly suggestive. By the way, what was your theory of the pistol being there?"

"I presumed that it had been dropped by the man in his flight."

Battle shook his head.

"Not dropped, Sir Oswald. There are two points against that. To begin with, there is only one set of footprints crossing the lawn just there—your own."

"I see," said Sir Oswald thoughtfully.

"Can you be sure of that, Battle?" put in George.

"Quite sure, sir. There is one other set of tracks crossing the lawn, Miss Wade's, but they are a good deal farther to the left."

He paused, and then went on: "And there's the dent in the ground. The pistol must have struck the ground with some force. It all points to its having been thrown."

"Well, why not?" said Sir Oswald. "Say the man fled down the path to the left. He'd leave no footprints on the path and he'd hurl the pistol away from him into the middle of the lawn, eh, Lomax?"

George agreed by a nod of the head.

"It's true that he'd leave no footprints on the path,"

said Battle, "but from the shape of the dent and the way the turf was cut, I don't think the pistol was thrown from that direction. I think it was thrown from the terrace here."

"Very likely," said Sir Oswald. "Does it matter, Superintendent?"

"Ah, yes, Battle," broke in George. "Is it—er—strictly relevant?"

"Perhaps not, Mr. Lomax. But we like to get things just so, you know. I wonder now if one of you gentlemen would take this pistol and throw it. Will you, Sir Oswald? That's very kind. Stand just here in the window. Now fling in into the middle of the lawn."

Sir Oswald complied, sending the pistol flying through the air with a powerful sweep of his arm. Jimmy Thesiger drew near with breathless interest. The Superintendent lumbered off after it like a well-trained retriever. He reappeared with a beaming face.

"That's it, sir. Just the same kind of mark. Although, by the way, you sent it a good ten yards farther. But then, you're a very powerfully built man, aren't you, Sir Oswald? Excuse me, I thought I heard someone at the door."

The Superintendent's ears must have been very much sharper than anyone else's. Nobody else had heard a sound, but Battle was proved right, for Lady Coote stood outside, a medicine glass in her hand.

"Your medicine, Oswald," she said, advancing into the room. "You forgot it after breakfast."

"I'm very busy, Maria," said Sir Oswald. "I don't want my medicine."

"You would never take it if it wasn't for me," said his wife serenely, advancing upon him. "You're just like a naughty little boy. Drink it up now."

And meekly, obediently, the great steel magnate drank it up!

Lady Coote smiled sadly and sweetly at everyone.

"Am I interrupting you? Are you very busy? Oh, look at those revolvers. Nasty, noisy, murdering things. To think, Oswald, that you might have been shot by the burglar last night."

"You must have been alarmed when you found he was missing, Lady Coote," said Battle.

"I didn't think of it at first," confessed Lady Coote. "This poor boy here"—she indicated Jimmy—"being shot—and everything so dreadful, but so exciting. It wasn't till Mr. Bateman asked me where Sir Oswald was that I remembered he'd gone out half an hour before for a stroll."

"Sleepless, eh, Sir Oswald?" asked Battle.

"I am usually an excellent sleeper," said Sir Oswald. "But I must confess that last night I felt unusually restless. I thought the night air would do me good."

"You came out through this window, I suppose?"

Was it his fancy, or did Sir Oswald hesitate for a moment before replying.

"Yes."

"In your pumps too," said Lady Coote, "instead of putting thick shoes on. What would you do without me to look after you?"

She shook her head sadly.

"I think, Maria, if you don't mind leaving us—we have still a lot to discuss."

"I know, dear, I'm just going."

Lady Coote withdrew, carrying the empty medicine glass as though it were a goblet out of which she had just administered a death potion.

"Well, Battle," said George Lomax, "it all seems clear enough. Yes, perfectly clear. The man fires a shot, disabling Mr. Thesiger, flings away the weapon, runs along the terrace and down the gravel path."

"Where he ought to have been caught by my men," put in Battle.

"Your men, if I may say so, Battle, seem to have been singularly remiss. They didn't see Miss Wade come in. If they could miss her coming in, they could easily miss the thief going out."

Superintendent Battle opened his mouth to speak, then seemed to think better of it. Jimmy Thesiger looked at him curiously. He would have given a lot to know just what was in Superintendent Battle's mind.

"Must have been a champion runner," was all the Scotland Yard man contented himself with saying.

"How do you mean, Battle?"

"Just what I say, Mr. Lomax. I was round the corner of the terrace myself not fifty seconds after the shot was fired. And for a man to run all that distance towards me and get round the corner of the path before I appeared round the side of the house—well, as I say, he must have been a champion runner."

"I am at a loss to understand you, Battle. You have some idea of your own which I have not yet—er—grasped. You say the man did not go across the lawn and now you hint—What exactly do you hint? That the man did not go down the path? Then in your opinion—er—where *did* he go?"

For answer, Superintendent Battle jerked an eloquent thumb upwards.

"Eh?" said George.

The Superintendent jerked harder than ever. George raised his head and looked at the ceiling.

"Up there," said Battle. "Up the ivy again."

"Nonsense, Superintendent. What you are suggesting is impossible."

"Not at all impossible, sir. He'd done it once. He could do it twice."

"I don't mean impossible in that sense. But if the man wanted to escape, he'd never bolt back into the house."

"Safest place for him, Mr. Lomax."

"But Mr. O'Rourke's door was still locked on the inside when we came to him."

"And how did you get to him? Through Sir Stanley's room. That's the way our man went. Lady Eileen tells me she saw the door knob of Mr. O'Rourke's door move. That was when our friend was up there the first time. I suspect the key was under Mr. O'Rourke's pillow. But his exit is clear enough the second time—through the communicating door and through Sir Stanley's room, which, of course, was empty. Like everyone else, Sir Stanley, is rushing downstairs to the library. Our man's got a clear course."

"And where did he go then?"

Superintendent Battle shrugged his burly shoulders and became evasive.

"Plenty of ways open. Into an empty room on the other side of the house and down the ivy again—out through a side door—or, just possibly, if it was an inside job, he—well, stayed in the house."

George looked at him in shocked surprise.

"Really, Battle, I should—I should feel it very deeply if one of my servants—er—I have the most perfect reliance on them—it would distress me very much to have to suspect—"

"Nobody's asking you to suspect anyone, Mr. Lomax. I'm just putting all the possibilities before you. The servants may be all right—probably are."

"You have disturbed me," said George. "You have disturbed me greatly."

His eyes appeared more protuberant than ever.

To distract him, Jimmy poked delicately at a curious blackened object on the table.

"What's this?" he asked.

"That's exhibit Z," said Battle. "The last of our little lot. It is, or rather it has been, a glove."

He picked it up, the charred relic, and manipulated it with pride.

"Where did you find it?" asked Sir Oswald.

Battle jerked his head over his shoulder.

"In the grate—nearly burnt, but not quite. Queer; looks as though it had been chewed by a dog."

"It might possibly be Miss Wade's," suggested Jimmy. "She has several dogs."

The Superintendent shook his head.

"This isn't a lady's glove—no, not even the large kind of loose glove ladies wear nowadays. Fit it on, sir, a moment."

He adjusted the blackened object over Jimmy's hand.

"You see—it's large even for you."

"Do you attach importance to this discovery?" inquired Sir Oswald coldly.

"You never know, Sir Oswald, what's going to be important or what isn't."

There was a sharp tap at the door and Bundle entered.

"I'm so sorry," she said apologetically, "but Father has just rung up. He says I must come home because everybody is worrying him."

She paused.

"Yes, my dear Eileen?" said George encouragingly, perceiving that there was more to come.

"I wouldn't have interrupted you—only that I thought it might perhaps have something to do with all this. You see, what has upset Father is that one of our footmen is missing. He went out last night and hasn't come back."

"What is the man's name?" It was Sir Oswald who took up the cross-examination.

"John Bauer."

"An Englishman?"

"I believe he calls himself a Swiss—but I think he's a German. He speaks English perfectly, though."

"Ah!" Sir Oswald drew in his breath with a long, satisfied hiss. "And he has been at Chimneys—how long?"

"Just under a month."

Sir Oswald turned to the other two.

"Here is our missing man. You know, Lomax, as well as I do, that several foreign Governments are after the thing. I remember the man now perfectly—tall, well-drilled fellow. Came about a fortnight before we left. A clever move. Any new servants here would be closely scrutinized, but at Chimneys, five miles away—" He did not finish the sentence.

"You think the plan was laid so long beforehand?"

"Why not? There are millions in that formula, Lomax. Doubtless Bauer hoped to get access to my private papers at Chimneys, and to learn something of forthcoming arrangements from them. It seems likely that he may have had an accomplice in this house—someone who put him wise to the lie of the land and who saw to the doping of O'Rourke. But Bauer was the man Miss Wade saw climbing down the ivy—the big, powerful man."

He turned to Superintendent Battle.

"Bauer was your man, Superintendent. And, somehow or other, you let him slip through your fingers."

CHAPTER XXIV

Bundle Wonders

THERE was no doubt that Superintendent Battle was taken aback. He fingered his chin thoughtfully.

"Sir Oswald is right, Battle," said George. "This is the man. Any hope of catching him?"

"There may be, sir. It certainly looks—well, suspicious. Of course the man may turn up again—at Chimneys, I mean."

"Do you think it likely?"

"No, it isn't," confessed Battle. "Yes, it certainly looks as though Bauer were the man. But I can't quite see how he got in and out of these grounds unobserved."

"I have already told you my opinion of the men you posted," said George. "Hopelessly inefficient—I don't want to blame you, Superintendent, but—" His pause was eloquent.

"Ah, well," said Battle lightly, "my shoulders are broad."

He shook his head and sighed.

"I must get to the telephone at once. Excuse me, gentlemen. I'm sorry, Mr. Lomax—I feel I've rather bungled this business. But it's been puzzling, more puzzling than you know."

He strode hurriedly from the room.

"Come into the garden," said Bundle to Jimmy. "I want to talk to you."

They went out together through the window. Jimmy stared down at the lawn, frowning.

"What's the matter?" asked Bundle.

Jimmy explained the circumstances of the pistol throwing.

"I'm wondering," he ended, "what was in old Battle's mind when he got Coote to throw the pistol. Something, I'll swear. Anyhow, it landed up about ten yards farther than it should have done. You know, Bundle, Battle's a deep one."

"He's an extraordinary man," said Bundle. "I want to tell you about last night."

She retailed her conversation with the Superintendent. Jimmy listened attentively.

"So the Countess is No. 1," he said thoughtfully. "It all hangs together very well. No. 2—Bauer—comes over from Chimneys. He climbs up into O'Rourke's room, knowing that O'Rourke has had a sleeping draught administered to him—by the Countess somehow or other. The arrangement is that he is to throw down the papers to the Countess, who will be waiting below. Then she'll nip back through the library and up to her room. If Bauer's caught leaving the grounds, they'll find nothing on him. Yes, it was a good plan—but it went wrong. No sooner is the Countess in the library than she hears me coming and has to jump behind the screen. Jolly awkward for her, because she can't warn her accomplice. No. 2 pinches the papers looks out of the window, sees, as he thinks, the Countess waiting, pitches the papers down to her and proceeds to climb down the ivy, where he finds a nasty surprise in the shape of me waiting for him. Pretty nervy work for the Countess waiting behind her screen. All things considered, she told a pretty good story. Yes, it all hangs together very well."

"Too well," said Bundle decidedly.

"Eh?" said Jimmy, surprised.

"What about No. 7—No. 7, who never appears, but lives in the background. The Countess and Bauer? No, it's not so simple as that. Bauer was here last night, yes. But he was only here in case things went wrong—as they have done. His part is the part of scapegoat; to draw all attention from No. 7—the boss."

"I say, Bundle," said Jimmy anxiously, "you haven't been reading too much sensational literature, have you?"

Bundle threw him a glance of dignified reproach.

"Well," said Jimmy, "I'm not yet like the Red Queen. I can't believe six impossible things before breakfast."

"It's after breakfast," said Bundle.

"Or even after breakfast. We've got a perfectly good hypothesis which fits the facts—and you won't have it at any price, simply because like the old riddle, you want to make things more difficult."

"I'm sorry," said Bundle, "but I cling passionately to a mysterious No. 7 being a member of the house-party."

"What does Bill think?"

"Bill," said Bundle coldly, "is impossible."

"Oh!" said Jimmy. "I suppose you've told him about the Countess? He ought to be warned. Heaven knows what he'll go blabbing about otherwise."

"He won't hear a word against her," said Bundle. "He's—oh, simply idiotic. I wish you'd drive it home to him about that mole."

"You forget I wasn't in the cupboard," said Jimmy. "And anyway I'd rather not argue with Bill about his lady friend's mole. But surely he can't be such an ass as not to see that everything fits in?"

"He's every kind of ass," said Bundle bitterly. "You made the greatest mistake, Jimmy, in ever telling him at all."

"I'm sorry," said Jimmy. "I didn't see it at the time—but I do now. I was a fool, but dash it all, old Bill—"

"You know what foreign adventuresses are," said Bundle. "How they get hold of one."

"As a matter of fact, I don't," said Jimmy. "One has never tried to get hold of me." And he sighed.

For a moment or two there was silence. Jimmy was turning things over in his mind. The more he thought about them, the more unsatisfactory they seemed.

"You say that Battle wants the Countess let alone," he said at last.

"Yes."

"The idea being that through her he will get at some-one else?"

Bundle nodded.

Jimmy frowned deeply as he tried to see where this

led. Clearly Battle had some very definite idea in his mind.

"Sir Stanley Digby went up to town early this morning, didn't he?" he said.

"Yes."

"O'Rourke with him?"

"Yes, I think so."

"You don't think—no, that's impossible?"

"What?"

"That O'Rourke can be mixed up in this in any way?"

"It's possible," said Bundle thoughtfully. "He's got what one calls a very vivid personality. No, it wouldn't surprise me if—oh, to tell the truth, nothing would surprise me! In fact, there's only one person I'm really sure isn't No. 7."

"Who's that?"

"Superintendent Battle."

"Oh! I thought you were going to say George Lomax."

"Ssh, here he comes."

George was, indeed, bearing down upon them in an unmistakable manner. Jimmy made an excuse and slipped away. George sat down by Bundle.

"My dear Eileen, must you really leave us?"

"Well, Father seems to have got the wind up rather badly. I think I'd better go home and hold his hand."

"This little hand will indeed be comforting," said George, taking it and pressing it playfully. "My dear Eileen, I understand your reasons and I honour you for them. In these days of changed and unsettled conditions—"

"He's off," thought Bundle desperately.

"—when family life is at a premium—all the old standards falling!—it becomes our class to set an example—to show that we, at least, are unaffected by modern conditions. They call us the Die Hards—I am proud of the term—I repeat I am proud of the term! There are things that *should* die hard—dignity, beauty, modesty, the sanctity of family life, filial respect—who dies if these shall live? As I was saying, my dear Eileen,

I envy you the privileges of your youth. Youth! What a wonderful thing! What a wonderful word! And we do not appreciate it until we grow to—er—maturer years. I confess, my dear child, that I have in the past been disappointed by your levity. I see now it was but the careless and charming levity of a child. I perceive now the serious and earnest beauty of your mind. You will allow me, I hope, to help you with your reading?"

"Oh, thank you," said Bundle faintly.

"And you must never be afraid of me again. I was shocked when Lady Caterham told me that you stood in awe of me. I can assure you that I am a very humdrum sort of person."

The spectacle of George being modest struck Bundle spellbound. George continued.

"Never be shy with me, dear child. And do not be afraid of boring me. It will be a great delight to me to —if I may say so—form your budding mind. I will be your political mentor. We have never needed young women of talent and charm in the Party more than we need them to-day. You may well be destined to follow in the footsteps of your aunt, Lady Caterham."

This awful prospect knocked Bundle out completely. She could only stare helplessly at George. This did not discourage him—on the contrary. His main objection to women was that they talked too much. It was seldom that he found what he considered a really good listener. He smiled benignantly at Bundle.

"The butterfly emerging from the chrysalis. A wonderful picture. I have a very interesting work on political economy. I will look it out now, and you can take it to Chimneys with you. When you have finished it, I will discuss it with you. Do not hesitate to write to me if any point puzzles you. I have many public duties, but by unsparing work I can always make time for the affairs of my friends. I will look for the book."

He strode away. Bundle gazed after him with a dazed expression. She was roused by the unexpected advent of Bill.

"Look here," said Bill, "what the hell was Codders holding your hand for?"

"It wasn't my hand," said Bundle wildly. "It was my budding mind."

"Don't be an ass, Bundle."

"Sorry, Bill, but I'm a little worried. Do you remember saying that Jimmy ran a grave risk coming down here?"

"So he does," said Bill. "It's frightfully hard to escape from Codders once he's got interested in you. Jimmy will be caught in the toils before he knows where he is."

"It's not Jimmy who's got caught—it's me," said Bundle wildly. "I shall have to meet endless Mrs. Macattas, and read political economy and discuss it with George, and Heavens knows where it will end!"

Bill whistled.

"Poor old Bundle. Been laying it on a bit thick, haven't you?"

"I must have done. Bill, I feel horribly entangled."

"Never mind," said Bill consolingly. "George doesn't really believe in women standing for Parliament, so you won't have to stand up on platforms and talk a lot of junk, or kiss dirty babies in Bermondsey. Come and have a cocktail. It's nearly lunch time."

Bundle got up and walked by his side obediently.

"And I do so hate politics," she murmured piteously.

"Of course you do. So do all sensible people. It's only people like Codders and Pongo who take them seriously and revel in them. But all the same," said Bill, reverting suddenly to a former point, "you oughtn't to let Codders hold your hand."

"Why on earth not?" said Bundle. "He's known me all my life."

"Well, I don't like it."

"Virtuous William— Oh, I say, look at Superintendent Battle."

They were just passing in through a side door. A cupboard-like room opened out of the little hallway. In it were kept golf clubs, tennis racquets, bowls and other features of country house life. Superintendent Battle was conducting a minute examination of various golf clubs. He looked up a little sheepishly at Bundle's exclamation.

"Going to take up golf, Superintendent Battle?"

"I might do worse, Lady Eileen. They say it's never too late to start. And I've got one good quality that will tell at any game."

"What's that?" asked Bill.

"I don't know when I'm beaten. If everything goes wrong, I turn to and start again!"

And with a determined look on his face, Superintendent Battle came out and joined them, shutting the door behind him.

CHAPTER XXV

Jimmy Lays His Plans

JIMMY THESIGER was feeling depressed. Avoiding George, whom he suspected of being ready to tackle him on serious subjects, he stole quietly away after lunch. Proficient as he was in details of the Santa Fé boundary dispute, he had no wish to stand an examination on it this minute.

Presently what he hoped would happen came to pass. Loraine Wade, also unaccompanied, strolled down one of the shady garden paths. In a moment Jimmy was by her side. They walked for some minutes in silence and then Jimmy said tentatively:

"Loraine?"

"Yes?"

"Look here, I'm a bad chap at putting things—but what about it? What's wrong with getting a special license and being married and living together happy ever afterwards?"

Loraine displayed no embarrassment at this surprising proposal. Instead she threw back her head and laughed frankly.

"Don't laugh at a chap," said Jimmy reproachfully.

"I can't help it. You were so funny."

"Loraine—you are a little devil."

"I'm not. I'm what's called a thoroughly nice girl."

"Only to those who don't know you—who are taken in by your delusive appearance of meekness and decorum."

"I like your long words."

"All out of cross-word puzzles."

"So educative."

"Loraine dear, don't beat about the bush. Will you or won't you?"

Loraine's face sobered. It took on its characteristic appearance of determination. Her small mouth hardened and her little chin shot out aggressively.

"No, Jimmy. Not while things are as they are at present—all unfinished."

"I know we haven't done what we set out to do," agreed Jimmy. "But all the same—well, it's the end of a chapter. The papers are safe at the Air Ministry. Virtue triumphant. And—for the moment—nothing doing."

"So—let's get married?" said Loraine with a slight smile.

"You've said it. Precisely the idea."

But again Loraine shook her head.

"No, Jimmy. Until this thing's rounded up—until we're safe—"

"You think we're in danger?"

"Don't you?"

Jimmy's cherubic pink face clouded over.

"You're right," he said at last. "If that extraordinary rigmarole of Bundle's is true—and I suppose, incredible as it sounds, it must be true—then we're not safe till we've settled with—No. 7!"

"And the others?"

"No—the others don't count. It's No. 7 with his own ways of working that frightens me. Because I don't know who he is or where to look for him."

Loraine shivered.

"I've been frightened," she said in a low voice. "Ever since Gerry's death. . . ."

"You needn't be frightened. There's nothing for you

to be frightened about. You leave everything to me. I tell you, Loraine—*I'll get No. 7 yet*. Once we get him—well, I don't think there'll be much trouble with the rest of the gang, whoever they are."

"If you get him—and suppose he gets you?"

"Impossible," said Jimmy cheerfully. "I'm much too clever. Always have a good opinion of yourself—that's my motto."

"When I think of the things that might have happened last night—" Loraine shivered.

"Well, they didn't," said Jimmy. "We're both here, safe and sound—though I must admit my arm is confoundedly painful."

"Poor boy."

"Oh, one must expect to suffer in a good cause. And what with my wounds and my cheerful conversation, I've made a complete conquest of Lady Coote."

"Oh! Do you think that important?"

"I've an idea it may come in useful."

"You've got some plan in your mind, Jimmy. What is it?"

"The young hero never tells his plans," said Jimmy firmly. "They mature in the dark."

"You are an idiot, Jimmy."

"I know. I know. That's what everyone says. But I can assure you, Loraine, there's a lot of brain-work going on underneath. Now what about your plans? Got any?"

"Bundle has suggested that I should go to Chimneys with her for a bit."

"Excellent," said Jimmy approvingly. "Nothing could be better. I'd like an eye kept on Bundle anyway. You never know what mad thing she won't be up to next. She's so frightfully unexpected. And the worst of it is, she's so astonishingly successful. I tell you, keeping Bundle out of mischief is a whole-time job."

"Bill ought to look after her," suggested Loraine.

"Bill's pretty busy elsewhere."

"Don't you believe it," said Loraine.

"What? Not the Countess? But the lad's potty about her."

Loraine continued to shake her head.

"There's something there I don't quite understand. But it's not the Countess with Bill—it's Bundle. Why, this morning Bill was talking to me when Mr. Lomax came out and sat down by Bundle. He took her hand or something, and Bill was off like—like a rocket."

"What a curious taste some people have," observed Mr. Thesiger. "Fancy anyone who was talking to you wanting to do anything else. But you surprise me very much, Loraine. I thought our simple Bill was enmeshed in the toils of the beautiful foreign adventuress. Bundle thinks so, I know."

"Bundle may," said Loraine, "but I tell you, Jimmy, it isn't so."

"Then what's the big idea?"

"Don't you think it possible that Bill is doing a bit of sleuthing on his own?"

"Bill? He hasn't got the brains."

"I'm not so sure. When a simple, muscular person like Bill does set out to be subtle, no one ever gives him credit for it."

"And in consequence he can put in some good work. Yes, there's something in that. But all the same I'd never have thought it of Bill. He's doing the Countess's little woolly lamb to perfection. I think you're wrong, you know, Loraine. The Countess is an extraordinarily beautiful woman—not my type, of course," put in Mr. Thesiger hastily—"and old Bill has always had a heart like an hotel."

Loraine shook her head, unconvinced.

"Well," said Jimmy, "have it your own way. We seem to have more or less settled things. You go back with Bundle to Chimneys, and for heaven's sake keep her from poking about in that Seven Dials place again. Heaven knows what will happen if she does."

Loraine nodded.

"And now," said Jimmy, "I think a few words with Lady Coote would be advisable."

Lady Coote was sitting on a garden seat doing wool-work. The subject was a disconsolate and somewhat misshapen young woman weeping over an urn.

Lady Coote made room for Jimmy by her side, and he promptly, being a tactful young man, admired her work.

"Do you like it," said Lady Coote, pleased. "It was begun by my Aunt Selina the week before she died. Cancer of the liver, poor thing."

"How beastly," said Jimmy.

"And how is the arm?"

"Oh, it's feeling quite all right. Bit of a nuisance and all that, you know."

"You'll have to be careful," said Lady Coote in a warning voice. "I've known blood-poisoning set in—and in that case you might lose your arm altogether."

"Oh! I say, I hope not."

"I'm only warning you," said Lady Coote.

"Where are you hanging out now?" inquired Mr. Thesiger. "Town—or where?"

Considering that he knew the answer to his query perfectly well, he put the question with a praiseworthy amount of ingenuousness.

Lady Coote sighed heavily.

"Sir Oswald has taken the Duke of Alton's place. Letherbury. You know it, perhaps?"

"Oh, rather. Topping place, isn't it?"

"Oh, I don't know," said Lady Coote. "It's a very large place, and gloomy, you know. Rows of picture galleries with such forbidding looking people. What they call Old Masters are very depressing, I think. You should have seen a little house we had in Yorkshire, Mr. Thesiger. When Sir Oswald was plain Mr. Coote. Such a nice lounge hall and a cheerful drawing-room with an ingle-nook—a white striped paper with a frieze of wistaria I chose for it, I remember. Satin stripe, you know, not moiré. Much better taste, I always think. The dining-room faced northeast, so we didn't get much sun in it, but with a good bright scarlet paper and a set of those comic hunting prints—why, it was as cheerful as Christmas."

In the excitement of these reminiscences, Lady Coote dropped several little balls of wool, which Jimmy dutifully retrieved.

"Thank you, my dear," said Lady Coote. "Now, what was I saying? Oh!—about houses—yes, I do like a cheerful house. And choosing things for it gives you an interest."

"I suppose Sir Oswald will be buying a place of his own one of these days," suggested Jimmy. "And then you can have it just as you like."

Lady Coote shook her head sadly.

"Sir Oswald talks of a firm doing it—and you know what that means."

"Oh! But they'd consult you!"

"It would be one of those grand places—all for the antique. They'd look down on the things I call comfortable and homey. Not but that Sir Oswald wasn't very comfortable and satisfied in his home always, and I daresay his tastes are just the same underneath. But nothing will suit him now but the best! He's got on wonderfully, and naturally he wants something to show for it, but many's the time I wonder where it will end."

Jimmy looked sympathetic.

"It's like a runaway horse," said Lady Coote. "Got the bit between its teeth and away it goes. It's the same with Sir Oswald. He's got on, and he's got on, till he can't stop getting on. He's one of the richest men in England now—but does that satisfy him? No, he wants still more. He wants to be—I don't know what he wants to be! I can tell you, it frightens me sometimes!"

"Like the Persian Johnny," said Jimmy, "who went about wailing for fresh worlds to conquer."

Lady Coote nodded acquiescence without much knowing what Jimmy was talking about.

"What I wonder is—will his stomach stand it?" she went on tearfully. "To have him an invalid—with his ideas—oh, it won't bear thinking of."

"He looks very hearty," said Jimmy, consolingly.

"He's got something on his mind," said Lady Coote. "Worried, that's what he is. *I* know."

"What's he worried about?"

"I don't know. Perhaps something at the works. It's a great comfort for him having Mr. Bateman. Such an earnest young man—and so conscientious."

"Marvellously conscientious," agreed Jimmy.

"Oswald thinks a lot of Mr. Bateman's judgment. He says that Mr. Bateman is always right."

"That was one of his worst characteristics years ago," said Jimmy feelingly.

Lady Coote looked slightly puzzled.

"That was an awfully jolly week-end I had with you at Chimneys," said Jimmy. "I mean it would have been awfully jolly if it hadn't been for poor old Gerry kicking the bucket. Jolly nice girls."

"I find girls very perplexing," said Lady Coote. "Not romantic, you know. Why, I embroidered some handkerchiefs for Sir Oswald with my own hair when we were engaged."

"Did you?" said Jimmy. "How marvellous. But I suppose girls haven't got long enough hair to do that nowadays."

"That's true," admitted Lady Coote. "But, oh, it shows in lots of other ways. I remember when I was a girl, one of my—well, my young men—picked up a handful of gravel, and a girl who was with me said at once that he was treasuring it because my feet had trodden on it. Such a pretty idea, I thought. Though it turned out afterwards that he was taking a course of mineralogy—or do I mean geology?—at a technical school. But I liked the idea—and stealing a girl's handkerchief and treasuring it—all those sort of things."

"Awkward if the girl wanted to blow her nose," said the practical Mr. Thesiger.

Lady Coote laid down her wool-work and looked searchingly but kindly at him.

"Come now," she said, "isn't there some nice girl that you fancy? That you'd like to work and make a little home for?"

Jimmy blushed and mumbled.

"I thought you got on very well with one of those girls at Chimneys that time—Vera Daventry."

"Socks?"

"They do call her that," admitted Lady Coote. "I can't think why. It isn't pretty."

"Oh, she's a topper," said Jimmy. "I'd like to meet her again."

"She's coming down to stay with us next week-end."

"Is she?" said Jimmy, trying to infuse a large amount of wistful longing into the two words.

"Yes. Would—would you like to come?"

"I *would*," said Jimmy heartily. "Thanks ever so much, Lady Coote."

And reiterating fervent thanks, he left her.

Sir Oswald presently joined his wife.

"What has that young jackanapes been boring you about?" he demanded. "I can't stand that young fellow?"

"He's a dear boy," said Lady Coote. "And so brave. Look how he got wounded last night."

"Yes, messing around where he'd no business to be."

"I think you're very unfair, Oswald."

"Never done an honest day's work in his life. A real waster if there ever was one. He'd never get on if he had his way to make in the world."

"You must have got your feet damp last night," said Lady Coote. "I hope you won't get pneumonia. Freddie Richards died of it the other day. Dear me, Oswald, it makes my blood run cold to think of you wandering about with a dangerous burglar loose in the grounds. He might have shot you. I've asked Mr. Thesiger down for next week-end, by the way."

"Nonsense," said Sir Oswald. "I won't have that young man in my house, do you hear, Maria?"

"Why not?"

"That's my business."

"I'm so sorry, dear," said Lady Coote placidly. "I've asked him now, so it can't be helped. Pick up that ball of pink wool, will you, Oswald?"

Sir Oswald complied, his face black as thunder. He looked at his wife and hesitated. Lady Coote was placidly threading her wool needle.

"I particularly don't want Thesiger down next week-end," he said at last. "I've heard a good deal about him from Bateman. He was at school with him."

"What did Mr. Bateman say?"

"He'd no good to say of him. In fact, he warned me very seriously against him."

"He did, did he?" said Lady Coote thoughtfully.

"And I have the highest respect for Bateman's judgment. I've never known him wrong."

"Dear me," said Lady Coote. "What a mess I seem to have made of things. Of course, I should never have asked him if I had known. You should have told me all this before, Oswald. It's too late now."

She began to roll up her work very carefully. Sir Oswald looked at her, made as if to speak, then shrugged his shoulders. He followed her into the house. Lady Coote, walking ahead, wore a very faint smile on her face. She was fond of her husband, but she was also fond—in a quiet, unobtrusive, wholly womanly manner—of getting her own way.

CHAPTER XXVI

Mainly About Golf

"THAT friend of yours is a nice girl, Bundle," said Lord Caterham.

Loraine had been at Chimneys for nearly a week, and had earned the high opinion of her host—mainly because of the charming readiness she had shown to be instructed in the science of the mashie shot.

Bored by his winter abroad, Lord Caterham had taken up golf. He was an execrable player and in consequence was profoundly enthusiastic over the game. He spent most of his mornings lofting mashie shots over various shrubs and bushes—or, rather, essaying to loft them, hacking large bits out of the velvety turf and generally reducing MacDonald to despair.

"We must lay out a little course," said Lord Caterham, addressing a daisy. "A sporting little course. Now then, just watch this one, Bundle. Off the right knee, slow back, keep the head still and use the wrists."

The ball, heavily topped, scudded across the lawn and disappeared into the unfathomed depths of a great bank of rhododendrons.

"Curious," said Lord Caterham. "What did I do then, I wonder? As I was saying, Bundle, that friend of yours is a very nice girl. I really think I am inducing her to take quite an interest in the game. She hit some excellent shots this morning—really quite as good as I could do myself."

Lord Caterham took another careless swing and removed an immense chunk of turf. MacDonald, who was passing, retrieved it and stamped it firmly back. The look he gave Lord Caterham would have caused anyone but an ardent golfer to sink through the earth.

"If MacDonald has been guilty of cruelty to Cootes, which I strongly suspect," said Bundle, "he's being punished now."

"Why shouldn't I do as I like in my own garden?" demanded her father. "MacDonald ought to be interested in the way my game is coming on—the Scotch are a great golfing nation."

"You poor old man," said Bundle. "You'll never be a golfer—but at any rate it keeps you out of mischief."

"Not at all," said Lord Caterham. "I did the long sixth in five the other day. The pro was very surprised when I told him about it."

"He would be," said Bundle.

"Talking of Cootes, Sir Oswald plays a fair game—a very fair game. Not a pretty style—too stiff. But straight down the middle every time. But curious how the cloven hoof shows—won't give you an six-inch putt! Makes you put it in every time. Now I don't like that."

"I suppose he's a man who likes to be sure," said Bundle.

"It's contrary to the spirit of the game," said her father. "And he's not interested in the theory of the thing either. Says he just plays for exercise and doesn't bother about style. Now, that secretary chap, Bateman, is quite different. It's the theory interests him. I was

slicing badly with my spoon; and he said it all came
from too much right arm; and he evolved a very interesting theory. It's all left arm in golf—the left arm is
the arm that counts. He says he plays tennis left handed
but golf with ordinary clubs because there his supe-
riority with the left arm tells."

"And did he play very marvellously?" inquired Bundle.

"No, he didn't," confessed Lord Caterham. "But
then he may have been off his game. I see the theory
all right and I think there's a lot in it. Ah! Did you
see that one, Bundle? Right over the rhododendrons.
A perfect shot. Ah! If one could be sure of doing that
every time—Yes, Tredwell, what is it?"

Tredwell addressed Bundle.

"Mr. Thesiger would like to speak to you on the
telephone, my lady."

Bundle set off at full speed for the house, yelling
"Loraine, Loraine," as she did so. Loraine joined her
just as she was lifting the receiver.

"Hallo, is that you, Jimmy?"

"Hallo. How are you?"

"Very fit, but a bit bored."

"How's Loraine?"

"She's all right. She's here. Do you want to speak
to her?"

"In a minute. I've got a lot to say. To begin with,
I'm going down to the Cootes' for the week-end," he
said significantly. "Now, look here, Bundle, you don't
know how one gets hold of skeleton keys, do you?"

"Haven't the foggiest. Is it really necessary to take
skeleton keys to the Cootes'?"

"Well, I had a sort of idea they'd come in handy.
You don't know the sort of shop one gets them at?"

"What you want is a kindly burglar friend to show
you the ropes."

"I do, Bundle, I do. And unfortunately, I haven't
got one. I thought perhaps your bright brain might
grapple successfully with the problem. But I suppose
I shall have to fall back upon Stevens as usual. He'll

be getting some funny ideas in his head soon about me —first a blue-nosed automatic—and now skeleton keys. He'll think I've joined the criminal classes."

"Jimmy?" said Bundle.

"Yes?"

"Look here—be careful, won't you? I mean if Sir Oswald finds you nosing around with skeleton keys— well, I should think he could be very unpleasant when he likes."

"Young man of pleasing appearance in the dock! All right, I'll be careful. Pongo's the fellow I'm really frightened of. He sneaks around so on those flat feet of his. You never hear him coming. And he always did have a genius for poking his nose in where he wasn't wanted. But trust to the boy hero."

"Well, I wish Loraine and I were going to be there to look after you."

"Thank you, nurse. As a matter of fact, though, I have a scheme—"

"Yes?"

"Do you think you and Loraine might have a convenient car breakdown near Letherbury to-morrow morning? It's not so very far from you, is it?"

"Forty miles. That's nothing."

"I thought it wouldn't be—to you! Don't kill Loraine though. I'm rather fond of Loraine. All right, then —somewhere round about quarter to half past twelve."

"So that they invite us to lunch?"

"That's the idea. I say, Bundle, I ran into that girl Socks yesterday and what do you think—Terence O'Rourke is going to be down there this week-end!"

"Jimmy, do you think he—"

"Well— suspect everyone, you know. That's what they say. He's a wild lad, and daring as they make them. I wouldn't put it past him to run a secret society. He and the Countess might be in this together. He was out in Hungary last year."

"But he could pinch the formula any time."

"That's just what he couldn't. He'd have to do it under circumstances where he couldn't be suspected. But the retreat up the ivy and into his own bed—well, that would be rather neat. Now for instructions. After a few polite nothings to Lady Coote, you and Loraine are to get hold of Pongo and O'Rourke by hook or by crook and keep them occupied till lunch time. See? It oughtn't to be difficult for a couple of beautiful girls like you."

"You're using the best butter, I see."

"A plain statement of fact."

"Well, at any rate, your instructions are duly noted. Do you want to talk to Loraine now?"

Bundle passed over the receiver and tactfully left the room.

CHAPTER XXVII

Nocturnal Adventure

JIMMY THESIGER arrived at Letherbury on a sunny autumn afternoon and was greeted affectionately by Lady Coote and with cold dislike by Sir Oswald. Aware of the keen match-making eye of Lady Coote upon him, Jimmy took pains to make himself extremely agreeable to Socks Daventry.

O'Rourke was there in excellent spirits. He was inclined to be official and secretive about the mysterious events at the Abbey, about which Socks catechized him freely, but his official reticence took a novel form— namely that of embroidering the tale of events in such a fantastic manner that nobody could possibly guess what the truth might have been.

"Four masked men with revolvers? Is that really so?" demanded Socks severely.

"Ah! I'm remembering how that there was the round half dozen of them to hold me down and force the stuff down my throat. Sure, and I thought it was poison, and I done for entirely."

"And what was stolen, or what did they try and steal?"

"What else but the crown jewels of Russia that were

brought to Mr. Lomax secretly to deposit in the Bank of England."

"What a bloody liar you are," said Socks without emotion.

"A liar? I? And the jewels brought over by aeroplane with my best friend as pilot. This is secret history I'm telling you, Socks. Will you ask Jimmy Thesiger there if you don't believe me. Not that I'd be putting any trust in what he'd say."

"Is it true," said Socks, "that George Lomax came down without his false teeth? That's what I want to know."

"There were two revolvers," said Lady Coote. "Nasty things. I saw them myself. It's a wonder this poor boy wasn't killed."

"Oh, I was born to be hanged," said Jimmy.

"I hear that there was a Russian countess there of subtle beauty," said Socks. "And that she vamped Bill."

"Some of the things she said about Buda Pesth were too dreadful," said Lady Coote. "I shall never forget them. Oswald, we must send a subscription."

Sir Oswald grunted.

"I'll make a note of it, Lady Coote," said Rupert Bateman.

"Thank you, Mr. Bateman. I feel one ought to do something as a thank offering. I can't imagine how Sir Oswald escaped being shot—letting alone die of pneumonia."

"Don't be foolish, Maria," said Sir Oswald.

"I've always had a horror of cat burglars," said Lady Coote.

"Think of having the luck to meet one face to face. How thrilling!" murmured Socks.

"Don't you believe it," said Jimmy. "It's damned painful." And he patted his right arm gingerly.

"How is the poor arm?" inquired Lady Coote.

"Oh, pretty well all right now. But it's been the most confounded nuisance having to do everything with the left hand. I'm no good whatever with it."

"Every child should be brought up to be ambidextrous," said Sir Oswald.

"Oh!" said Socks, somewhat out of her depth. "Is that like seals?"

"Not amphibious," said Mr. Bateman. "Ambidextrous means using either hand equally well."

"Oh!" said Socks, looking at Sir Oswald with respect. "Can you?"

"Certainly; I can write with either hand."

"But not with both at once?"

"That would not be practical," said Sir Oswald shortly.

"No," said Socks thoughtfully. "I suppose that would be a bit too subtle."

"It would be a grand thing now in a Government department," observed Mr. O'Rourke, "if one could keep the right hand from knowing what the left hand was doing."

"Can you use both hands?"

"No, indeed. I'm the most right-handed person that ever was."

"But you deal cards with your left hand," said the observant Bateman. "I noticed the other night."

"Oh, but that's different entirely," said Mr. O'Rourke easily.

A gong with a sombre note pealed out and everyone went upstairs to dress for dinner.

After dinner Sir Oswald and Lady Coote, Mr. Bateman and Mr. O'Rourke played bridge and Jimmy passed a flirtatious evening with Socks. The last words Jimmy heard as he retreated up the staircase that night were Sir Oswald saying to his wife:

"You'll never make a bridge player, Maria."

And her reply:

"I know, dear. So you always say. You owe Mr. O'Rourke another pound, Oswald. That's right."

It was some two hours later that Jimmy crept noiselessly (or so he hoped) down the stairs. He made one brief visit to the dining-room and then found his way to Sir Oswald's study. There, after listening intently for a minute or two, he set to work. Most of the drawers of the desk were locked, but a curiously shaped bit of wire in Jimmy's hand soon saw to that. One by one the drawers yielded to his manipulations.

Drawer by drawer he sorted through methodically, being careful to replace everything in the same order. Once or twice he stopped to listen, fancying he heard some distant sound. But he remained undisturbed.

The last drawer was looked through. Jimmy now knew—or could have known had he been paying attention—many interesting details relating to steel; but he had found nothing of what he wanted—a reference to Herr Eberhard's invention or anything that could give him a clue to the identity of the mysterious No. 7. He had, perhaps, hardly hoped that he would. It was an off-chance and he had taken it—but he had not expected much result—except by sheer luck.

He tested the drawers to make sure that he had relocked them securely. He knew Rupert Bateman's powers of minute observation and glanced round the room to make sure that he had left no incriminating trace of his presence.

"That's that," he muttered to himself softly. "Nothing there. Well, perhaps I'll have better luck to-morrow morning—if the girls only play up."

He came out of the study, closing the door behind him and locking it. For a moment he thought he heard a sound quite near him, but decided he had been mistaken. He felt his way noiselessly along the great hall. Just enough light came from the high vaulted windows to enable him to pick his way without stumbling into anything.

Again he heard a soft sound—he heard it quite certainly this time and without the possibility of making a mistake. He was not alone in the hall. Somebody else was there, moving as stealthily as he was. His heart beat suddenly very fast.

With a sudden spring he jumped to the electric switch and turned on the lights. The sudden glare made him blink—but he saw plainly enough. Not four feet away stood Rupert Bateman.

"My goodness, Pongo," cried Jimmy, "you did give me a start. Slinking about like that in the dark."

"I heard a noise," explained Mr. Bateman severely. "I thought burglars had got in and I came down to see."

Jimmy looked thoughtfully at Mr. Bateman's rubber-soled feet.

"You think of everything, Pongo," he said genially. "Even a lethal weapon."

His eye rested on the bulge in the other's pocket.

"It's as well to be armed. One never knows whom one may meet."

"I am glad you didn't shoot," said Jimmy. "I'm a bit tired of being shot at."

"I might easily have done so," said Mr. Bateman.

"It would be dead against the law if you did," said Jimmy. "You've got to make quite sure the beggar's house-breaking, you know, before you pot at him. You mustn't jump to conclusions. Otherwise you'd have to explain why you shot a guest on a perfectly innocent errand like mine."

"By the way, what did you come down for?"

"I was hungry," said Jimmy. "I rather fancied a dry biscuit."

"There are some biscuits in a tin by your bed," said Rupert Bateman.

He was staring at Jimmy very intently through his horn-rimmed spectacles.

"Ah! That's where the staff work has gone wrong, old boy. There's a tin there with 'Biscuits for Starving Visitors' on it. But when the starving visitor opened it—nothing inside. So I just toddled down to the dining-room."

And with a sweet, ingenuous smile, Jimmy produced from his dressing-gown pocket a handful of biscuits.

There was a moment's pause.

"And now I think I'll toddle back to bed," said Jimmy. "Night-night, Pongo."

With an affectation of nonchalance, he mounted the staircase. Rupert Bateman followed him. At the doorway of his room, Jimmy paused as if to say good-night once more.

"It's an extraordinary thing about these biscuits," said Mr. Bateman. "Do you mind if I just—"

"Certainly, laddie, look for yourself."

Mr. Bateman strode across the room, opened the biscuit box and stared at its emptiness.

"Very remiss," he murmured. "Well, good-night."

He withdrew. Jimmy sat on the edge of his bed listening for a minute.

"That was a narrow shave," he murmured to himself. "Suspicious sort of chap, Pongo. Never seems to sleep. Nasty habit of his prowling around with a revolver."

He got up and opened one of the drawers of the dressing-table. Beneath an assortment of ties lay a pile of biscuits.

"There's nothing for it." said Jimmy. "I shall have to eat all the damned things. Ten to one, Pongo will come prowling round in the morning."

With a sigh, he settled down to a meal of biscuits for which he had no inclination whatever.

CHAPTER XXVIII

Suspicions

IT was just on the appointed hour of twelve o'clock that Bundle and Loraine entered the park gates, having left the Hispano at an adjacent garage.

Lady Coote greeted the two girls with surprise, but distinct pleasure, and immediately pressed them to stay to lunch.

O'Rourke, who had been reclining in an immense arm-chair, began at once to talk with great animation to Loraine, who was listening with half an ear to Bundle's highly technical explanation of the mechanical troubles which had affected the Hispano.

"And we said," ended Bundle, "how marvellous that the brute should have broken down just here! Last time it happened was on a Sunday at a place called Little Spedlington under the Hill. And it lived up to its name, I can tell you."

"That would be a grand name on the films," remarked O'Rourke.

"Birthplace of the simple country maiden," suggested Socks.

"I wonder now," said Lady Coote, "where Mr. Thesiger is?"

"He's in the billiard-room, I think," said Socks. "I'll fetch him."

She went off, but had hardly gone a minute when Rupert Bateman appeared on the scene, with the harassed and serious air usual with him.

"Yes, Lady Coote? Thesiger said you were asking for me. How do you do, Lady Eileen——"

He broke off to greet the two girls, and Loraine immediately took the field.

"Oh, Mr. Bateman! I've been wanting to see you. Wasn't it you who was telling me what to do for a dog when he is continually getting sore paws?"

The secretary shook his head.

"It must have been someone else, Miss Wade. Though, as a matter of fact, I do happen to know——"

"What a wonderful young man you are," interrupted Loraine. "You know about everything."

"One should keep abreast of modern knowledge," said Mr. Bateman seriously. "Now about your dog's paws——"

Terence O'Rourke murmured *sotto voce* to Bundle:

"'Tis a man like that that writes all those little paragraphs in the weekly papers. 'It is not generally known that to keep a brass fender uniformly bright,' etc.; 'The dorper beetle is one of the most interesting characters in the insect world'; 'The marriage customs of the Fingalese Indians,' and so on."

"General information, in fact."

"And what more horrible two words could you

have?" said Mr. O'Rourke, and added piously: "Thank the heavens above I'm an educated man and know nothing whatever upon any subject at all."

"I see you've got clock golf here," said Bundle to Lady Coote.

"I'll take you on at it, Lady Eileen," said O'Rourke.

"Let's challenge those two," said Bundle. "Loraine, Mr. O'Rourke and I want to take you and Mr. Bateman on at clock golf."

"Do play, Mr. Bateman," said Lady Coote, as the secretary showed a momentary hesitation. "I'm sure Sir Oswald doesn't want you."

The four went out on the lawn.

"Very cleverly managed, what?" whispered Bundle to Loraine. "Congratulations on our girlish tact."

The round ended just before one o'clock, victory going to Bateman and Loraine.

"But I think you'll agree with me, partner," said Mr. O'Rourke, "that we played a more sporting game."

He lagged a little behind with Bundle.

"Old Pongo's a cautious player—he takes no risks. Now, with me it's neck or nothing. And a fine motto through life, don't you agree, Lady Eileen?"

"Hasn't it ever landed you in trouble?" asked Bundle, laughing.

"To be sure it has. Millions of times. But I'm still going strong. Sure, it'll take the hangman's noose to defeat Terence O'Rourke."

Just then Jimmy Thesiger strolled round the corner of the house.

"Bundle, by all that's wonderful!" he exclaimed.

"You've missed competing in the Autumn Meeting," said O'Rourke.

"I'd gone for a stroll," said Jimmy. "Where did these girls drop from?"

"We came on our flat feet," said Bundle. "The Hispano let us down."

And she narrated the circumstances of the breakdown.

Jimmy listened with sympathetic attention.

"Hard luck," he vouchsafed. "If it's going to take some time, I'll run you back in my car after lunch."

A gong sounded at that moment and they all went in. Bundle observed Jimmy covertly. She thought she had noticed an unusual note of exultance in his voice. She had the feeling that things had gone well.

After lunch they took a polite leave of Lady Coote, and Jimmy volunteered to run them down to the garage in his car. As soon as they had started the same word burst simultaneously from both girls' lips:

"Well?"

Jimmy chose to be provoking.

"Well?"

"Oh, pretty hearty, thanks. Slight indigestion owing to over indulgence in dry biscuits."

"But what has happened?"

"I tell you. Devotion to the cause made me eat too many dry biscuits. But did our hero flinch? No, he did not."

"Oh, Jimmy," said Loraine reproachfully, and he softened.

"What do you really want to know?"

"Oh, everything. Didn't we do it well? I mean, the way we kept Pongo and Terence O'Rourke in play."

"I congratulate you on the handling of Pongo. O'Rourke was probably a sitter—but Pongo is made of other stuff. There's only one word for that lad—it was in the *Sunday Newsbag* cross-word last week. Word of ten letters meaning everywhere at once. Ubiquitous. That describes Pongo down to the ground. You can't go anywhere without running into him—and the worst of it is you never hear him coming."

"You think he's dangerous?"

"Dangerous? Of course he's not dangerous. Fancy Pongo being dangerous. He's an ass. But, as I said just now, he's an ubiquitous ass. He doesn't even seem to need sleep like ordinary mortals. In fact, to put it bluntly, the fellow's a damned nuisance."

And, in a somewhat aggrieved manner, Jimmy described the events of the previous evening.

Bundle was not very sympathetic.

"I don't know what you think you're doing anyway, mouching round here."

"No. 7," said Jimmy crisply. "That's what I'm after. No. 7."

"And you think you'll find him in this house?"

"I thought I might find a clue."

"And you didn't?"

"Not last night—no."

"But this morning," said Loraine, breaking in suddenly. "Jimmy, you did find something this morning. I can see it by your face."

"Well, I don't know if it is anything. But during the course of my stroll—"

"Which stroll didn't take you far from the house, I imagine."

"Strangely enough, it didn't. Round trip in the interior, we might call it. Well, as I say, I don't know whether there's anything in it or not. But I found this."

With the celerity of a conjuror he produced a small bottle and tossed it over to the girls. It was half full of a white powder.

"What do you think it is?" asked Bundle.

"A white crystalline powder, that's what it is," said Jimmy. "And to any reader of detective fiction those words are both familiar and suggestive. Of course, if it turns out to be a new kind of patent tooth-powder, I shall be chagrined and annoyed."

"Where did you find it?" asked Bundle sharply.

"Ah!" said Jimmy, "that's my secret."

And from that point he would not budge in spite of cajolery and insult.

"Here we are at the garage," he said. "Let's hope the high-mettled Hispano has not been subjected to any indignities."

The gentleman at the garage presented a bill for five shillings and made a few vague remarks about loose nuts. Bundle paid him with a sweet smile.

"It's nice to know we all get money for nothing sometimes," she murmured to Jimmy.

The three stood together in the road, silent for the moment as they each pondered the situation.

"I know," said Bundle suddenly.

"Know what?"

"Something I meant to ask you—and nearly forgot. Do you remember that glove that Superintendent Battle found—the half-burnt one?"

"Yes."

"Didn't you say that he tried it on your hand?"

"Yes—it was a shade big. That fits in with the idea of its being a big, hefty man who wore it."

"That's not at all what I'm bothering about. Never mind the size of it. George and Sir Oswald were both there too, weren't they?"

"Yes."

"He could have given it to either of them to fit on?"

"Yes, of course—"

"But he didn't. He chose you. Jimmy, don't you see what that means?"

Mr. Thesiger stared at her.

"I'm sorry, Bundle. Possibly the jolly old brain isn't functioning as well as usual, but I haven't the faintest idea what you're talking about."

"Don't you see, Loraine?"

Loraine looked at her curiously, but shook her head. "Does it mean anything in particular?"

"Of course it does. Don't you see—Jimmy had his right hand in a sling."

"By Jove, Bundle," said Jimmy slowly. "It was rather odd now I come to think of it; it's being a left hand glove, I mean. Battle never said anything."

"He wasn't going to draw attention to it. By trying it on you it might pass without notice being drawn to it, and he talked about the size just to put everybody off. But surely it must mean that the man who shot at you held the pistol in his *left* hand."

"So we've got to look for a left-handed man," said Loraine thoughtfully.

"Yes, and I'll tell you another thing. That was what Battle was doing looking through the golf clubs. He was looking for a left-handed man's."

"By Jove," said Jimmy suddenly.

"What is it?"

"Well, I don't suppose there's anything in it, but it's rather curious."

He retailed the conversation at tea the day before.

"So Sir Oswald Coote is ambidextrous?" said Bundle.

"Yes. And I remember now on that night at Chimneys—you know, the night Gerry Wade died—I was watching the bridge and thinking idly how awkwardly someone was dealing—and then realizing that it was because they were dealing with the left hand. Of course, it must have been Sir Oswald."

They all three looked at each other. Loraine shook her head.

"A man like Sir Oswald Coote! It's impossible. What could he have to gain by it?"

"It seems absurd," said Jimmy. "And yet—"

"No. 7 has his own ways of working," quoted Bundle softly. "Supposing this is the way Sir Oswald has really made his fortune?"

"But why stage all that comedy at the Abbey when he'd had the formula at his own works."

"There might be ways of explaining that," said Loraine. "The same line of argument you used about Mr. O'Rourke. Suspicion had to be diverted from him and placed in another quarter."

Bundle nodded eagerly.

"It all fits in. Suspicion is to fall on Bauer and the Countess. Who on earth would ever dream of suspecting Sir Oswald Coote?"

"I wonder if Battle does," said Jimmy slowly.

Some chord of memory vibrated in Bundle's mind. *Superintendent Battle plucking an ivy leaf off the millionaire's coat.*

Had Battle suspected all the time?

CHAPTER XXIX

Singular Behaviour of George Lomax

"MR. LOMAX is here, my lord."

Lord Caterham started violently, for, absorbed in the intricacies of what not to do with the left wrist, he had not heard the butler approach over the soft turf. He looked at Tredwell more in sorrow than in anger.

"I told you at breakfast, Tredwell, that I should be particularly engaged this morning."

"Yes, my lord, but—"

"Go and tell Mr. Lomax that you have made a mistake, that I am out in the village, that I am laid up with the gout, or, if all else fails, that I am dead."

"Mr. Lomax, my lord, has already caught sight of your lordship when driving up the drive."

Lord Caterham sighed deeply.

"He would. Very well, Tredwell, I am coming." In a manner highly characteristic, Lord Caterham was always most genial when his feelings were in reality the reverse. He greeted George now with a heartiness quite unparalleled.

"My dear fellow, my dear fellow. Delighted to see you. Absolutely delighted. Sit down. Have a drink. Well, well, this is splendid!"

And having pushed George into a large arm-chair, he sat down opposite him and blinked nervously.

"I wanted to see you very particularly," said George.

"Oh!" said Lord Caterham faintly, and his heart sank, whilst his mind raced actively over all the dread possibilities that might lie behind that simple phrase.

"*Very* particularly," said George with heavy emphasis.

Lord Caterham's heart sank lower than ever. He felt that something was coming worse than anything he had yet thought of.

"Yes?" he said, with a courageous attempt at non-chalance.

"Is Eileen at home?"

Lord Caterham felt reprieved, but slightly surprised.

"Yes, yes," he said. "Bundle's here. Got that friend of hers with her—the little Wade girl. Very nice girl— *very* nice girl. Going to be quite a good golfer one day. Nice easy swing—"

He was chatting garrulously on when George interrupted with ruthlessness:

"I am glad Eileen is at home. Perhaps I might have an interview with her presently?"

"Certainly, my dear fellow, certainly." Lord Caterham still felt very surprised, but was still enjoying the sensation of reprieve. "If it doesn't bore you."

"Nothing could bore me less," said George. "I think, Caterham, if I may say so, that you hardly appreciate the fact that Eileen is grown up. She is no longer a child. She is a woman, and if I may say so, a very charming and talented woman. The man who succeeds in winning her love will be extremely lucky. I repeat it —extremely lucky."

"Oh, I daresay," said Lord Caterham. "But she's very restless, you know. Never content to be in one place for more than two minutes together. However, I daresay young fellows don't mind that nowadays."

"You mean that she is not content to stagnate. Eileen has brains, Caterham; she is ambitious. She interests herself in the questions of the day, and brings her fresh and vivid young intellect to bear upon them."

Lord Caterham stared at him. It occurred to him that what was so often referred to as "the strain of modern life," had begun to tell upon George. Certainly his description of Bundle seemed to Lord Caterham ludicrously unlike.

"Are you sure you are feeling quite well?" he asked anxiously.

George waved the inquiry aside impatiently.

"Perhaps, Caterham, you begin to have some inkling of my purpose in visiting you this morning. I am not a man to undertake fresh responsibilities lightly. I have a proper sense, I hope, of what is due to the position I hold. I have given this matter my deep and earnest consideration. Marriage, especially at my age, is not to be undertaken without full—er—consideration. Equality of birth, similarity of tastes, general suitability, and the same religious creed—all these things are necessary and the pros and cons have to be weighed and considered. I can, I think, offer my wife a position in society that is not to be despised. Eileen will grace that position admirably. By birth and breeding she is fitted for it, and her brains and her acute political sense cannot but further my career to our mutual advantage. I am aware, Caterham, that there is—er—some disparity in years. But I can assure you that I feel full of vigour—in my prime. The balance of years should be on the husband's side. And Eileen has serious tastes—an older man will suit her better than some young jackanapes without either experience or *savoir-faire*. I can assure you, my dear Caterham, that I will cherish her—er—exquisite youth; I will cherish it—er—it will be appreciated. To watch the exquisite flower of her mind unfolding—what a privilege! And to think that I never realized—"

He shook his head deprecatingly and Lord Caterham, finding his voice with difficulty, said blankly:

"Do I understand you to mean—ah, my dear fellow, you can't want to marry Bundle?"

"You are surprised. I suppose to you it seems sudden. I have your permission, then, to speak to her?"

"Oh, yes," said Lord Caterham. "If it's permission you want—of course you can. But you know, Lomax, I really shouldn't if I were you. Just go home and think it over like a good fellow. Count twenty. All that sort of thing. Always a pity to propose and make a fool of yourself."

"I daresay you mean your advice kindly, Caterham, though I must confess that you put it somewhat strangely. But I have made up my mind to put my fortune to the test. I may see Eileen?"

"Oh, it's nothing to do with me," said Lord Caterham hastily; "Eileen settles her own affairs. If she came to me to-morrow and said she was going to marry the

chauffeur, I shouldn't make any objections. It's the only
way nowadays. Your children can make life damned
unpleasant if you don't give in to them in every way.
I say to Bundle, 'Do as you like, but don't worry me,'
and really, on the whole, she is amazingly good about
it."

George stood up, intent upon his purpose.

"Where shall I find her?"

"Well, really, I don't know," said Lord Caterham
vaguely. "She might be anywhere. As I told you just
now, she's never in the same place for two minutes
together. No repose."

"And I suppose Miss Wade will be with her? It
seems to me, Caterham, that the best plan would be for
you to ring the bell and ask your butler to find her,
saying that I wish to speak to her for a few minutes."

Lord Caterham pressed the bell obediently.

"Oh, Tredwell," he said, when the bell was answered, "just find her ladyship, will you? Tell her Mr.
Lomax is anxious to speak to her in the drawing-room."

"Yes, my lord."

Tredwell withdrew. George seized Lord Caterham's
hand and wrung it warmly, much to the latter's discomfort.

"A thousand thanks," he said. "I hope soon to bring
you good news."

He hastened from the room.

"Well," said Lord Caterham. "Well!"

And after a long pause:

"What *has* Bundle been up to?"

The door opened again.

"Mr. Eversleigh, my lord."

As Bill hastened in, Lord Caterham caught his hand
and spoke earnestly.

"Hullo, Bill. You're looking for Lomax, I suppose?
Look here, if you want to do a good turn, hurry into
the drawing-room and tell him the Cabinet have called
an immediate meeting, or get him away somehow. It's
really not fair to let the poor devil make an ass of himself all for some silly girl's prank."

"I've not come for Codders," said Bill. "Didn't know

he was here. It's Bundle I want to see. Is she anywhere about?"

"You can't see her," said Lord Caterham. "Not just now, at any rate. George is with her."

"Well—what does it matter?"

"I think it does rather," said Lord Caterham. "He's probably spluttering horribly at this minute, and we mustn't do anything to make it worse for him."

"But what is he saying?"

"Heaven's knows," said Lord Caterham. "A lot of damned nonsense, anyway. Never say too much, that was always my motto. Grab the girl's hand and let events take their course."

Bill stared at him.

"But look here, sir, I'm in a hurry. I must talk to Bundle—"

"Well, I don't suppose you'll have to wait long. I must confess I'm rather glad to have you here with me —I suppose Lomax will insist on coming back and talking to me when it's all over."

"When what's all over? What is Lomax supposed to be doing?"

"Hush," said Lord Caterham. "He's proposing."

"Proposing? Proposing what?"

"Marriage. To Bundle. Don't ask me why. I suppose he's come to what they call the dangerous age. I can't explain it any other way."

"Proposing to Bundle? The dirty swine. At his age."

Bill's face grew crimson.

"He says he's in the prime of life," said Lord Caterham cautiously.

"He? Why, he's decrepit—senile! I—" Bill positively choked.

"Not at all," said Lord Caterham coldly. "He's five years younger than I am."

"Of all the damned cheek! Codders and Bundle! A girl like Bundle! You oughtn't to have allowed it."

"I never interfere," said Lord Caterham.

"You ought to have told him what you thought of him."

"Unfortunately modern civilization rules that out,"

said Lord Caterham regretfully. "In the Stone Age now —but, dear me, I suppose even then I shouldn't be able to do it—being a small man."

"Bundle! Bundle! Why, I've never dared to ask Bundle to marry me because I knew she'd only laugh. And George—a disgusting wind-bag, an unscrupulous, hypocritical old hot-air merchant—a foul, poisonous self advertiser—"

"Go on," said Lord Caterham. "I'm enjoying this."

"My God!" said Bill simply and with feeling. "Look here, I must be off."

"No, no, don't go. I'd much rather you stayed. Besides, you want to see Bundle."

"Not now. This has driven everything else out of my head. You don't know where Jimmy Thesiger is by any chance? I believe he was staying with the Cootes. Is he there still?"

"I think he went back to town yesterday. Bundle and Loraine were over there on Saturday. If you'll only wait—"

But Bill shook his head energetically and rushed from the room. Lord Caterham tiptoed out into the hall, seized a hat and made a hurried exit by the side door. In the distance he observed Bill streaking down the drive in his car.

"That young man will have an accident," he thought.

Bill, however, reached London without any mischance, and proceeded to park his car in St. James's Square. Then he sought out Jimmy Thesiger's rooms. Jimmy was at home.

"Hullo, Bill. I say, what's the matter? You don't look your usual bright little self."

"I'm worried," said Bill. "I was worried anyway, and then something else turned up and gave me a jolt."

"Oh!" said Jimmy. "How lucid. What's it all about? Can I do anything?"

Bill did not reply. He sat staring at the carpet and looking so puzzled and uncomfortable that Jimmy felt his curiosity aroused.

"Has anything very extraordinary occurred, William?" he asked gently.

"Something damned odd. I can't make head or tail of it?"

"The Seven Dials business?"

"Yes—the Seven Dials business. I got a letter this morning."

"A letter? What sort of a letter?"

"A letter from Ronny Devereux's executors."

"Good Lord! After all this time!"

"It seems he left instructions. If he was to die suddenly, a certain sealed envelope was to be sent to me exactly a fortnight after his death."

"And they've sent it to you?"

"Yes."

"You've opened it?"

"Yes."

"Well—what did it say?"

Bill turned a glance upon him, such a strange and uncertain one that Jimmy was startled.

"Look here," he said. "Pull yourself together, old man. It seems to have knocked the wind out of you, whatever it is. Have a drink."

He poured out a stiff whisky and soda and brought it over to Bill, who took it obediently. His face still bore the same dazed expression.

"It's what's in the letter," he said. "I simply can't believe it, that's all."

"Oh, nonsense," said Jimmy. "You must get into the habit of believing six impossible things before breakfast. I do it regularly. Now then, let's hear all about it. Wait a minute."

He went outside.

"Stevens?"

"Yes, sir."

"Just go out and get me some cigarettes, will you? I've run out."

"Very good, sir."

Jimmy waited till he heard the front door close. Then he came back into the sitting-room. Bill was just in the act of setting down his empty glass. He looked better, more purposeful and more master of himself.

"Now then," said Jimmy. "I've sent Stevens out so

that we can't be overheard. Are you going to tell me all about it?"

"It's so incredible."

"Then it's sure to be true. Come on, out with it."

Bill drew a deep breath.

"I will. I'll tell you everything."

CHAPTER XXX

An Urgent Summons

LORAINE, playing with a small and delectable puppy, was somewhat surprised when Bundle rejoined her after an absence of twenty minutes, in a breathless state and with an indescribable expression on her face.

"Whoof," said Bundle, sinking on to a garden seat. "Whoof."

"What's the matter?" asked Loraine, looking at her curiously.

"George is the matter—George Lomax."

"What's he been doing?"

"Proposing to me. It was awful. He spluttered and he stuttered, but he would go through with it—he must have learnt it out of a book, I think. There was no stopping him. Oh, how I hate men who splutter! And, unfortunately, I didn't know the reply."

"You must have known what you wanted to do."

"Naturally I'm not going to marry an apoplectic idiot like George. What I mean is, I didn't know the correct reply from the book of etiquette. I could only just say flatly: 'No, I won't.' What I ought to have said was something about being very sensible of the honour he had done me and so on and so on. But I got so rattled that in the end I jumped out of the window and bolted."

"Really, Bundle, that's not like you."

"Well, I never dreamt of such a thing happening. George—who I always thought hated me—and he did too. What a fatal thing it is to pretend to take an interest in a man's pet subject. You should have heard the drivel George talked about my girlish mind and the pleasure it would be to form it. My mind! If George knew one quarter of what was going on in my mind, he'd faint with horror!"

Loraine laughed. She couldn't help it.

"Oh, I know it's my own fault. I let myself in for this. There's Father dodging round that rhododendron. Hallo, Father."

Lord Caterham approached with a hangdog expression.

"Lomax gone, eh?" he remarked with somewhat forced geniality.

"A nice business you let me in for," said Bundle. "George told me he had your full approval and sanction."

"Well," said Lord Caterham, "what did you expect me to say? As a matter of fact, I didn't say that at all, or anything like it."

"I didn't really think so," said Bundle. "I assumed that George had talked you into a corner and reduced you to such a state that you could only nod your head feebly."

"That's very much what happened. How did he take it? Badly?"

"I didn't wait to see," said Bundle. "I'm afraid I was rather abrupt."

"Oh, well," said Lord Caterham, "perhaps that was the best way. Thank goodness in the future Lomax won't always be running over as he has been in the habit of doing, worrying me about things. Everything is for the best they say. Have you seen my jigger anywhere?"

"A mashie shot or two would steady my nerves, I think," said Bundle. "I'll take you on for sixpence, Loraine."

An hour passed very peacefully. The three returned to the house in a harmonious spirit. A note lay on the hall table.

"Mr. Lomax left that for you, my lord," explained Tredwell. "He was much disappointed to find that you had gone out."

Lord Caterham tore it open. He uttered a pained ejaculation and turned upon his daughter. Tredwell had retired.

"Really, Bundle, you might have made yourself clear, I think."

"What do you mean?"

"Well, read this."

Bundle took it and read:

"MY DEAR CATERHAM—I am sorry not to have had a word with you. I thought I made it clear that I wanted to see you again after my interview with Eileen. She, dear child, was evidently quite unaware of the feelings I entertained towards her. She was, I am afraid, much startled. I have no wish to hurry her in any way. Her girlish confusion was very charming, and I entertain an even higher regard for her, as I much appreciate her maidenly reserve. I must give her time to become accustomed to the idea. Her very confusion shows that she is not wholly indifferent to me and I have no doubts of my ultimate success.

"Believe me, dear Caterham,
"Your sincere friend,
"GEORGE LOMAX."

"Well," said Bundle. "Well, I'm damned!"

Words failed her.

"The man must be mad," said Lord Caterham. "No one could write those things about you, Bundle, unless they were slightly touched in the head. Poor chap, poor chap. But what persistence! I don't wonder he got into the Cabinet. It would serve him right if you did marry him, Bundle."

The telephone rang and Bundle moved forward to answer it. In another minute George and his proposal were forgotten, and she was beckoning eagerly to Loraine. Lord Caterham went off to his own sanctum.

"It's Jimmy," said Bundle. "And he's tremendously excited about something."

"Thank goodness I've caught you," said Jimmy's voice. "There's no time to be lost. Loraine's there, too?"

"Yes, she's here."

"Well, look here, I haven't got time to explain everything—in fact, I can't through the telephone. But Bill has been round to see me with the most amazing story you ever heard. If it's true—well, if it's true, it's the biggest scoop of the century. Now, look here, this is what you've got to do. Come up to town at once, both of you. Garage the car somewhere and go straight to the Seven Dials Club. Do you think that when you get there you can get rid of that footman fellow?"

"Alfred? Rather. You leave that to me."

"Good. Get rid of him and watch out for me and Bill. Don't show yourselves at the windows, but when we drive up, let us in at once. See?"

"Yes."

"That's all right then. Oh, Bundle, don't let on that you're going up to town. Make some other excuse. Say you're taking Loraine home. How would that do?"

"Splendidly. I say, Jimmy, I'm thrilled to the core."

"And you might as well make your will before starting."

"Better and better. But I wish I knew what it was all about."

"You will as soon as we meet. I'll tell you this much. We're going to get ready the hell of a surprise for No. 7!"

Bundle hung up the receiver and turned to Loraine, giving her a rapid résumé of the conversation. Loraine rushed upstairs and hurriedly packed her suitcase, and Bundle put her head round her father's door.

"I'm taking Loraine home, Father."

"Why? I had no idea she was going to-day."

"They want her back," said Bundle vaguely. "Just telephoned. Bye-bye."

"Here, Bundle, wait a minute. When will you be home?"

"Don't know. Expect me when you see me."

With this unceremonious exit Bundle rushed upstairs, put a hat on, slipped into her fur coat and was ready to start. She had already ordered the Hispano to be brought round.

The journey to London was without adventure, except such as was habitually provided by Bundle's driving. They left the car at a garage and proceeded direct to the Seven Dials Club.

The door was opened to them by Alfred. Bundle pushed her way past him without ceremony and Loraine followed.

"Shut the door, Alfred," said Bundle. "Now, I've come here especially to do you a good turn. The police are after you."

"Oh, my lady!"

Alfred turned chalk white.

"I've come to warn you because you did me a good turn the other night," went on Bundle rapidly. "There's a warrant out for Mr. Mosgorovsky, and the best thing you can do is to clear out of here as quick as you can. If you're not found here, they won't bother about you. Here's ten pounds to help you get away somewhere."

In three minutes' time an incoherent and badly scared Alfred had left 14 Hunstanton Street with only one idea in his head—never to return.

"Well, I've managed that all right," said Bundle with satisfaction.

"Was it necessary to be so—well, drastic?" Loraine demurred.

"It's safer," said Bundle. "I don't know what Jimmy and Bill are up to, but we don't want Alfred coming back in the middle of it and wrecking everything. Hallo, here they are. Well, they haven't wasted much time. Probably watching round the corner to see Alfred leave. Go down and open the door to them, Loraine."

Loraine obeyed. Jimmy Thesiger alighted from the driving seat.

"You stop there for a moment, Bill," he said. "Blow the horn if you think anyone's watching the place."

He ran up the steps and banged the door behind him. He looked pink and elated.

"Hallo, Bundle, there you are. Now then, we've got to get down to it. Where's the key of the room you got into last time?"

"It was one of the downstairs keys. We'd better bring the lot up."

"Right you are, but be quick. Time's short."

The key was easily found, the baize-lined door swung back and the three entered. The room was exactly as Bundle had seen it before, with the seven chairs grouped round the table. Jimmy surveyed it for a minute or two in silence. Then his eye went to the two cupboards.

"Which is the cupboard you hid in, Bundle?"

"This one."

Jimmy went to it and flung the door open. The same collection of miscellaneous glassware covered the shelves.

"We shall have to shift all this stuff," he murmured. "Run down and get Bill, Loraine. There's no need for him to keep watch outside any longer."

Loraine ran off.

"What are you going to do?" inquired Bundle impatiently.

Jimmy was down on his knees, trying to peer through the crack of the other cupboard door.

"Wait till Bill comes and you shall hear the whole story. This is his staff work—and a jolly creditable bit of work it is. Hallo—what's Loraine flying up the stairs for as though she'd got a mad bull after her?"

Loraine was indeed racing up the stairs as fast as she could. She burst in upon them with an ashen face and terror in her eyes.

"Bill—Bill—oh, Bundle—Bill!"

"What about Bill?"

Jimmy caught her by the shoulder.

"For God's sake, Loraine, what's happened?"

Loraine was still gasping.

"Bill—I think he's dead—he's in the car still—but he doesn't move or speak. I'm sure he's dead."

Jimmy muttered an oath and sprang for the stairs, Bundle behind him, her heart pounding unevenly and an awful feeling of desolation spreading over her.

Bill—dead? Oh, no! Oh, no! Not that. Please God—not that.

Together she and Jimmy reached the car, Loraine behind them.

Jimmy peered under the hood. Bill was sitting as he had left him, leaning back. But his eyes were closed and Jimmy's pull at his arm brought no response.

"I can't understand it," muttered Jimmy. "But he's not dead. Cheer up, Bundle. Look here, we've got to get him into the house. Let's pray to goodness no policeman comes along. If anybody says anything, he's our sick friend we're helping into the house."

Between the three of them they got Bill into the house without much difficulty, and without attracting much attention, save for an unshaven gentleman, who said sympathetically:

"Genneman's 'ad a couple, I shee," and nodded his head sapiently.

"Into the little back room downstairs," said Jimmy. "There's a sofa there."

They got him safely on to the sofa and Bundle knelt down beside him and took his limp wrist in her hand.

"His pulse is beating," she said. "What *is* the matter with him?"

"He was all right when I left him just now," said Jimmy. "I wonder if someone's managed to inject some stuff into him. It would be easily done—just a prick. The man might have been asking him the time. There's only one thing for it. I must get a doctor at once. You stay here and look after him."

He hurried to the door, then paused.

"Look here—don't be scared, either of you. But I'd better leave you my revolver. I mean—just in case. I'll be back just as soon as I possibly can."

He laid the revolver down on the little table by the sofa, then hurried off. They heard the front door bang behind him.

The house seemed very still now. The two girls

stayed motionless by Bill. Bundle still kept her finger on his pulse. It seemed to be beating very fast and irregularly.

"I wish we could do something," she whispered to Loraine. "This is awful."

Loraine nodded.

"I know. It seems ages since Jimmy went and yet it's only a minute and a half."

"I keep hearing things," said Bundle. "Footsteps and boards creaking upstairs—and yet I know it's only imagination."

"I wonder why Jimmy left us the revolver," said Loraine. "There can't really be danger."

"If they could get Bill—" said Bundle and stopped. Loraine shivered.

"I know—but we're in the house. Nobody can get in without our hearing them. And anyway we've got the revolver."

Bundle turned her attention back again to Bill.

"I wish I knew what to do. Hot coffee. You give them that sometimes."

"I've got some smelling-salts in my bag," said Loraine. "And some brandy. Where is it? Oh, I must have left it in the room upstairs."

"I'll get it," said Bundle. "They might do some good."

She sped quickly up the stairs, across the gaming room and through the open door into the meeting place. Loraine's bag was lying on the table.

As Bundle stretched out her hand to take it, she heard a noise from behind her. Hidden behind the door a man stood ready with a sand-bag in his hand. Before Bundle could turn her head, he had struck.

With a faint moan, Bundle slipped down, an unconscious heap, upon the floor.

CHAPTER XXXI

The Seven Dials

VERY slowly Bundle returned to consciousness. She was aware of a dark, spinning blackness, the centre of which was a violent, throbbing ache. Punctuating this were sounds. A voice that she knew very well saying the same thing over and over again.

The blackness spun less violently. The ache was now definitely located as being in Bundle's own head. And she was sufficiently herself to take an interest in what the voice was saying.

"Darling, darling Bundle. Oh, darling Bundle. She's dead; I know she's dead. Oh, my darling. Bundle, darling, darling Bundle. I do love you so. Bundle—darling —darling—"

Bundle lay quite still with her eyes shut. But she was now fully conscious. Bill's arms held her closely.

"Bundle, darling— Oh, dearest, darling Bundle. Oh, my dear love. Oh, Bundle—Bundle. What shall I do? Oh, darling one—my Bundle—my own dearest, sweetest Bundle. Oh, God, what shall I do? I've killed her. I've killed her."

Reluctantly—very reluctantly—Bundle spoke.

"No, you haven't, you silly idiot," she said.

Bill gave a gasp of utter amazement.

"Bundle—you're alive?"

"Of course I'm alive."

"How long have you been—I mean when did you come to?"

"About five minutes ago."

"Why didn't you open your eyes—or say something?"

"Didn't want to. I was enjoying myself."

"Enjoying yourself?"

"Yes. Listening to all the things you were saying.

You'll never say them so well again. You'll be too beastly self-conscious."

Bill had turned a dark brick-red.

"Bundle—you really didn't mind? You know, I *do* love you so. I have for ages. But I never have dared tell you so."

"You silly juggins," said Bundle. "Why?"

"I thought you'd only laugh at me. I mean—you've got brains and all that—you'll marry some bigwig."

"Like George Lomax?" suggested Bundle.

"I don't mean a fatuous ass like Codders. But some really fine chap who'll be worthy of you—though I don't think anyone could be that," ended Bill.

"You're rather a dear, Bill."

"But, Bundle, seriously, could you ever? I mean, could you ever bring yourself to?"

"Could I ever bring myself to do what?"

"Marry me. I know I'm awfully thick-headed—but I do love you, Bundle. I'd be your dog or your slave or your anything."

"You're very like a dog," said Bundle. "I like dogs. They're so friendly and faithful and warmhearted. I think that perhaps I could just bring myself to marry you, Bill—with a great effort, you know."

Bill's response to this was to relinquish his grasp of her and recoil violently. He looked at her with amazement in his eyes.

"Bundle—you don't mean it?"

"There's nothing for it," said Bundle. "I see I shall have to relapse into unconsciousness again."

"Bundle—darling—" Bill caught her to him. He was trembling violently. "Bundle—do you really mean it—do you?—you don't know how much I love you."

"Oh, Bill," said Bundle.

There is no need to describe in detail the conversation of the next ten minutes. It consisted mostly of repetitions.

"And do you really love me," said Bill, incredulously, for the twentieth time as he at last released her.

"Yes—yes—yes. Now do let's be sensible. I've got

a racking head still, and I've been nearly squeezed to death by you. I want to get the hang of things. Where are we and what's happened?"

For the first time, Bundle began to take stock of her surroundings. They were in the secret room, she noted, and the baize door was closed and presumably locked. They were prisoners, then!

Bundle's eyes came back to Bill. Quite oblivious of her question he was watching her with adoring eyes.

"Bill, darling," said Bundle, "pull yourself together. We've got to get out of here."

"Eh?" said Bill. "What? Oh, yes. That'll be all right. No difficulty about that."

"It's being in love makes you feel like that," said Bundle. "I feel rather the same myself. As though everything's easy and possible."

"So it is," said Bill. "Now that I know you care for me—"

"Stop it," said Bundle. "Once we begin again any serious conversation will be hopeless. Unless you pull yourself together and become sensible, I shall very likely change my mind."

"I shan't let you," said Bill. "You don't think that once having got you I'd be such a fool as to let you go, do you?"

"You would not coerce me against my will, I hope," said Bundle grandiloquently.

"Wouldn't I?" said Bill. "You just watch me do it, that's all."

"You really are rather a darling, Bill. I was afraid you might be too meek, but I see there's going to be no danger of that. In another half hour you'd be ordering me about. Oh, dear, we're getting silly again. Now, look here, Bill, we've got to get out of here."

"I tell you that'll be quite all right. I shall—"

He broke off, obedient to a pressure from Bundle's hand. She was leaning forward, listening intently. Yes, she had not been mistaken. A step was crossing the outer room. The key was thrust into the lock and turned. Bundle held her breath. Was it Jimmy coming to rescue them—or was it someone else?

The door opened and the black-bearded Mr. Mosgorovsky stood on the threshold.

Immediately Bill took a step forward, standing in front of Bundle.

"Look here," he said, "I want a word with you privately."

The Russian did not reply for a minute or two. He stood stroking his long, silky, black beard and smiling quietly to himself.

"So," he said at last, "it is like that. Very well. The lady will be pleased to come with me."

"It's all right, Bundle," said Bill. "Leave it to me. You go with this chap. Nobody's going to hurt you. I know what I'm doing."

Bundle rose obediently. That note of authority in Bill's voice was new to her. He seemed absolutely sure of himself and confident of being able to deal with the situation. Bundle wondered vaguely what it was that Bill had—or thought he had—up his sleeve.

She passed out of the room in front of the Russian. He followed her, closing the door behind him and locking it.

"This way, please," he said.

He indicated the staircase and she mounted obediently to the floor above. Here she was directed to pass into a small, frowsy room, which she took to be Alfred's bedroom.

Mosgorovsky said: "You will wait here quietly, please. There must be no noise."

Then he went out, closing the door behind him and locking her in.

Bundle sat down on a chair. Her head was aching badly still and she felt incapable of sustained thought. Bill seemed to have the situation well in hand. Sooner or later, she supposed, someone would come and let her out.

The minutes passed. Bundle's watch had stopped, but she judged that over an hour had passed since the Russian had brought her here. What was happening? What, indeed, *had* happened?

At last she heard footsteps on the stairs. It was Mosgorovsky once more. He spoke very formally to her.

"Lady Eileen Brent, you are wanted at an emergency meeting of the Seven Dials Society. Please follow me."

He led the way down the stairs and Bundle followed him. He opened the door of the secret chamber and Bundle passed in, catching her breath in surprise as she did so.

She was seeing for the second time what she had only had a glimpse of the first time through her peephole. The masked figures were sitting round the table. As she stood there, taken aback by the suddenness of it, Mosgorovsky slipped into his place, adjusting his clock mask as he did so.

But this time the chair at the head of the table was occupied. No. 7 was in his place.

Bundle's heart beat violently. She was standing at the foot of the table directly facing him and she stared and stared at the mocking piece of hanging stuff, with the clock dial on it, that hid his features.

He sat quite immovable and Bundle got an odd sensation of power radiating from him. His inactivity was not the inactivity of weakness—and she wished violently, almost hysterically, that he would speak—that he would make some sign, some gesture—not just sit there like a gigantic spider in the middle of its web waiting remorselessly for its prey.

She shivered and as she did so Mosgorovsky rose. His voice, smooth, silky, persuasive, seemed curiously far away.

"Lady Eileen, you have been present unasked at the secret councils of this society. It is therefore necessary that you should identify yourself with our aims and ambitions. The place 2 o'clock, you may notice, is vacant. It is that place that is offered to you."

Bundle gasped. The thing was like a fantastic nightmare. Was it possible that she, Bundle Brent, was being asked to join a murderous secret society? Had the same proposition been made to Bill, and had he refused indignantly?

"I can't do that," she said bluntly.

"Do not answer precipitately."

She fancied that Mosgorovsky, beneath his clock mask, was smiling significantly into his beard.

"You do not as yet know, Lady Eileen, what it is you are refusing."

"I can make a pretty good guess," said Bundle.

"Can you?"

It was the voice of 7 o'clock. It awoke some vague chord of memory in Bundle's brain. Surely she knew that voice?

Very slowly No. 7 raised a hand to his head and fumbled with the fastening of the mask.

Bundle held her breath. At last—she was going to *know*.

The mask fell.

Bundle found herself looking into the expressionless, wooden face of Superintendent Battle.

CHAPTER XXXII

Bundle Is Dumfounded

"THAT'S right," said Battle, as Mosgorovsky leapt up and came round to Bundle. "Get a chair for her. It's been a bit of a shock, I can see."

Bundle sank down on a chair. She felt limp and faint with surprise. Battle went on talking in a quiet, comfortable way wholly characteristic of him.

"You didn't expect to see me, Lady Eileen. No, and no more did some of the others sitting round this table. Mr. Mosgorovsky's been my lieutenant in a manner of speaking. He's been in the know all along. But most of the others have taken their orders blindly from him."

Still Bundle said no word. She was—a most unusual state of affairs for her—simply incapable of speech.

Battle nodded at her comprehendingly, seeming to understand the state of her feelings.

"You'll have to get rid of one or two preconceived

ideas of yours, I'm afraid, Lady Eileen. About this society, for instance—I know it's common enough in books—a secret organization of criminals with a mysterious super-criminal at the head of it whom no one ever sees. That sort of thing may exist in real life, but I can only say that I've never come across anything of the sort, and I've had a good deal of experience one way or another.

"But there's a lot of romance in the world, Lady Eileen. People, especially young people, like reading about such things, and they like still better really *doing* them. I'm going to introduce you now to a very creditable band of amateurs that has done remarkably fine work for my Department, work that nobody else could have done. If they've chosen rather melodramatic trappings, well, why shouldn't they? They've been willing to face real danger—danger of the very worst kind— and they've done it for these reasons: love of danger for its own sake—which to my mind is a very healthy sign in these Safety First days—and an honest wish to serve their country.

"And now, Lady Eileen, I'm going to introduce you. First of all, there's Mr. Mosgorovsky, whom you already know in a manner of speaking. As you're aware, he runs the club and he runs a host of other things too. He's our most valuable Secret Anti-Bolshevist Agent in England. No. 5 is Count Andras of the Hungarian Embassy, a very near and dear friend of the late Mr. Gerald Wade. No. 4 is Mr. Hayward Phelps, an American journalist, whose British sympathies are very keen and whose aptitude for scenting 'news' is remarkable. No. 3—"

He stopped, smiling, and Bundle stared dumfounded into the sheepish, grinning face of Bill Eversleigh.

"No. 2," went on Battle in a graver voice, "can only show an empty place. It is the place belonging to Mr. Ronald Devereux, a very gallant young gentleman who died for his country if any man ever did. No. 1—well, No. 1 was Mr. Gerald Wade, another very gallant gentleman who died in the same way. His place was taken—not without some grave misgivings on my part

—by a lady—a lady who has proved her fitness to have it and who has been a great help to us."

The last to do so, No. 1, removed her mask, and Bundle looked without surprise into the beautiful, dark face of Countess Radzky.

"I might have known," said Bundle resentfully, "that you were too completely the beautiful foreign adventuress to be anything of the kind really."

"But you don't know the real joke," said Bill. *"Bundle this is Babe St. Maur*—you remember my telling you about her and what a ripping actress she was—and she's about proved it."

"That's so," said Miss St. Maur in pure transatlantic nasal. "But it's not a terrible lot of credit to me, because Poppa and Momma came from the part of Yurrup—so I got the patter fairly easy. Gee, but I nearly gave myself away once at the Abbey, talking about gardens."

She paused and then said abruptly:

"It's—it's not been just fun. You see, I was kinder engaged to Ronny, and when he handed in his checks—well, I had to do something to track down the skunk who murdered him. That's all."

"I'm completely bewildered," said Bundle. "Nothing is what it seems."

"It's very simple, Lady Eileen," said Superintendent Battle. "It began with some of the young people wanting a bit of excitement. It was Mr. Wade who first got on to me. He suggested the formation of a band of what you might call amateur workers to do a bit of secret service work. I warned him that it might be dangerous —but he wasn't the kind to weigh that in the balance. I made it plain to him that any one who came in must do so on that understanding. But, bless you, that wasn't going to stop any of Mr. Wade's friends. And so the thing began."

"But what was the object of it all?" asked Bundle.

"We wanted a certain man—wanted him badly. He wasn't an ordinary crook. He worked in Mr. Wade's world, a kind of Raffles, but much more dangerous than any Raffles ever was or could be. He was out for big stuff, international stuff. Twice already valuable secret inventions had been stolen, and clearly stolen by someone who had inside knowledge. The professionals had had a try—and failed. Then the amateurs took on —and succeeded."

"Succeeded?"

"Yes—but they didn't come out of it unscathed. The man was dangerous. Two lives fell victim to him and he got away with it. But the Seven Dials stuck to it. And as I say, they succeeded. Thanks to Mr. Eversleigh, the man was caught at last red-handed."

"Who was he?" asked Bundle. "Do I know him?"

"You know him very well, Lady Eileen. His name is Mr. Jimmy Thesiger, and he was arrested this afternoon."

CHAPTER XXXIII

Battle Explains

SUPERINTENDENT BATTLE settled to explain. He spoke comfortably and cozily.

"I didn't suspect him myself for a long time. The first hint of it I had was when I heard what Mr. Devereux's last words had been. Naturally, you took them to mean that Mr. Devereux was trying to send word to Mr. Thesiger that the Seven Dials had killed him. That's what the words seemed to mean on their face value. But of course I knew that that couldn't be so. It was the Seven Dials that Mr. Devereux wanted told—and what he wanted them told was something about Mr. Jimmy Thesiger.

"The thing seemed incredible, because Mr. Devereux and Mr. Thesiger were close friends. But I remembered something else—that these thefts must have been committed by someone who was absolutely in the know. Someone who, if not in the Foreign Office himself, was in the way of hearing all its chit-chat. And I found it very hard to find out where Mr. Thesiger got his money. The income his father left him was a small one, yet he was able to live at a most expensive rate. Where did the money come from?

"I knew that Mr. Wade had been very excited by something that he had found out. He was quite sure that he was on the right track. He didn't confide in anyone about what he thought that track was, but he did say something to Mr. Devereux about being on the point of making sure. That was just before they both went down to Chimneys for that week-end. As you know, Mr. Wade died there—apparently from an overdose of a sleeping draught. It seemed straight-forward enough, but Mr. Devereux did not accept that explanation for a minute. He was convinced that Mr. Wade had been very cleverly put out of the way and that someone in the house must actually be the criminal we were all after. He came, I think, very near confiding in Mr. Thesiger, for he certainly had no suspicions of him at that moment. But something held him back.

"Then he did rather a curious thing. He arranged seven clocks upon the mantelpiece, throwing away the eighth. It was meant as a symbol that the Seven Dials would revenge the death of one of their members—and he watched eagerly to see if anyone betrayed themselves or showed signs of perturbation."

"And it was Jimmy Thesiger who poisoned Gerry Wade?"

"Yes, he slipped the stuff into a whisky and soda which Mr. Wade had downstairs before retiring to bed. That's why he was already feeling sleepy when he wrote that letter to Miss Wade."

"Then the footman, Bauer, hadn't anything to do with it?" asked Bundle.

"Bauer was one of our people, Lady Eileen. It was thought likely that our crook would go for Herr Eberhard's invention and Bauer was got into the house to watch events on our behalf. But he wasn't able to do much. As I say, Mr. Thesiger administered the fatal dose easily enough. Later, when everyone was asleep, a bottle, glass and empty chloral bottle were placed by Mr. Wade's bedside by Mr. Thesiger. Mr. Wade was unconscious then, and his fingers were probably pressed round the glass and the bottle so that they should be found there if any questions should arise. I don't know what effect the seven clocks on the mantelpiece made on Mr. Thesiger. He certainly didn't let on anything to Mr. Devereux. All the same, I think he had a bad five minutes now and again thinking of them. And I think he kept a pretty wary eye on Mr. Devereux after that.

"We don't know exactly what happened next. No one saw much of Mr. Devereux after Mr. Wade's death. But it is clear that he worked along the same lines that he knew Mr. Wade had been working on and reached the same result—namely, that Mr. Thesiger was the man. I fancy, too, that he was betrayed in the same way."

"You mean?"

"Through Miss Loraine Wade, Mr. Wade was devoted to her—I believe he hoped to marry her—she wasn't really his sister, of course—and there is no doubt that he told her more than he should have done. But Miss Loraine Wade was devoted body and soul to Mr. Thesiger. She would do anything he told her. She passed on the information to him. In the same way, later, Mr. Devereux was attracted to her, and probably warned her against Mr. Thesiger. So Mr. Devereux in turn was silenced—and died trying to send word to the Seven Dials that his murderer was Mr. Thesiger."

"How ghastly," cried Bundle. "If I had only known."

"Well, it didn't seem likely. In fact, I could hardly credit it myself. But then we came to the affair at the Abbey. You will remember how awkward it was—specially awkward for Mr. Eversleigh here. You and Mr. Thesiger were hand in glove. Mr. Eversleigh had already been embarrassed by your insisting on being brought to this place, and when he found that you had actually overheard what went on at a meeting, he was dumfounded."

The Superintendent paused and a twinkle came into his eye.

"So was I, Lady Eileen. I never dreamed of such a

thing being possible. You put one over on me there all right.

"Well, Mr. Eversleigh was in a dilemma. He couldn't let you into the secret of the Seven Dials without letting Mr. Thesiger in also—and that would never do. It all suited Mr. Thesiger very well, of course, for it gave him a bona fide reason for getting himself asked to the Abbey, which made things much easier for him.

"I may say that the Seven Dials had already sent a warning letter to Mr. Lomax. That was to ensure his applying to me for assistance, so that I should be able to be on the spot in a perfectly natural manner. I made no secret of my presence, as you know."

And again the Superintendent's eyes twinkled.

"Well, ostensibly, Mr. Eversleigh and Mr. Thesiger were to divide the night into two watches. Really, Mr. Eversleigh and Miss St. Maur did so. She was on guard at the library window when she heard Mr. Thesiger coming and had to dart behind the screen.

"And now comes the cleverness of Mr. Thesiger. Up to a point he told a perfectly true story, and I must admit that with the fight and everything, I was distinctly shaken—and began to wonder whether he had had anything to do with the theft at all, or whether we were completely on the wrong track. There were one or two suspicious circumstances that pointed in an entirely different direction, and I can tell you I didn't know what to make of things, when something turned up to clinch matters.

"I found the burnt glove in the fireplace with the teeth marks on it—and then—well—I knew that I'd been right after all. But, upon my word, he was a clever one."

"What actually happened?" said Bundle. "Who was the other man?"

"There wasn't any other man. Listen, and I'll show you how in the end I reconstructed the whole story. To begin with, Mr. Thesiger and Miss Wade are in this together. And they have a rendezvous for an exact time. Miss Wade comes over in her car, climbs through the fence and comes up to the house. She's got a perfectly good story if any one stops her—the one she told eventually. But she arrived unmolested on the terrace just after the clock had struck two.

"Now, I may say to begin with that she was seen coming in. My men saw her, but they had orders to stop nobody coming in—only going out. I wanted, you see, to find out as much as possible. Miss Wade arrives on the terrace, and at that minute a parcel falls at her feet and she picks it up. A man comes down the ivy and she starts to run. What happens next? The struggle—and presently the revolver shots. What will everyone do? Rush to the scene of the fight. And Miss Loraine Wade could have left the grounds and driven off with the formula safely in her possession.

"But things don't happen quite like that. Miss Wade runs straight into my arms. And at that moment the game changes. It's no longer attack but defence. Miss Wade tells her story. It is perfectly true and perfectly sensible.

"And now we come to Mr. Thesiger. One thing struck me at once. The bullet wound alone couldn't have caused him to faint. Either he had fallen and hit his head—or—well, he hadn't fainted at all. Later we had Miss St. Maur's story. It agreed perfectly with Mr. Thesiger's—there was only one suggestive point. Miss St. Maur said that after the lights were turned out and Mr. Thesiger went over to the window, he was so still that she thought he must have left the room and gone outside. Now, if any one is in the room, you can hardly help hearing their breathing if you are listening for it. Supposing, then, that Mr. Thesiger *had* gone outside. Where next? Up the ivy to Mr. O'Rourke's room—Mr. O'Rourke's whisky and soda having been doped the night before. He gets the papers, throws them down to the girl, climbs down the ivy again, and—starts the fight. That's easy enough when you come to think of it. Knock the tables down, stagger about, speak in your own voice and then in a hoarse half-whisper. And then, the final touch, the two revolver shots. His own Colt automatic, bought openly the day before, is fired at an imaginary assailant. Then, with his left gloved

hand, he takes from his pocket the small Mauser pistol
and shoots himself through the fleshy part of the right
arm. He flings the pistol through the window, tears off
the glove with his teeth, and throws it into the fire.
When I arrive he is lying on the floor in a faint."

Bundle drew a deep breath.

"You didn't realize all this at the time, Superintendent Battle?"

"No, that I didn't. I was taken in as much as anyone
could be. It wasn't till long afterwards that I pieced it
all together. Finding the glove was the beginning of it.
Then I made Sir Oswald throw the pistol through the
window. It fell a good way farther on than it should
have done. But a man who is right-handed doesn't
throw nearly as far with the left hand. Even then it was
only suspicion—and a very faint suspicion at that.

"But there was one point struck me. The papers were
obviously thrown down for someone to pick up. If
Miss Wade was there by accident, who was the real person? Of course, for those who weren't in the know, that
question was answered easily enough—the Countess.
But there I had the pull over you. *I knew the Countess
was all right.* So what follows? Why, the idea that the
papers had actually been picked up by the person they
were meant for. And the more I thought of it, the more
it seemed to me a very remarkable coincidence that
Miss Wade should have arrived at the exact moment
she did."

"It must have been very difficult for you when I came
to you full of suspicion about the Countess."

"It was, Lady Eileen. I had to say something to
put you off the scent. And it was very difficult for Mr.
Eversleigh here, with the lady coming out of a dead
faint and no knowing what she might say."

"I understand Bill's anxiety now," said Bundle. "And
the way he kept urging her to take time and not talk
till she felt quite all right."

"Poor old Bill," said Miss St. Maur. "That poor baby
had to be vamped against his will—getting madder'n a
hornet every minute."

"Well," said Superintendent Battle, "there it was. I

suspected Mr. Thesiger—but I couldn't get definite proof. On the other hand, Mr. Thesiger himself was rattled. He realized more or less what he was up against in the Seven Dials—but he wanted badly to know who No. 7 was. He got himself asked to the Cootes under the impression that Sir Oswald Coote was No. 7."

"I suspected Sir Oswald," said Bundle, "especially when he came in from the garden that night."

"I never suspected him," said Battle. "But I don't mind telling you that I *did* have my suspicions of that young chap, his secretary."

"Pongo?" said Bill. "Not old Pongo?"

"Yes, Mr. Eversleigh, old Pongo as you call him. A very efficient gentleman and one that could have put anything through if he'd a mind to. I suspected him partly because he'd been the one to take the clocks into Mr. Wade's room that night. It would have been easy for him to put the bottle and glass by the bedside then. And then, for another thing, he was left-handed. That glove pointed straight to him—if it hadn't been for one thing—"

"What?"

"The teeth marks—only a man whose right hand was incapacitated would have needed to tear off that glove with his teeth."

"So Pongo was cleared."

"So Pongo was cleared, as you say. I'm sure it would be a great surprise to Mr. Bateman to know he was ever suspected."

"It would," agreed Bill. "A solemn card—a silly ass like Pongo. How you could ever think—"

"Well, as far as that goes, Mr. Thesiger was what you might describe as an empty-headed young ass of the most brainless description. One of the two was playing a part. When I decided that it was Mr. Thesiger, I was interested to get Mr. Bateman's opinion of him. All along, Mr. Bateman had the gravest suspicions of Mr. Thesiger and frequently said as much to Sir Oswald."

"It's curious," said Bill, "but Pongo always is right. It's maddening."

"Well, as I say," went on Superintendent Battle, "we

got Mr. Thesiger fairly on the run, badly rattled over this Seven Dials business and uncertain just where the danger lay. That we got him in the end was solely through Mr. Eversleigh. He knew what he was up against, and he risked his life cheerfully. But he never dreamt that you would be dragged into it, Lady Eileen."

"My God, no," said Bill with feeling.

"He went round to Mr. Thesiger's rooms with a cooked-up tale," continued Battle. "He was to pretend that certain papers of Mr. Devereaux's had come into his hands. Those papers were to suggest a suspicion of Mr. Thesiger. Naturally, as the honest friend, Mr. Eversleigh rushed round, sure that Mr. Thesiger would have an explanation. We calculated that if we were right, Mr. Thesiger would try and put Mr. Eversleigh out of the way, and we were fairly certain as to the way he'd do it. Sure enough, Mr. Thesiger gave his guest a whisky and soda. During the minute or two that his host was out of the room, Mr. Eversleigh poured that into a jar on the mantelpiece, but he had to pretend, of course, that the drug was taking effect. It would be slow, he knew, not sudden. He began his story, and Mr. Thesiger at first denied it all indignantly, but as soon as he saw (or thought he saw) that the drug was taking effect, he admitted everything and told Mr. Eversleigh that he was the third victim.

"When Mr. Eversleigh was nearly unconscious, Mr. Thesiger took him down to the car and helped him in. The hood was up. He must already have telephoned to you unknown to Mr. Eversleigh. He made a clever suggestion to you. You were to say that you were taking Miss Wade home.

"You made no mention of a message from him. Later, when your body was found here, Miss Wade would swear that you had driven her home and gone up to London with the idea of penetrating into this house by yourself.

"Mr. Eversleigh continued to play his part, that of the unconscious man. I may say that as soon as the two young men had left Jermyn Street, one of my men gained admission and found the doctored whisky, which contained enough hydro-chloride of morphia to kill two men. Also the car they were in was followed. Mr. Thesiger drove out of town to a well-known golf course, where he showed himself for a few minutes, speaking of playing a round. That, of course, was for an alibi, should one be needed. He left the car with Mr. Eversleigh in it a little way down the road. Then he drove back to town and to the Seven Dials Club. As soon as he saw Alfred leave, he drove up to the door, spoke to Mr. Eversleigh as he got out in case you might be listening and came into the house and played his little comedy.

"When he pretended to go for a doctor, he really only slammed the door and then crept quietly upstairs and hid behind the door of this room, where Miss Wade would presently send you up on some excuse. Mr. Eversleigh, of course, was horrorstruck when he saw you, but he thought it best to keep up the part he was playing. He knew our people were watching the house, and he imagined that there was no immediate danger intended to you. He could always 'come to life' at any moment. When Mr. Thesiger threw his revolver on the table and apparently left the house it seemed safer than ever. As for the next bit——" He paused, looking at Bill. "Perhaps you'd like to tell that, sir."

"I was still lying on that bally sofa," said Bill, "trying to look done in and getting the fidgets worse and worse. Then I heard someone run down the stairs, and Loraine got up and went to the door. I heard Thesiger's voice, but not what he said. I heard Loraine say: 'That's all right—it's gone splendidly.' Then he said: 'Help me carry him up. It will be a bit of a job, but I want them both together there—a nice little surprise for No. 7.' I didn't quite understand what they were jawing about, but they hauled me up the stairs somehow or other. It *was* a bit of a job for them. I made myself a dead weight all right. They heaved me in here, and then I heard Loraine say: 'You're sure it's all right. She won't come round?' And Jimmy said—the damned blackguard: 'No fear. I hit with all my might.'

"They went away and locked the door, and then I

opened my eyes and saw you. My God, Bundle, I shall never feel so perfectly awful again. I thought you were dead."

"I suppose my hat saved me," said Bundle.

"Partly," said Superintendent Battle. "But partly it was Mr. Thesiger's wounded arm. He didn't realize it himself—but it had only half its usual strength. Still, that's all no credit to the Department. We didn't take the care of you we ought to have done, Lady Eileen— and it's a black blot on the whole business."

"I'm very tough," said Bundle. "And also rather lucky. What I can't get over is Loraine being in it. She was such a gentle little thing."

"Ah!" said the Superintendent. "So was the Pentonville murderess that killed five children. You can't go by that. She's got bad blood in her—her father ought to have seen the inside of a prison more than once."

"You've got her too?"

Superintendent Battle nodded.

"I daresay they won't hang her—juries are soft-hearted. But young Thesiger will swing all right—and a good thing too—a more utterly depraved and callous criminal I never met.

"And now," he added. "If your head isn't aching too badly, Lady Eileen. What about a little celebration? There's a nice little restaurant round the corner."

Bundle heartily agreed.

"I'm starving. Superintendent Battle. Besides," she looked round, "I've got to get to know all my colleagues."

"The Seven Dials," said Bill, "Hurrah! Some fizz is what we need. Do they run to fizz at this place, Battle?"

"You won't have anything to complain of, sir. You leave it to me."

"Superintendent Battle," said Bundle, "you are a wonderful man. I'm sorry you're married already. As it is, I shall have to put up with Bill."

CHAPTER XXXIV

Lord Caterham Approves

"FATHER," said Bundle, "I've got to break a piece of news to you. You're going to lose me."

"Nonsense," said Lord Caterham. "Don't tell me that you're suffering from galloping consumption or a weak heart or anything like that, because I simply don't believe it."

"It's not death," said Bundle. "It's marriage."

"Very nearly as bad," said Lord Caterham. "I suppose I shall have to come to the wedding, all dressed up in tight, uncomfortable clothes, and give you away. And Lomax may think it necessary to kiss me in the vestry."

"Good heavens! You don't think I'm going to marry George, to you?" cried Bundle.

"Well, something like that seemed to be in the wind last time I saw you," said her father. "Yesterday morning, you know."

"I'm going to be married to some one a hundred times nicer than George," said Bundle.

"I hope so, I'm sure," said Lord Caterham. "But one never knows. I don't feel you're really a good judge of character, Bundle. You told me that young Thesiger was a cheerful inefficient, and from all I hear now it seems that he was one of the most efficient criminals of the day. The sad thing is that I never met him. I was thinking of writing my reminiscences soon—with a special chapter on murderers I have met—and by a purely technical oversight, I never met this young man."

"Don't be silly," said Bundle. "You know you haven't got the energy to write reminiscences or anything else."

"I wasn't actually going to write them myself," said Lord Caterham. "I believe that's never done. But I met a very charming girl the other day and that's her special job. She collects the material and does all the actual writing."

"And what do you do?"

"Oh, just give her a few facts for half an hour every day. Nothing more than that." After a slight pause, Lord Caterham said: "She was a nice-looking girl—very restful and sympathetic."

"Father," said Bundle, "I have a feeling that without me you will run into deadly danger."

"Different kinds of danger suit different kinds of people," said Lord Caterham.

He was moving away, when he turned back and said over his shoulder:

"By the way, Bundle, who *are* you marrying?"

"I was wondering," said Bundle, "when you were going to ask me that. I'm going to marry Bill Eversleigh."

The egoist thought it over for a minute. Then he nodded in complete satisfaction.

"Excellent," he said. "He's scratch, isn't he? He and I can play together in the foursomes in the Autumn Meeting."

THE MYSTERIOUS WORLD OF AGATHA CHRISTIE

the intriguing situations and the breathtaking final deduction.
Acknowledged as the world's most popular mystery writer of all
time, Dame Agatha Christie's books have thrilled millions of
readers for generations. With her care and attention to characters,
it's no wonder that Agatha Christie is the world's best-selling
mystery writer.

☐	25678	SLEEPING MURDER	$3.50
☐	24144	A HOLIDAY FOR MURDER	$2.95
☐	23908	POIROT INVESTIGATES	$2.95
☐	24038	THE SECRET ADVERSARY	$2.95
☐	23776	DEATH ON THE NILE	$2.95
☐	24093	THE MYSTERIOUS AFFAIR AT STYLES	$2.95
☐	25493	THE POSTERN OF FATE	$3.50
☐	23905	THE SEVEN DIALS MYSTERY	$2.95

Prices and availability subject to change without notice.

Buy them at your local bookstore or use this handy coupon for ordering:

Bantam Books, Inc., Dept. AC, 414 East Golf Road, Des Plaines, Ill. 60016

Please send me the books I have checked above. I am enclosing $_____
(please add $1.25 to cover postage and handling). Send check or money order
—no cash or C.O.D.'s please.

Mr/Mrs/Miss _____

Address_____

City_____ State/Zip_____

AC—12/85

Please allow four to six weeks for delivery. This offer expires 6/86.